SENS...

Amanda Quick

MW00987989

"DON'T TOUCH HER. DON'T TOUCH HER. FOR GOD'S SAKE, DO NOT TOUCH HER!"

This was his only coherent thought, an increasingly frantic litany, as her lips burned beneath his.

Suddenly her eyelids snapped open. With a sound of utter horror her lips broke free. "Oh, my Lord!"

She jerked away, tumbling off the rail and landing flat on her back. He followed her, vaulting over the stile and standing above her as she stared wild-eyed up at him.

"I didn't touch you!" he shouted.

"I know that!" she shouted back, and began thrashing about, trying to get upright.

In her frenzy her skirt hiked high above her knees, displaying lace-trimmed undergarments—Lily Bede, lace? Pins flew from her head and a cascade of gleaming black corkscrew curls fell around her neck and shoulders in an inky fantasy of abandonment.

"You might want to fix your—petticoats," he whispered.

She hitched up her chin and looked him squarely in the eye. Fascinated, he waited to see what she would do next. . . .

AS YOU DESIRE

"Romance with strength, wit, and intelligence. Connie Brockway delivers!"
—*New York Times* bestselling author Tami Hoag

"Priceless! A jewel of a love story in a fascinating setting. *As You Desire* will turn its fortunate finders into avid Brockway keepers—and seekers!"
—Kathleen Eagle

"Erudite and witty, Connie Brockway's fast-paced humor delights and entertains. I loved it!"
—Pamela Morsi

A DANGEROUS MAN

"A winner! Everything readers want in a romance and more. She writes the kind of romance I love."
—Amanda Quick

"Connie Brockway's delightful characters and emotional story will surely captivate readers. Her refreshing, dynamic characters and the heartfelt emotions she portrays are what make *A Dangerous Man* special."
—*Romantic Times*

"Fresh, innovative, and instantly captivating."
—Catherine Anderson, author of *Annie's Song*

Dell Books by Connie Brockway

A DANGEROUS MAN

AS YOU DESIRE

ALL THROUGH THE NIGHT

MY DEAREST ENEMY

Connie Brockway

MY DEAREST ENEMY

A DELL BOOK

Published by
Dell Publishing
a division of
Bantam Doubleday Dell Publishing Group, Inc.
1540 Broadway
New York, New York 10036

ISBN: 0-440-22375-X

Printed in the United States of America

Published simultaneously in Canada

August 1998

10 9 8 7 6 5 4 3

OPM

Acknowledgments

As always, this book is the result of kind people taking an interest and helping me out with the facts and the fancy. Thank you, Chandra Tauer and Rachel Brockway for describing, in graphic detail, what it feels like to have an asthma attack. Thank you, Maggie Crawford, for editing and polishing. Your talents are much appreciated. Thank you, Damaris Rowland, my wonderful and wonderfully supportive agent. As always, my gratitude to the trolls for providing me fodder. And most of all, thank you, Jennifer Suarino, Lily's model—only infinitely prettier and twice as smart.

Chapter One

The news of Horatio Algernon Thorne's death came accompanied by a letter from him.

Avery James Thorne   March 1, 1887
Bloomsbury, London

Avery,

My physicians tell me I haven't long to live and that I should put my affairs in order. This I intend to do. By ensuring this letter arrives in your hand before the reading of my will I do you the favor of forewarning you of its contents. You may thank my sense of familial obligation for this courtesy, a sensibility with which you apparently have little experience.

You have probably assumed that upon my death and as your cousin Bernard's only living male relative you would become his guardian. You are mistaken and I will now tell you why.

First and foremost, you are too like your father. In spite

of my best efforts to correct your temperamental similarity to him, you have remained irresponsible as well as willful, and combative. These last two qualities may have stood you in good stead had you been robust and hearty, as I was in my youth, and might have made you a leader of men. But physically you are a poor specimen and no man willingly takes orders from a weakling.

I judge you would be a dangerous example to Bernard, particularly at this point in his life when he shows the same unfortunate inclination toward physical feebleness. Do not think I do not remember the many times you used your illness as an excuse to lie abed in the school's infirmary, or the letters you had your tutors write asking that you be released early from terms on account of your wretched weakness. You would be too likely to molly-coddle Bernard and as the heir to a great fortune he must overcome this tendency.

Thus, in your stead, I have appointed bank trustees whom I have known personally for many years to act as Bernard's guardian.

Now, as to you, Avery. As I have said, I am conscious of my familial duty. For the next five years you will receive a reasonable monthly allowance either from these same bank trustees or from one Miss Lillian Bede who, upon my death, has been offered the management of Mill House and who will, at the end of five years, inherit the estate should it demonstrably profit under her management. If she does not show a profit, you shall inherit.

Why I have made this proviso is no concern of yours. Mill House is mine to bestow as and where I see fit.

However, should you recall that I once suggested you might one day own the estate, I feel obliged as a gentleman to inform you that I have not forgotten that which you may have construed as a promise. I am still perfectly confident you still shall do so. Miss Bede is, after all, a nineteen-year-old female and if this pricks your manly pride, so much the better.

Consider your inheritance on hiatus while you, hopefully, become worthy of it. Not that I expect you shall spend much time regretting the loss of such a responsibility. Indeed, you are probably happy to be given this reprieve. You seem as indifferent toward your inheritance as you are toward your cousin.

At the end of five years you shall be appointed Bernard's legal guardian. In the interim I commend you from my grave to commit yourself to humility, thrift, and your family obligations.

Horatio Algernon Thorne

"And I commend you to a fiery hell." Avery pushed himself away from the battered desk occupying one wall of his rented apartments. His gaze traveled over the few mismatched furnishings that came with the let, other people's castoffs, endurable only because he'd known that someday he would have something of his own. Someday he would have Mill House.

Fifteen years ago, a week after an influenza epidemic had taken both his parents, he'd arrived in

Devon to meet his guardian, his uncle Horatio. He'd
been seven.

He remembered coming onto the shell drive from
the cypress-lined lane. He'd stuck his head out the
window, taken one look at the stone manor house
glowing like amber on a bed of summer green, and
fallen passionately in love.

Horatio, amused by Avery's wide-eyed infatuation
and as yet unacquainted with Avery's "intolerable
wheezing," had yielded to an uncharacteristic whim
and promised it to him. Well could Horatio afford
such munificence. Mill House meant nothing to Horatio; it was simply another house he owned that had
come with the acreage to a farm purchased by his father.

Even allowing for Avery's infrequent visits thereafter—two rare Christmas holidays, a few weeks during
one incomparable autumn—he'd held the image of
Mill House firmly in his mind's eye. And during those
lengthy convalescence periods that he'd spent in Harrow's infirmary, he'd fled his pain by mentally walking
Mill House's halls.

He'd waited for it most of his life. Like the most
devoted suitor he'd admired and wanted, never revealing the extent of his passion lest it be used against
him. And now that careful indifference would appear
to be his undoing. His house was being offered to
some nineteen-year-old suffragist!

His fingers closed tighter on the envelope and his
lips curled in a bitter smile. Long ago, as a matter of

survival, he'd developed a tough spirit to make up for his physical frailty. He'd become adept at taking it like a man, like the gentleman he'd determined to become. Whatever blows dealt him, both physical and emotional, whether from the fates, his guardian, or other lads, he'd accepted with fierce dignity and a biting quip. It had earned him the respect and admiration of the other lads, if no one else.

Indeed, he'd often pleaded with the schoolmasters not to write Horatio regarding any downward turn in his physical condition. He knew full well it would only disgust his guardian. Gauging from Horatio's letter, his wishes had not always been heeded.

All he'd ever owned had been a keen mind, his status as a gentleman, and the promise of a house. And now that was being "put on hiatus" while it went to this . . . Lillian Bede.

He was vaguely familiar with the name. He remembered seeing an artist's rendition of her in one of the newspapers. A tall, black-browed gypsy-looking girl, the darling of the suffragists.

How had this little baggage wormed her way into Horatio's good graces and why would she accept such an insane challenge? Certainly what Horatio had said was true: no slip of a girl could for five years manage an estate like Mill House. Not successfully.

Five years. Avery dropped his head against the back of the swivel chair. He spun slowly around in a circle, forcing himself to think, but no matter how he abjured himself to be calm, the anger continued to boil within him. *Five damn years.*

He was sick to death of taking it. Carefully, he ripped the letter into little pieces. Pride was a costly commodity but in this case it was the only commodity he owned. He opened his thin hand, watched the scraps flutter to the floor, and knew what he had to do.

The dark walnut door to the hushed innermost office of Gilchrist and Goode, Solicitors, banged open and Lily Bede burst unceremoniously from the interior. She held up the envelope in her hand. A thin layer of sweat coated her palms and bled from her fingertips into the thick vellum.

She looked around. No one followed her out into the anteroom, not the lovely widow, the spindly little boy, or the handsome, middle-aged daughter. Doubtless they were still sitting around the solicitors' table, mouths agape. Only one person affected by the terms of Horatio Algernon Thorne's will had been absent for its reading: Avery Thorne, the presumed heir to Mill House and, should she decide to accept the terms of this bizarre will, her . . . ward? Charge?

At the thought, Lily's legs began to tremble.

She spotted a small bench beneath an open window and lurched gratefully to it, sinking down on the hard surface. This morning she'd been searching for some way to pay the rent on her mean little attic room. This afternoon she was being offered a manor.

And what amounted to the guardianship of a grown man.

Her light-headedness returned. Who could have foreseen this? She'd met Horatio Thorne only once, three years ago, after her parents' untimely deaths. A tight-lipped, fierce-looking old man, he'd come, so he said, out of respect for his dear departed wife—her aunt—to offer Lily financial aid.

Penniless, Lily had swallowed her pride and used his money to go to one of the new women's colleges. Upon completing her education she'd discovered that a superior education did not necessarily translate into superior employment. In fact, she hadn't any employment at all. When she'd received the surprising request to attend the reading of Horatio's will, she'd been pitifully relieved.

She'd hoped for a small bequest; instead she'd been offered a tiger's tail. She looked down at the envelope she clutched. Why? She ripped it open and withdrew several sheets of paper.

Miss Bede,   *March 1, 1887*

As you know, I disapproved of my wife's brother-in-law, your father. He should have legalized his relationship with your mother by marrying her and thus legitimized you. Out of respect for my wife I attempted to alleviate this wrong by assisting you financially.

Imagine my shock and disappointment when I saw your name printed in a newspaper! The article—about this so-

called Women's Movement—quoted you lambasting the institution of "legalized slavery called marriage."

Considering your own situation, I would think that you, of all people, would support the sacred institution that protects women. As for your claim that women are capable of doing whatever a man does, only better—balderdash! Alas, I know full well the uselessness of preaching to young, headstrong people. So I will offer you instead a lesson through experience.

I offer you the chance to prove your claim by making Mill House a going concern. If, at the end of five years, you succeed you shall inherit it and all its assets. You will have achieved your ambition and can live completely independent of masculine influence. And you will have the redoubtable pleasure of proving a dead man wrong. But, should you fail, the house will go to my nephew, Avery Thorne.

Avery Thorne is currently as little capable of managing the estate as you, though he, at least ostensibly, possesses the masculine qualities necessary to do so. Unfortunately he has not yet demonstrated these qualities. Hence the two-fold nature of my proposition.

Avery is in need of self-discipline and humility. By making you responsible for his financial maintenance, I hope to provide the groundwork for both.

Of course, should you already see the error of your ways you may cry off. Avery will inherit Mill House and you, upon your public concession that a woman's place is in the home under the care of a man, shall be awarded a handsome yearly stipend. But, should your name ever again be *associated with those suffragist creatures, you will be imme-diately dispossessed.*

Respectfully,
Horatio Algernon Thorne

Lily crumpled the letter into a tight little ball, tak-ing savage delight in the process. The interfering, self-important . . . ! Her lips flattened, heat rose in her cheeks. How dare he make judgements about her fam-ily?

She may have been a bastard but her parents had at least sheltered her from pious snobs like Horatio Thorne. As for marriage—marriage was no guarantee of security, safety, or happiness. Marriage only guar-anteed that a woman was legal chattel, subject to the whims and brutality of a man. Even her children be-came his legal property. Why, her own brother and sister—she shied away from the hurtful thought, re-turning to the matter at hand.

She couldn't possibly accept Horatio's proposal. She was amazed the old fox had managed to make the conditions of such a will legal. Surely someone would contest it. Horatio's daughter? The widowed daugh-ter-in-law? Certainly this Avery Thorne.

But, she thought, her stomach once more coiling in apprehension and hope, if no one *did* contest it and she were to oversee the estate and do it successfully . . . The concept tantalized. She would not have to worry about when she would next eat, if she could pay the rent. Even more incredibly, she might meet people with the same ideas and convictions that she had. Perhaps she would even meet a soul mate, a man who would not take her heart and offer her slavery.

Her slight smile faded from her lips. She was being nonsensical. Of course someone would contest the will.

A shadow fell across the sheet of paper she clutched. The scent of lilacs filled her nostrils. She looked up.

Horatio's daughter-in-law, Evelyn Thorne, stood silently before her in the sunlight shining through the window. Her lightly clasped hands trembled. The sun washed the color from her skin and bleached her fair hair, giving her the appearance of a noontide specter, too timid to haunt the night.

"You'll want to collect your things," Evelyn said in her soft, hesitant voice. "You might send for the driver. That is, if you think that's right."

Lily gazed at her without understanding.

A tentative smile flickered over Evelyn's face. "You are going to come to Mill House, aren't you?" She paused. "It seems a waste to maintain two separate establishments."

Her friendliness when Lily had expected only resentment was irresistible. She returned Evelyn's smile with a rueful one of her own. "No one could possibly call my rented room an 'establishment,' Mrs. Thorne."

Evelyn's cheeks grew pink.

"Forgive me," Lily said, rising to her feet. She stood a head taller than Evelyn and now, this close, one could discern the finest net of lines at the corners of her lovely gray eyes, a delicate crepe on her slender neck. She was older than Lily had first surmised, nearer thirty-five than twenty-five.

Lily stuffed the letter into her skirt pocket. "I have been set up for failure, Mrs. Thorne. I can't possibly fulfill the terms of your father-in-law's will. I have no idea how to begin handling an estate."

"I understand," Evelyn concurred. "I would not dream of interfering but should I hazard a guess, I would assume Mill House must have certain systems in place to keep it running." She swallowed.

Lily studied Evelyn thoughtfully. She was right. Presumably, the operations at Mill House hadn't come grinding to a halt since Horatio's death. If she just had the time to figure out how things worked . . .

"But what about Mr. Thorne's daughter? She looks a formidable sort of woman. Won't she resent a stranger's coming into her home and taking over the management, especially someone as inexperienced as I?"

"Francesca?" Evelyn's eyes widened. "She's never used it as more than a temporary home. I assure you, Francesca doesn't care who lives in the house or handles the estate. Besides, Horatio has provided her, as well as my son and I, with ample means."

"Well, there's still the matter of Mr. Avery

Thorne," Lily said. "Mill House could be his. He will doubtless contest the will." She warmed to her subject. "He'll only need to appear in court to have the judicial system deem him right, regardless of the issue, by virtue of his gender alone. He—"

"He has left for Africa, Miss Bede," Evelyn cut in gently. "This past Friday."

"What?"

"We had a letter from him. He intends to spend the next five years traveling."

"Traveling," Lily echoed dumbly.

"Yes. He . . . he stated his, um, disappointment with the terms of the will and his confidence that he shall assume ownership of Mill House upon his return five years hence."

Evelyn held a hand out. "At least Avery won't be contesting the will if he's not in England. So, until we discover his plans, won't you be more comfortable at home?"

"Home?" Lily said. She could not believe Avery Thorne had relinquished his claim on Mill House without a fight. Perhaps the house meant nothing to him. Perhaps he did not need a home as desperately as she did.

Evelyn flushed and her lashes fluttered. "I—we'll vacate the premises of course. As soon as you wish."

"No!" Lily said in shock. "Please. Even if I were inclined to accept the will's terms, I could never do so knowing that my windfall had resulted in your eviction."

"Oh, we can take up residence at the town house. It's very . . . fashionable. Quite grand."

"But it isn't your *home*," Lily insisted.

"Well, I could no longer live at Mill House knowing that in doing so we'd kept you from accepting it." There was a stubborn smoothness to Evelyn's clear brow. "I suppose . . ." Evelyn flashed her an anxious glance. "That is perhaps, if we helped with the expenses, we might . . ."

"Yes?" Lily prodded.

"We might *all* live there?"

Lily stared.

"At home," Evelyn clarified.

Home. The word swept through Lily with a tidal wave of longing. She'd never had a home, just rented garrets, lofts in the city, and borrowed cottages.

She considered her options. She could receive a princely stipend for as many years as she could keep silent on a subject about which she had decidedly strong opinions or she could take a chance.

"Yes," she said faintly. "I believe we could. But first I have some affairs to settle. I will come to Mill House by week's end."

She would never have been able to keep quiet anyway.

Chapter Two

"Almost there, Miss Bede," the driver said with a wink before turning his attention back to his horse.

Lily told herself not to gape. After all, she'd been in manor houses before. Several of her father's friends maintained fabulous estates. But, she thought with a wide grin, she'd never seen a manor that could some-day be hers.

The hack came round the cypress alley into the drive and she forgot her self-admonition. She gaped.

Mill House was lovely. Only a hundred years old, it had been built of a locally quarried buff stone. The hand-hewn blocks glowed the color of clover honey in the warm mid-morning light. Tall windows were set in the south-facing front facade, their regimented sym-metry flanking a simple, raised entry, their gleaming glass throwing back a rare reflection of flawless blue sky.

True to its rural origins, no trees or gardens crowded the house. Only a single ancient cypress towered behind one corner. Lacing through a green field dotted with lady's mantle and cowslip, a small, lively river flowed beneath steep, mossy banks. Beyond that, Lily could make out a plowman harrowing a field. She closed her eyes, inhaling deeply. The rich odor of the freshly turned loam scented the air. Exquisite.

The driver drew the carriage to a halt, sprang from his seat, and came round to hand her down. As if on cue, the door opened and a severely dressed middle-aged man appeared at the top of the stairs. His face was country homely, the features bunched closely together in the center of his face, his gray hair a thicket of wiry brush.

In the dim hall behind him a seemingly endless row of people assembled: young, old, mostly women, a few young lads, some in aprons, others in rough garb. Servants.

Her parents had never employed more than a daily.

Lily mounted the exterior steps and the older man hastened forward. "Allow me to introduce myself. I'm Jacob Flowers, Miss Bede."

"And what is your position, Mr. Flowers?"

"I am the butler. I oversee the indoor staff, miss," he said. He waved his hand toward the line of people. "This staff. May I present them?"

Aware of countless eyes fastened on her, Lily could only nod. Mr. Flowers ushered her ahead of him. He fired off names as they passed servants who fell into bows and curtsies like tin rabbits being hit by pellets at a country fair shooting gallery.

By the time they'd reached the last kitchen girl—an apple-cheeked lass with a suspiciously taut apron—Lily's head was spinning.

"How many?" she asked.

"Twenty-nine, Miss Bede," Mr. Flowers announced proudly, "and that don't count the outdoor staff."

" 'Course"—his eye fell like a scepter on the pregnant maid—"we'll soon be twenty-eight."

"So many people to care for one building?" she asked. "What do they all do?" Rough hands, daubs of charcoal, and the smell of strong lye told the tale of the women's employment easily enough, but Lily wondered about the six tall, immaculately groomed young men in white gloves. "What do *they* do?"

"Carry silver trays and fetch packages from town." At Lily's still puzzled expression, Mr. Flowers added, "Serve at dinner parties, hold carriage horses, lower the hall chandelier. And raise it, of course."

"Of course," she murmured. She looked back down the line. Every face was turned toward her, some shuttered, some curious, a few with that daunting look of familiarity, the one that so clearly stated, "You aren't my better, gypsy get, you aren't even my equal."

Her heartbeat began a frightened race. She scoured her mind for something to say.

"In the weeks to come," she began, her voice quavering, "things shall change at Mill House. Those whose work I consider superfluous will be let go, of course, with letters of recommendation."

"What you mean 'superfluous?' " a voice asked.

"I mean those whose skills are unnecessary in the simple day-to-day running of this estate."

"Don't worry, Peg. There'll always be a call for your particular skills, lass," a male voice called out followed by a spat of laughter. Lily's gaze settled on a brash-looking lad.

"Leave," she said.

"What? You can't—"

"I can. You are no longer in my employ."

For a long minute she and he stared each other into the ground. Thank God, her skirts hid the shaking of her legs. Finally, with a choked oath, the lad broke line and stomped through the still-open front door. The rest regarded his departing back with open-mouthed incredulity.

"Henceforth in this house, *my* house, every woman's work shall be valued and a tweenie will be treated as respectfully as a chef."

"Here now, let's not get carried away," the small white-haired cook with the unlikely name of Mrs. Kettle muttered.

"I want Mill House to be a success, not only for my sake, but for the sake of all women. For if a woman like me, without name, station or birth, can through her own perseverance and hard work win an estate the likes of Mill House, what is within your grasp?

"I tell you plainly, I need your help. I cannot do this alone. If you are not up to the task, if you cannot give me your unswerving loyalty, there is no place for you here."

"I'll stand by you, miss!" the pregnant maid said in a quavering voice.

"Good!" said Lily. "The rest of you, think of what I've said. Consider your future and by week's end we will see where we stand. You're all dismissed."

As one the ranks broke. The servants milled past, disappearing down halls, through doors, and up stairways, leaving Lily alone with Mr. Flowers.

"I don't approve, miss," he said, scowling fiercely. "I feel obligated to tell you I don't approve them communist tactics in my household."

Lily met the man's eye squarely. She drew a deep breath. "It isn't your household, Mr. Flowers, it's mine. But seeing how you disapprove of me and my . . . tactics, I feel sure you will be only too happy to know that I will not be requiring the services of a butler."

"Wha—?"

"You're dismissed, Mr. Flowers."

For a second she thought he would argue, but he only sputtered, turned, and stomped away.

She closed her eyes, stunned by her audacity. Her knees felt watery with relief.

"I say, you'd have my vote," a throaty female voice spoke close beside her. "That is, if I had one."

Heat consumed Lily. She opened her eyes to find Horatio's middle-aged spinster daughter, Francesca, standing beside her.

No one could have looked less like a spinster. Her ash blond hair curled above her pale, drowsy eyes and

teased the corners of lips too uniformly rose pink to
be natural. She didn't dress like a spinster, either. Her
peacock blue taffeta gown whispered sensuously as she
moved closer.

"I'm Francesca Thorne," she said. "I'm sorry Evie
isn't here to greet you. She was called down to Eton
yesterday. Bernard is unwell—no need for concern, he
has bad lungs and occasionally is taken with these attacks. He'll be fine as long as he stays calm. Evie, in
case you hadn't noticed, is excessively calming."

Lily nodded.

"She asked me to give you a proper greeting,"
Francesca said. "Greetings, Miss Bede." Her three-
point smile tipped mockingly.

"Miss Thorne, I'm sorry if I appear precipitate—"

"Call me Francesca," she said. "I admit I was all set
to go off to Paris but after that performance—" Again
that mysterious smile. "Well, I think I'll just stay on a
while. That's allowable, isn't it?"

"Of course." Lily cast a troubled look at Francesca's elaborate coiffure and expensive gown.

"You mustn't worry about me and my little staff,
Miss Bede," Francesca said, catching the direction of
her glance. "Father would have liked to think I was
entirely dependent on him for my income. Suffice to
say that Father was wrong." She shrugged. "Evelyn is
another matter. After her husband's death, Evelyn
packed up Bernard and a few belongings and decamped. She landed here and here she's since lived. Of
course, you can always send her packing."

Lily, genuinely shocked, pulled away from the older woman. "I wouldn't do that!"

"Why not?" Francesca asked. "Men do it all the time."

"Just another reason in a fistful of reasons why women are better off without them."

"Pray, dear God, remember," Francesca's hand flew to her chest as her eyes rose heavenward, "*she* said it, not *I*! Any celestial reckoning should exclude me. Come, Miss Bede, I've ordered tea in my room upstairs. This way, please."

Lily trailed behind Francesca, her avid gaze taking in the house's lovely accoutrements: an oriental runner, a malachite inlaid table, a priceless Sevres vase overflowing with shaggy bronze chrysanthemums. In spite of Francesca's provocations, things were going better than she'd anticipated. She'd met nearly everyone affected by Horatio Thorne's will and none of them seemed likely to cause trouble except—

"Except for Avery Thorne," she murmured. She'd spent a great deal of time thinking about the would-be heir to Mill House. Unpleasant thoughts, as his name always brought a tincture of guilt with it. And guilt, she'd discovered, often was trailed by suspicion. "He's up to something. I know it."

"I didn't hear you, Miss Bede," Francesca said.

"I believe Avery Thorne is attempting to preempt my bid for Mill House." Curse her penchant for speaking her thoughts aloud.

Francesca, however, didn't appear offended. "And what makes you think that?"

Lily considered prevaricating but then, this woman might provide some insight into Avery Thorne. "His desire to see not simply the world, but the most inaccessible part of the world," she said. "I believe that by putting himself beyond my reach Avery Thorne is attempting to make me lose Mill House."

Francesca looked baffled. "But how?"

"By making it appear that I am negligent in my duty to provide him an adequate living during the tenure of my guardianship. By making it impossible to deliver to him the allowance I am compelled, by the terms of this will, to provide." Lily folded her hands primly at her waist, her smile grim. "He shan't be successful. My parents had friends throughout the world. I assure you, if Avery Thorne is within a day's march of one, he'll get his allowance."

"I think you're mistaken." Francesca sounded sincere. "Avery is not the type to bother with plots."

She sighed, her expression fond if rueful. "He would never do anything underhanded. For whatever unaccountable reasons, Avery has always labored under the delusion that he is the quintessential gentleman. He's not. He's had scant experience with polite society and it shows, sometimes to a lamentable degree. Indeed, his 'gentlemanliness' is a matter of honor not etiquette—though he'd be the first to argue that point."

"He is a man, Miss Thorne, and as a man," Lily

instructed, "he is capable of anything when it comes to getting his way."

Francesca turned her hands up, defeated, as Lily knew she must be, by the weight of such unassailable logic.

"Forgive me, Miss Thorne," Lily hurriedly said, "for speaking so insensitively about your home. I realize it must be difficult to see it 'put up for grabs' as it were and I think you're being splendidly gracious about it."

Francesca swung around. "Oh, dear, no. It isn't and never has been my home. Nor Evie's, really. As I said, she's lived here only since her husband Gerald died."

"I'm sorry."

"You'd be the only one." Francesca hooked her arm through Lily's and led her up a curving staircase. "My dear brother spent years trying to get poor Evie with child—a male child. Upon hearing he'd succeeded, old Ger promptly drank himself into a standing stupor, insisted that his stallion be saddled—because a man who has just produced a son can hardly ride a gelding, can he?—and rode off to inform the neighborhood. He broke his neck before his son's first wails had died away."

"But that's tragic," Lily exclaimed.

"Gerald was a great bullying monster. Evie is still recovering from her marriage to him. You might as well hear it from me rather than the servants. Oh, dear. I've shocked you, haven't I?"

"Not really," Lily answered.

She'd heard the same story countless times before. Women seldom sought divorce on the grounds of abuse. Proof of such rarely fell short of physical disfigurement. And few women took the option of leaving their spouses, since it often meant leaving their children as well. As her mother had left her children.

She forced her chin up. It had been a long while since she'd thought of her half-brother and sister.

Francesca glanced at her curiously but Lily forbade comment. They'd reached the top of the stairs and arrived on a landing with halls shooting off from either end.

"Here begins the grand tour," Francesca said and then began in a false, clipped accent. "Mill House has twenty-two rooms. Or maybe more. Perhaps fewer. I've never counted them. I do know, however, that there are eight bedrooms. I'm sure that at one time or another I've slept in them all." Her glance was purposefully suggestive.

Lily returned her look complacently. Despite her mother's diligent shielding, she'd still been raised amidst a very loose society. Francesca would have to do better than that if she wished to shock her. "Then perhaps you might advise me on which has the best mattress?"

Francesca's startled glance turned abruptly into a burst of laughter. "Yes, I shall definitely have to stay."

Francesca ushered her through an arched doorway into a small gallery. A number of portraits faced the windows, a distinct family resemblance declared itself in intense, improbably blue-green eyes and sensualist's lips.

They stopped before a recent oil of an adolescent male built like a scarecrow. He had the Thorne eyes and the Thorne lips and a large nose with what looked like a break to it. The artist had chosen—in Lily's opinion unwisely—to position him in an aristocratic pose, one large-boned hand on his hip and one leg forward. Unfortunately, it only accented his spindly calves and knobby wrists.

"Who is that?" Lily asked.

"*That* is the only Thorne who really has any attachment to Mill House. *That* is Avery Thorne."

That skinny, large-nosed, *boy* was Avery Thorne? *That* was the other contender for Mill House?

"This was painted five years ago," Francesca went on, "when he was seventeen. I haven't seen him for a few years now, but I have been told he's filled out."

"That's nice. Is he very . . . bright? I mean he looks a sullen sort of weed—" She broke off abruptly, blushing profusely.

"Here now," Francesca chuckled, "that's my darling cousin you're speaking about. But, to answer your question, yes, if the infrequent letters he wrote my father were any indication, he is bright. Decidedly bright."

Lily studied the portrait warily. The boy's nose had probably been broken being thrust where it had no business. His eyes were too deep-set . . . hooded. His mouth was sneering.

The thought intruded that perhaps she was being harsh on Avery Thorne for no other reason than she fully intended to beat him out of part of his inheritance. She dislodged it. Being a man, he'd have any number of opportunities to secure his future. She had one. *This one.*

Chapter Three

Avery picked up his pace, swatting at the mosquitoes draining blood from the back of his neck. This deep into the interior, the damn things grew as big as songbirds. He withdrew the gnawed stub of his cigar from between his teeth and blew a thick bluish cloud, hoping to discourage the less committed bloodsuckers.

As Avery entered the camp, his former college classmate, Karl Dhurmann, looked up from where he stirred a noxious-smelling stew. Propped against the trunk of a mahogany tree sat John Neigl, the American leader of their expedition. In spite of the heat, he was wrapped in blankets, the trembling in his body pronounced, his eyes half-closed.

He'd contracted malaria six weeks ago. The sunken-cheeked apparition he was now mocked any resemblance to the burly young man who'd led them so confidently forth. Luckily, they were only ten miles from Stanleyville, where Avery had spent the day booking John's passage back to Europe.

"How goes it, old man?" Avery asked.

"Simply grand," John said around his chattering teeth. "Did you get things arranged? Am I to go home?"

"Yes," Avery said. "You're going home." Noting the tension draining from John's taut face, Avery wondered for one moment where he would have been shipped had he been the one to succumb to malaria. Certainly no home awaited him, no haven where he had the right to be and where he would always find welcome. Not yet.

"That's not all I got." Avery withdrew a parcel from his pocket. "*I* have a package from England."

"From whom?" John asked and Avery was gratified to see a spark of interest in his dulled eyes.

In answer Avery tore open the wrapping. An envelope fell out, his name scrawled in a decisive hand upon its surface. On the back was written the name "Lillian Bede, Mill House, Devon, England."

"It's from that woman," he said.

"What woman?" Karl asked, his interest engaged. "You don't know any women. You're not a woman's sort of chap. Never were. Unless you were leading a secret double life during college, one as frail cantankerous scholar and the other as a debonair ladykiller."

"Wouldn't surprise me," John murmured. "Old Avery's some sort of damned human chameleon." His face gleamed in the camp light with oily perspiration.

"This Godawful journey doesn't seem to have done *him* any harm. I hate to have to remind you both, but *I* am supposed to be the vigorous, hirsute leader of this expedition. Avery's role was to have been the consumptive, albeit witty, chronicler."

Avery shrugged uncomfortably. There was no mistaking the bittersweet flavor of truth. Avery hadn't anticipated taking to such a dangerous existence. He'd certainly never expected to flourish in it.

"I'm sure the proper order of things will be restored once you're back on your feet, John." Uncomfortable with the turn of conversation, Avery held up the letter. "What I'd like to know is how in the bloody hell she managed to get this delivered out here?"

"Women have ways," Karl said mysteriously. He scraped the last of the tinned beef into the blackened pot with his knife and then wiped the blade clean on his tongue.

"Don't they teach simple table etiquette where you come from?" John asked petulantly.

Karl's only answer was the clicking of his pocket watch lid as he flicked it open and shut. He'd once told Avery that it reminded him that no hour was promised, no tomorrow assured. And that name and family and home, all a man owned, all a man held dear, could all vanish in minutes.

A civil war had resulted in the dissolution of Karl's country—and that of his entire aristocratic family.

As if he had read his thoughts and would not suffer

his pity, Karl said without looking up, "Why don't you read the damn letter."

Avery sliced open the envelope, puffed into the opening, and upended the packet. Eighteen ten-pound bills fluttered to the muddy ground. "What the bloody hell?"

"Perhaps the letter might explain," John suggested.

"Right," Avery said and read aloud, " *'Mr. Thorne, I have been assured that any persons traveling through the Congo will eventually come to a place called Stanleyville and that this letter shall there find your hand.*

" *'Perhaps, in the future, you would like to inform me of where I might send my correspondence? I am sure you will not have realized that should I fail to furnish you an adequate allowance I shall have broken the terms of my guardianship of you, thereby possibly endangering my own anticipated inheritance?'* "

How dare the chit question his honor? Avery thought incredulously. She was actually baiting him! Clearly she thought she could win this preposterous challenge that Horatio had forced her—forced all of them—into.

" *'Indeed,'* " he read on, " *'I am sure your continued inaccessibility is mere happenstance and not a concentrated effort to put yourself beyond my reach.'* "

"Why the suspicious, low-minded . . . female!" Avery burst out, winning a startled look from Karl. "Listen to this. *'Still, one can't be too careful when dealing with men.'* "

"*Men?*" His brows climbed. "I am a *gentleman*. Though I daresay Miss Bede—consorting with those suffragists as she does—will have had such scant traffic with gentlemen she might be incapable of recognizing one."

Karl stared at him with a bemused expression. "What a marvelous imagination," he muttered.

"I won't even attempt to recognize to whom or what you're referring."

"Good," Karl said. "Now about this letter . . ." he trailed off invitingly.

Avery read on.

" '*I shall deliver into your hands your quarterly allowance. Now, to business: I have looked over the bills you left outstanding upon your flight from London—*'

" 'Flight from London!' The insufferable chit makes it sound as if I were running away in the most nefarious manner imaginable."

A wheezing laugh erupted from John's throat. "I swear, I can't remember being so well entertained. A woman who can match your lethal sarcasm."

Avery chose to ignore this. After all, the man was ill. He turned the sheet over. " '*I have looked over the bills you left outstanding upon your flight from London and paid them. It is doubtless my plebian antecedents which have me drawing faint breath over settling an account of 50 pounds for a* <u>hunting jacket.</u> *Pray, sir, satisfy my curiosity. Could you not hunt in, say, a simple jacket? Or would the fox take exception?*

" '*Needless to say, I shall not be paying such bills again. I have decided to allot you a quarterly allowance of 180 pounds. Here then, is your first installment.*

" 'Should you find this is inadequate to meet your needs, I suggest you learn to need less.*

" 'Cordially yours,*

" 'Lillian Bede*

" 'Post script: You are welcome at Mill House for Christmas. Your trip to Africa has quite captured your cousin Bernard's imagination.' "

"What a wonderful woman," Karl declared. "I swear I shall propose as soon as I return to England."

Avery lifted an eyebrow in his friend's direction. "Nonsense. She's not your type at all."

"How would you know?" Karl scoffed.

"Because you, Karl, like any man of discernment, admire soft, feminine women and she's not. I saw an illustration of her in one of the wretched socialist rags. At best she's a scrawny, hollow-eyed croneling."

"Croneling?" John tilted his head in perplexity.

"Croneling. Noun. One who has yet to achieve cronehood. The adolescent phase of the British crone," Avery lectured.

"But the papers may have made her look ugly on purpose," John protested. Avery watched the renewed animation on his two friends' faces and offered a silent word of thanks to Lily Bede.

"John, old man, a beautiful woman can have anything she desires simply because of the symmetrical arrangement of her features, the chance of pigmentation of her eye, the shape of the pore which molds the texture of her hair. If she's a smart woman then she need only add to what nature bequeathed her by training her mouth to form more smiles than frowns. Having done this she can assure herself a life of being petted and cosseted and indulged."

"What is your point?" Karl asked.

"My point," Avery said, "is that as her letter attests, Miss Bede is an intelligent woman, if an annoying one. Therefore if she had even a modicum of good looks she would by now have used them to get herself wed."

John did not look convinced. "But perhaps the illustrator made her ugly because he did not like her politics."

"Yes. Her politics. Which only supports my theory regarding her lack of looks. Ask yourselves this, gentlemen," he said, his kind smile declaring his patience with his friends' obtuseness. "Have you ever seen a *good-looking* suffragist?"

Devon, England
August 1888

"Olly olly oxen free!" Lily leapt into the air, tucked her arms around her knees and landed in the center of the mill pond, making an enormous and enormously satisfying splash. She came up laughing, shaking her head, sending showers of diadem sparked water flying across the rippling surface of the pool.

From the edge of the bank, Bernard stared down at her in fascination.

"Your turn, old chum!" Lily called, lifting her arm and waving the boy on.

"Maybe I should wait until I swim better," Bernard said dubiously.

Lily scrunched up her nose. "You swim beautifully right now."

The boy's sallow face flushed with pleasure and Lily was glad of the inspiration that had led her to—not exactly sneak—but rather circumnavigate Evelyn's too intent supervision for these occasional swimming lessons.

Being the child of two nonconformists had its boons, Lily thought, floating on her back and waiting for Bernard to scramble down the bank. Swimming was one of them.

A moment later she heard Bernard making his entrance into the water. A gulp, a gasp—she waited. Her heartbeat jumped slightly, until she heard his breathing, even and unimpaired by the dreadful wheezing that sometimes tormented him.

"Do you really think I swim beautifully?" he asked shyly, dog-paddling to her side.

"Wonderfully," Lily avowed, flipping over and treading the water so that her chin bobbed in and out. "I doubt any one of the other boys at school can swim half so well. If they can swim at all." She grinned impishly. "It isn't exactly a pastime one associates with gentlemen."

"Well, *I* like it," Bernard declared. "And I am a gentleman . . . aren't I?"

"Decidedly."

Her confirmation brought a flood of relief to his worried-looking face.

"Is it so important to be a gentleman, Bernard?" she asked gently.

Her question brought an expression of shock to his narrow, pinched little face. "Of course. I am a Thorne. It's my heritage. It's—it's English. Without gentlemen the world would be an uncivilized place."

"Who says?" Lily teased.

But Bernard wasn't about to be teased about something so important. "Avery Thorne."

"Hmph." She should have known. Avery Thorne. Idol to small boys and tabloid readers across the nation.

"Is something wrong?" Bernard, ever sensitive to the emotions of those around him, was once more looking worried.

How she hated that expression on his ten-year-old face. If she had her way, it would not make another appearance this afternoon. Today they would both play hooky, she from all the cares and responsibilities of running an estate, and he from those of becoming a gentleman.

"Nope," she said.

The sun was warm on her face as she lay back to float in the cool water, her hair streaming around her like black silk. She grinned again and Bernard caught the infectious pleasure she felt in this simple activity. He smiled back.

"Want to learn how to dive?"

Lily, standing beside Francesca and Evelyn at the top step leading down to the drive, tapped the envelope she held against her chin. Below a lorry driver and the head gardener, Hob, man-handled a huge wooden box from the wagon's bed.

"Is that another letter from one of your former maids?" Francesca asked, glancing incuriously at the lorry. "However do you manage to pawn off all these girls as widows with infant children on unsuspecting households? Does no one think it odd that you've employed no less than twelve recently bereaved widows in the last two years?"

Lily didn't answer, paying only partial attention. They'd had this conversation before. Primarily young, unmarried pregnant women staffed Mill House.

Along with room, board, and a small salary, after the girls' babies were born Lily wrote them sterling letters of recommendation, gave them a nice bonus, and if necessary, manufactured replicant marriage licenses. She then shipped them off to various remote households that were in pressing need of servants. It was an entirely satisfactory arrangement all around. She wasn't sure why it so amused Francesca.

"Whatever do you think it can be?" Evelyn whispered, gesturing at the crate.

Lily glanced around, noting as she did an ivy vine

above the front door. She'd have to snip it. Her gaze traveled with fierce, proprietal pride over the rest of Mill House. The pink granite steps sparkled, the brass doorplate gleamed, the rich wooden patina of the door shone.

"Maybe it is some sort of bomb Lily's suffragist friends want stored," Francesca offered. "I swear I wouldn't put it past that Polly Makepeace."

Lily speared Francesca with a look of mild reproof. Polly Makepeace may not have the most agreeable personality but her commitment to various important women's causes was unquestionable.

"Did that letter come with it?" Evelyn asked.

Lily nodded.

"Well, why don't you read it?" Francesca suggested.

"It's not addressed to me. It's to Bernard," Lily said, unable to hide the frustration this fact engendered.

"Bernard," Francesca said, "went back to school last week. I'm sure he'd want us to read whatever direction comes with whatever this is so that whatever it is might be properly cared for."

"Yes," Evelyn agreed. "I believe Bernard would."

"Really?" Lily asked. The two women nodded vigorously. "Well, if you're sure I couldn't be accused of prying—"

"Oh, no!" Evelyn protested.

"You, Lily?" Francesca asked, her eyes wide with feigned shock. "Never."

Lily decided to be mollified. She opened the envelope and pulled out the sheet inside. "It's from *him*," she said with flat triumph.

No further explanation was necessary. Evelyn pursed her lips in the approved expression of censure and Francesca grinned.

Lily cleared her throat. "He begins, *'March 14, 1888. Dear Cousin and whoever else might chance to read this letter.'*" Lily snorted derisively. "*'I hope you enjoy Billy, as man-hating, crusty an aberration of nature ever to lurk upon earth. Billy here is actually a female. Please inform your dear guardian that any chance resemblance between old Billy here and, well, whomever is unintentional. Even the name 'Billy,' so similar in cadence to her name, is merely a curious coincidence.'*"

"Why are you snickering, Lily?" Evelyn asked in an affronted voice. "The blackguard is twitting you."

"I know," Lily said, finally giving vent to her laughter. "He is so *utterly* impossible. And obvious!"

"Read on," Francesca urged.

"*'So I really think it best that in the interests of chivalry we fellows switch Billy's gender since Billy is beyond caring. Billy here was terrorizing a village when he/she/it succumbed to a shot from my Ruger .44. A shot, I might modestly add, which has resulted in the local tribesmen declaring me a god.'* Ha!" Lily broke out.

"Lily, *please*," Francesca pleaded.

"Oh, all right." She continued. "*'It is quite nice being a god, Cousin. I suggest you try it someday, though I must point out that an elevation to god status is unlikely in your present circumstances. But be brave, Bernard, I assure you there are households in America and Africa and even Britain where a man still rules his fate.'* The smug, officious—"

"Here," Francesca said in exasperation, "let me finish it." She plucked the letter from Lily's hand, quickly scanning the sheet to find the place where Lily had left off. " *'Still, godhood has its drawbacks, one being that I'm promised to these fellows for the nonce. They want me to come on their annual pilgrimage to find their totem animal.*

" *'Unfortunately this means yet another year in which I will be unable to return to England. Perhaps next Christmas. In the meantime, you are in my thoughts and plans.*

" *'Give my regards to your mother, your aunt Francesca, and of course, She Who Must Be Obeyed.'* He closes, *'Your cousin, Avery Thorne.'* " Francesca folded the letter shut.

"What do you suppose 'Billy' *is*?" Evelyn's eyes riveted on the crate the two men were trying to open.

"Who knows? I just wish Mr. Thorne would stop gifting Bernard with mementos of his 'Fabulous Adventures,' " Lily said, aware she sounded petulant. "The place is getting full up with all his nonsense: Maori headdresses, fertility statues, animal corpses—"

"Careful, Lily," Francesca advised. "You sound jealous."

"I am," Lily admitted calmly. "Who wouldn't be jealous of someone who gets to muck about the world, writing stories, selling them to journals, and making pots of money for indulging his childish whims?"

Francesca shrugged noncommittally. She'd just returned from three months in Paris indulging whims of her own.

"*I'm* not jealous," Evelyn said. "I'm happy just as I am. I thought you were, too, Lily."

"I am," Lily said. "But I thought the purpose of Horatio Thorne's will was to impose five years of frugal, staid living on his nephew. Well, we've only three more years to go and I have yet to see any evidence that Mr. Thorne has been rehabilitated.

"If anything he seems to grow more irresponsible with each month. Why, he's risked his life any number of times in the past year—*if* the accounts he writes are any indication, which, of course, they aren't. How can anyone believe that an—an attenuated scarecrow is capable of all that feverish athleticism? Has the press ever run a picture of him? No. Of course not. It would rob Mr. Thorne's boasts of their credibility, wouldn't it, Evie?"

The young widow nodded obligingly.

"See, Francesca? Evelyn agrees with me."

"Evelyn always agrees with you," Francesca said in a bored voice, her attention diverted by the sight of the lorry driver rolling his sleeves up over brawny forearms. "I think his stories are very exciting."

"Nuthin' for it, Miss Lily," Hob said, wiping his forehead with the back of his hand. "She's sealed tight as a clam. I'll have to go see Drummond about getting some men to help us."

"Drat," said Lily. She hated the thought of asking the farm manager for anything. Drummond was a confirmed woman-hater. Unfortunately, he was also the best farm manager in the county.

"That would be a shame," Francesca said.

Upon hearing Francesca's sigh of disappointment, the lorry driver's head snapped up. His expression set into one of fierce, ruddy concentration and in a fit of masculine bravura he leapt atop the crate. Like a Neanderthal spearing a wooly mammoth, he began stabbing his crowbar into the crate, splintering the wood. Francesca laughed, the lorry driver heaved, and the front popped out, falling to the ground with a crash.

Yes, thought Lily with a tinge of admiration, *whatever else one said, one had to admit Francesca had a way with men*. Waving her hand in front of her face to clear away the dust, Lily descended the stairs and squinted inside.

"What is it?" Evelyn asked.

Lily gave the monstrous creature eyeing her with baleful glass eyes a considering glance. "I should say crocodile. Twelve feet if it's an inch." She gave a deep sigh. "Best put it next to the Cape Buffalo, Hob."

Chapter Four

" '*Dear Thorne.*' Do I detect a chill note in this salutation or am I being unduly sensitive?" Avery asked, removing the cigar from his mouth and looking at his audience: Karl, John, newly returned from eight months of convalescence, and a new companion they'd picked up in Turkey, Omar Salimann.

Karl and John gestured impatiently for him to continue, their faces striped in light cast by the torches jutting from the hotel's balcony walls. Below, a jumble of ghostly pale *feluccas*, *dahabiyas*, and *zeheri* crowded Alexandria's harbor.

" '*Dear Thorne, Here is your money.*' Definitely a chill. All right, all right. I'm reading. Though why this woman's tart epistles should interest you remains a mystery."

A patent lie, Avery allowed silently, tapping the ash from the cigar. He knew why. Not only did Lily Bede always manage to find him no matter what corner of the globe he landed in but she'd turned their correspondence into a sort of literary boxing match, one in which she occasionally appeared to be ahead in points.

Even Avery allowed that their comminuqués had become interesting and even—in a limited fashion, of course—important to him. Of course when a man went months without feminine contact, any trace of womanly interest, even one as questionable as Lily Bede's, was bound to be welcome.

"Stop staring at the letter, Thorne, unless Miss Bede has made some particularly salient sally?"

"No," Avery answered. "And you needn't sound so hopeful, John." He tilted the letter back into the glow of the torchlight and continued. " *'Once again Bernard insisted that I read your letter—and open your newest shipment—before sending it (the letter, Thorne, not the shipment) on to him. Please, Thorne, you needn't continue populating Mill House with the pathetic remnants of your supposedly death-defying encounters.*

" *'Your latest offering now resides along with the Cape Buffalo and—what was your charming appellation for that poor mangy feline? Oh, yes.—The Death Ghost of Nepal.*

" *'Do attempt to restrain your literary enthusiasm, Thorne. Poor Bernard took your tale of being mauled by this animal quite seriously.'* Fancy"—Avery involuntarily rolled his arm in its socket—"so did my shoulder."

"She does not believe that the tiger mauled you?" Omar finally spoke up from where he'd been silently sitting. "How does a mere female doubt the great Avery Thorne?"

Avery gave Omar a beatific smile. Omar had joined their group for the express purpose of traveling with "one of the world's greatest explorers."

"How indeed?" Avery queried and read on before Karl could interject any comment. " '*In the unlikely case there is a shred of truth in the tiger story, I feel that on Bernard's behalf I must advise you not to risk your life foolishly. As if there are sensible ways to risk one's life. Only to a man could one make such a statement with a straight face.*' "

"Ouch," said John. "That one smarted."

"Ha!" Avery declared. "That's just a cuff. Listen to this next. '*In case you have utterly lost track of time, being lost in that perennial state of adolescent wanderlust in which you function,*'—Shut up, Karl. Your snorting is distracting—'*I believe you ought to begin considering your impending responsibilities. I am not speaking of Mill House which I anticipate shall soon be no concern of yours.*' "

"She can't be serious," Karl said.

But she was, the irksome female. Avery clamped his cigar firmly between his teeth. Her obsession to obtain Mill House was getting out of hand and could only lead to her severe disappointment. He did not like to think of Lily Bede desolate—he owed her something for the years of entertainment she'd provided.

He'd begun to suspect she wanted Mill House as badly as he did. Which was too damn bad. Mill House was his, promised to him since childhood. *His*.

"You know," Karl said, watching Avery with a troubled expression, "it wouldn't be entirely disastrous if Miss Bede won Mill House. I can't imagine you'd like having to assume responsibility for—what do you call her?—'that acid-tongued, would-be female.'"

Avery groaned. "I hadn't thought of that, but of course, you're right. Well, there's the devil."

"I do not understand," Omar protested. "If Miss Bede loses this Mill House, why would Avery have to assume responsibility for her? From what you have told me, she will be provided for by Horatio Thorne's will."

"Only," Avery said, "if she makes a public statement recanting her stand on women's emancipation and thereafter leads a quiet, unassuming life, never again fraternizing with her sister malcontents."

He nodded at Karl, idly flicking the lid to his watch open and shut. "Tell him, Karl. You've been listening to her for three years, can this woman keep her mouth shut?"

"Not a chance."

"But how does this make you responsible for her?" Omar asked.

Avery waved the hand holding the cigar in the air. The end glowed in the semi-darkness. "Omar, dear chap, I am an English Gentleman."

John groaned. Karl snickered. Avery ignored them.

"For arcane reasons the English Gentleman has been bred to be nearly incapable of allowing pig-headed women to suffer the consequences of their actions. Do not bother to ask why. It is an enigma which has no answer."

"Please," Omar said, his exasperation evident. "I still do not understand."

Avery tried again. "When this little farce is over Miss Bede will be destitute. I cannot, because I am a gentleman, throw her out of Mill House. Thus, I shall have to undertake the care and feeding of her, a task which I am understandably reluctant to do. Can you imagine the daily prospect of breakfasting with a woman who refers to one's life as 'a monotonous litany of masculine posturing?'"

"I see," Omar said dubiously.

Avery took a deep puff off the cigar and let the flavorful smoke drift from his lips. For unknown reasons he wasn't nearly as upset as he would have assumed he'd be at making such a nasty discovery.

"Could you possibly finish the letter now?" John asked.

"Where was I? Oh, yes. Miss Bede had, in her usual subtle way, made known her intention of winning Mill House. That done she continues, *'I am speaking of Bernard. Though the lad is still plagued by sporadic bouts of the lung problems which worry his mother,'* "—Avery's brows dipped—" *'he continues to do well academically. Evelyn would withdraw him from school but the bank trustees tell us that they shall abide by Horatio's wishes and keep Bernard in school unless we can prove his condition is life-threatening. It is abominable that in this country a dead*

*man has more power than a live woman. You will doubtless
disagree.' "*

But he did not disagree. It *was* abominable. He well
remembered Horatio giving the same instructions regarding himself: *"The boy is to endure unless he col-
lapses." "There will be no one to molly-coddle a sickling on
my estates, so the boy stays in the school's infirmary." "Under no circumstances are the headmasters to indulge—"*

"Why are you scowling so, Avery?" John asked,
motioning for one of the turbaned servants to refresh
his drink.

Avery stubbed his cigar out in a crystal ashtray. "No
reason. *'Perhaps you could offer Bernard a word of encouragement. He quite considers you a hero.' "*

Lily Bede must be seriously concerned in order to
let pass an opportunity to give him a set-down.

" *'He particularly liked your story about being elevated
to god status. Indeed, so did I, since it bears out the theory I
have long held that we Europeans underestimate the sense
of humor of other peoples. Yours truly, Lillian Bede.' "*
Avery broke out laughing.

"I adore her," Karl declared, raising his tumbler in
a toast.

"You say that with every one of her letters," Avery
said, replacing the note in his jacket pocket.

"It's true. I have never heard a man put in his place
with such élan. It is masterful."

"Yes," Avery agreed smoothly, "and that's the problem. She would be master when she should be mistress."

Mill House, Devon
December 1891

"Good morning." Francesca took her seat at the breakfast table beside Evelyn. The newest member of the household, a curly-haired maid who was just now beginning to show the results of 'a trip behind the stable,' poured Francesca's tea.

"Good morning, Francesca," Lily replied absently, thumbing through a stack of envelopes.

The women fell into companionable silence, interrupted only by the genteel clink of fork tines against china and the crackle of logs blazing in the hearth. Lily looked around at her adopted family with a feeling of supreme contentment. Surely, these two women could be no dearer to her than the brother and sister she'd never seen. But then, she'd never get the opportunity to discover if that were true, would she?

The thought cast a shadow on her easy, companionable mood.

"Anything interesting?" Francesca asked.

"Not really," Lily said. "Mr. Camfield requests my opinion regarding his new sheep."

"I think our new neighbor is smitten with Lil," Francesca said.

"Nonsense," Lily said. Martin Camfield, the new owner of the adjacent farm, was not only a fine-looking man but one of the few of his gender that had the good sense to treat women as equals. "He merely wants my considered opinion and that's all."

"Mr. Camfield seems an enlightened sort of man," Francesca said nonchalantly. "The sort of man one could expect to act in a progressive manner. He wouldn't, say, be tied by convention."

"No, I dare say he wouldn't," Lily answered slowly, eyeing Francesca suspiciously.

"One could see oneself enjoying a modern sort of association with such a man."

Lily felt herself blush. That Francesca was giving voice to thoughts she herself had entertained only made her abashment worse. Martin Camfield might seek her opinion on sheep dip, but he certainly had never asked her to tea. But then, what man would? She was a bastard, without name or money. Each passing season saw her small, closely-guarded hopes for romance growing more improbable.

"Is there anything else in there?" Evelyn asked.

"Excuse me?"

"I asked what other news you had."

"Let's see. Mr. Drummond writes that I shall have to dredge the mill pond this winter and build new berms which, of course, I cannot afford. Polly Makepeace asks if the Women's Emancipation Coalition can hold its annual board meeting here come April."

"All those terrible women in their mannish outfits," Evelyn said with distaste and then after a quick glance at Lily's own bloomers added, "not that you look anything less than charming in your . . . those . . . that garment. Few women have your panache, dear."

"Thank you," Lily said. She was quite aware of how Evelyn viewed her clothing.

"It's not their clothing alone I object to," Evelyn went on. "I simply do not think they are the proper sorts of people for you to mingle with, Lil."

Lily stared. Evelyn occasionally surprised her with her unexpected impulses to mother her.

"I agree," Francesca declared, surprising Lily even more. "That Makepeace woman uses you shamelessly, Lily. She's jealous of you. You have all the attributes of a leader and she has none."

Disconcerted by Francesca's remarks, she nonetheless found them terribly sweet. And terribly unnecessary. Though Polly Makepeace did make use of her, Lily thought it was a small enough price to pay to salve her conscience. Managing the estate had consumed her attention for four years, years she could have been using to promote the equality of women. Lily considered her words carefully. She wouldn't hurt either woman for the world.

"Pshaw. I hardly threaten Polly Makepeace's designs to become the Coalition chairwoman. I'm barely involved in the organization anymore, much to my shame. All my time is taken up with the demands of Mill House."

"But to have her in our *home*, Lily! What do we really know about her?" Evelyn asked. "Or these others. They might not be nice people, dear. Who knows where they come from?"

Lily sighed. "Darlings, if you don't want them here,

by all means say so. But if your only objection is their suspect antecedents, I'm afraid polite company would consider me far more likely to taint then to be tainted."

"Oh, don't ever say that!" Evelyn exclaimed in horror. "We love you, Lily. I don't know what we'd do without you. You've made this house so comfortable, a relaxed home."

"I think the word you want is 'lax' not 'relaxed,' " Lily answered. Evelyn seemed to have experienced the last four years of Lily's proprietorship as one unending girls' slumber party. "And it is not me who makes Mill House a home, darling, it is you. Once the five years is up," Lily went on, striving for a calm expression, "I'll have to leave here."

"But why?" Evelyn cried. Francesca sipped her tea, her expression unusually grave.

"If I lose, I doubt whether Mr. Thorne will ask me to stay on." The very notion brought a wry smile to her lips. "And if I win, I cannot afford to maintain the farm. It needs an influx of cash which I do not have. I'll have to sell it."

Lily carefully hid her anguish. She loved Evelyn and Francesca and she loved Mill House. She loved its bright, warm kitchen and its silent dust-shrouded bed-chambers. She loved its unlikely ballroom and the incongruous stained-glass window hiding beneath the third floor eaves. She loved the ducks squabbling on the pond, the fat stupid-looking sheep that stared at her as she walked down the alley each morning, and her broken-down race horses.

Evelyn sniffed. "There must be some way."

"We'll worry about it when the time comes," Lily reassured her. "Look. A letter from Bernard. Here, Evie."

Now twelve, Bernard had reached that stage in life where a boy tries on adulthood for size. In Bernard's case it wasn't fitting too well. Though exceptionally tall for his age, he didn't weigh more than he had when he was six inches shorter. His skin was getting blotchy and his voice broke at the most disconcerting moments.

"What does he say?" Francesca asked.

Evelyn scanned the sheet. "He says he's coming to Mill House early this summer."

"He's been well?" Lily asked, trying to keep the worry from her voice. She couldn't imagine those heartless old goats allowing the boy to leave school early without a pressing reason.

"He assures me it's nothing serious. He's simply convinced the headmaster that an additional few weeks of rest will serve him well." Evelyn's brave face crumpled. "Oh, Lily. If he's not well we can keep him here, can't we?"

"Of course," Lily assured her, feeling helpless. Horatio's myriad notes and the instruction left in the bank trustees' hands ruled the boy's life.

"It will be good to have him here with us for the

summer, won't it?" Evelyn asked, pathetically grateful for Lily's assurance.

"Delightful," Francesca said. "One can't have too many men about."

"Francesca!" Evelyn chided. "She simply can't talk this way in front of Bernard."

"No, of course not. Do behave, Fran," Lily murmured distractedly. Her gaze had fallen on the final letter in the stack. It was from Avery Thorne and it was addressed to Miss Lillian Bede. Not She Who Must Be Obeyed, not the Emancipated Miss Bede, not Herself. A little tingle of trepidation raced through her; something was wrong. She tucked his letter away at the bottom of the stack to be read later.

Fifteen minutes later she stood at the window of her office looking outside. Beneath her window the Michaelmas roses were blooming, their creamy petals bright as snow against the green foliage. She opened the letter.

Adversary Mine,

Karl Dhurmann died yesterday. We were dog-sledding across the Greenland snowfields. He wasn't far ahead. Twenty yards or so. One minute he was there, the next gone. He'd fallen into a crevasse that had been breached by a drift of snow. It took us the day to retrieve him.

I thought you should know he died. He often stated his intention of marrying you. Your letters made him laugh and laughter was rare for Karl. He'd lost everything and died without country, home, or family. But you made him laugh.

I think he would want you to know he'd died and I thought perhaps you would spare him a smile for his ridiculous intention of marrying you, for his appreciation of your letters, or for whatever reason you like. I am not a religious man and your smile is as close to a prayer as he's likely to come.

Avery Thorne

Lily slowly folded the letter. For a long time she gazed outside her window and when she finally turned away, she did not leave the room. She wrote a letter.

Chapter Five

The childish, careful hand drew a smile from Avery.

Dear Cousin,

*I trust this letter finds you well. I have enjoyed indiffer-
ent health this year and shall go up early to Mill House this
summer.*

*Mother says we should take care to enjoy the manor
while it's still a Happy Home. She says that Miss Bede
means to sell Mill House if she comes into possession of it
though I don't think that likely since the fields flooded and
the entire crop of spring wheat was drowned.*

*Poor Miss Bede was greatly upset. Mother wrote that she
found her crying. Miss Bede is not a crying sort of female.*

*I wish I could do something for her but it will be ten
years before I can offer her my protection. Mother says Miss
Bede wants to protect herself. Why would she even want to
do such a thing do you suppose? Mother could offer no illumination. I believe Miss Bede is simply being brave.*

*I therefore must point out that if you were a gentleman,
you would offer her your protection. I'm sure you will do so
on your return which I very greatly hope will be soon.*

*I just read the serialization of your trip down the Ama-
zon. Sensational! Miss Bede is impressed, too, and you are
wrong about her thinking your trips are self-indulgent.
When I quizzed her about this she immediately wrote back
stating most emphatically that she could think of no man
who belongs in a jungle more than you.*

> *Your cousin,*
> *Bernard Thorne*

"So, she intends to sell my home, does she?"
Avery's slight smile faded. "And what the blazes does
the boy mean, *if* I were a gentleman?"

Absently he pulled Karl's gold timepiece from his
pocket. The five years of his "hiatus" were nearly up
and, as he'd expected, apparently Lily Bede was in desperate straits. Flooded out the spring crop, had she? It
would be a wonder if there was anything left of his
estate to refurbish after she was done with her tenancy.

Perhaps he ought to return to England early, see
just what sort of challenge awaited him before he took
over. Truth be told, he was tired of wandering. His
longing for a home had never been more pointed or
more insistent. Just a month or so early. What harm
could it do? Besides, he could then sort out what
should, or in her case *could*, be done with Lily Bede.

Yes, he thought pocketing the watch, there were any number of reasons why he should return to England now. He strode off down the wharf.

Mill House, Devon
May 1892

Lily raced down the hallway, muttering imprecations against Evelyn for having left that very morning for a week in Bath.

Why now of all times had that blasted school bowed to her repeated demands and allowed Bernard to come home? And how had Bernard made the long trip alone? She'd been dumbfounded when Teresa, as swollen as an October pumpkin and still two months from lying in, had grinned toothily that a *Mister* Thorne was waiting to receive her in the library.

Mister Thorne, indeed, and *receive* her? The boy was giving himself airs.

Blast Teresa anyway. She knew how the boy discomforted her. Last time Bernard had been home he'd dogged her footsteps from dawn to dusk. Lily recognized the signs of an incipient crush; she just had no idea what to do about one.

She didn't want to destroy his youthful, masculine confidence—and frankly Bernard, with his tall lanky body, narrow chest, and dark-ringed eyes, was going to need as much bolstering as he could get. She mustn't treat him like a boy. But not a man. Maybe a boyish man or a manly boy—

Blast! Now Lily, she thought, pausing at the threshold of the drawing room and patting her hair, he is twelve years old. Surely you can handle one boy-child barely into his double digits. Banter. Be avuncular and warm. But still, above all, refuse to acknowledge a soulful stare. Or anything else soulful, for that matter.

She took a deep breath, entered the library, and looked around. There he was, sitting in a big wingbacked chair turned toward the window. Dark, tumbled locks appeared above the back of the chair. The poor lad must have added even more inches to his ungainly body.

"Darling!" she greeted him. "I see you're making yourself comfortable. Excellent." There was no response.

He was shy, perhaps bolstering his courage before facing her. She pitied him. He'd arrived to find his mother gone, his aunt who-knows-where, and his only greeting from a woman on whom he had a crush. She remembered crushes. They hurt.

"Come now, m'lad." Her tone oozed with bonhomie. "What say you and I raid the larder? You must be starving after your journey and I know where Francesca hides her best bonbons from Bon Street." She waited. Not even a titter of laughter at her weak sally.

"We've been discussing what you might like for your birthday. It quite occupies our evenings of late." She edged closer. "Lead soldiers? Too childish. One of these new camera boxes? How about a fishing pole? Mill House boasts a most promising creek." She pulled out her trump card. "I hear your cousin Avery is a rabid angler."

He wouldn't be able to resist. Bernard's worship of Avery Thorne was a matter of record. Sure enough, she thought she detected a slight stirring from the chair.

"I know we haven't spent much time together lately and I regret that," she said softly. "But we can soon set that right. What better place to become reacquainted than on the banks of a pretty creek? What say you, sir? Come and let your auntie Lil greet you with a hug."

And now at last there was definite movement from the chair. Strong tanned hands, a thick gold signet ring adorning the smallest finger of the left, clutched the chair arms and pushed. A tall figure—exceedingly tall, broad-shouldered, straight, and masculine—rose and turned to face her.

"As pleasant as a hug sounds," the man drawled in soft, sardonic tones, "I'm afraid I'll make do with the bonbons . . . Auntie Lil."

Lillian Bede was stunning. The shock of her appearance capsized all his preconceptions and left Avery floundering for words.

Thank God, he'd already schooled his expression to blandness before turning. He wasn't sure he would have been able to say anything halfway intelligent had he seen her first and then, not two minutes into their first meeting, Lily Bede would have had the upper hand. Stunning or not, the one thing nearly five years of correspondence with this woman had taught him was that Lily Bede ought never, *ever*, to have the upper hand.

Broad across the cheeks and brow, her face narrowed to a small, squared jaw. Exotically tilted eyes studied him, fringed by such a wealth of lashes that they shadowed the clear whites. Her mouth was as full-lipped as an Egyptian's and as red as though she'd been sipping a cherry cordial. Clouds of tightly coiling, inky black hair had been pulled atop her head, accenting her long, slender throat and adding height to an already impressive figure.

Stunning, Avery thought once more. *Lily Bede*. It wasn't right.

She lifted her hand to her throat, in a gesture both alluring and defensive, drawing his attention to her garb. She wore what looked like a man's plain linen shirt and a dark, gored wool—by God, she was wearing bloomers! In spite of—or maybe because of—the severe, masculine garb, she looked exotic and out of place, like an odalisque in sackcloth.

Abruptly he realized that he'd been dumbly eyeing her for a full minute. Of course, she was taking her time studying him, too. But the expression in her eyes was hardly appreciative.

"You'll forgive me," she said at last, "I thought you were someone else." Her charmingly precise upper class accent only emphasized her foreign appearance.

He must be mad. Lily Bede, first stunning, now charming. "I'm delighted to make your ac—"

"Is there much luggage?" she asked.

"No. Not much." He crossed the room toward her. Her skin was the color of Tahitian sand and when she tipped her head to look up at him he could see a scar beneath one straight, dark brow. "As I was about to say, I'm delighted to finally meet you, Miss Bede. I appreciate your—"

"I don't think you and I need waste time with social niceties." She took a step back. "Where's Bernard?"

Play lady of the manor with him, would she? "I don't know," he answered. "Have you misplaced him?"

"I?" Startled, her eyes widened. They were as black as Turkish coffee, clear and rich. Abruptly they narrowed. "Listen, sir. I don't appreciate familiarity from Bernard's escort and I doubt Harrow's deans will either. Who are you, anyway? The football coach?"

Good God. The chit didn't know who he was. He felt as though she'd struck him. True, he would never have picked her out of a crowd as the author of the astringent letters that had followed him through four continents, but he'd only an ill-remembered newspaper caricature to guide him. She had no such excuse. His damn picture hung in the upper hall—he went still. At least, it had.

Forgetting his resolve to remain cool, calm, and impeccably polite, he strode past her into the hall. Behind him, he heard the rustle of her blasted bloomers.

"I say, you can't just—"

He ignored her, bent on discovering the whereabouts of his portrait. It was the only portrait of him in existence, done at his uncle's insistence. True, it had never meant a bloody thing to him before but it had lately—very lately—gained considerable importance. It was the principle of the thing. How dare she have it taken down?

"Just who do you think you are?" Lily panted, struggling to keep up, her heavy bloomers swishing angrily. "I'll have your job for this!"

He stalked down the central hall, vaguely aware of a certain elegant paucity in the rooms he passed, a bare but gleaming ebony table, the well worn oriental runner with the frayed binding, the smell of beeswax and lemon oil. He mounted the curving staircase and turned into the wing where some of the family's countless pictures had always hung. There, right beside his great grandmother, Catherine Montrose, it should have—

He stopped. There, where it had always been, clear as day, hung his portrait. It wasn't even tilted.

With a scowl, Avery turned. Lily Bede stood a foot behind him, hand on hips, spots of carnelian edging each cheekbone.

"If you're not out of my house in two minutes, I shall have you thrown out." The upper-crust accent still rode high, but the imperious Lady Bountiful attitude had fallen into the ditches.

Throw him out of *her* house? Her gaze locked with

his as he moved closer. She didn't retreat. She would, Avery realized, go toe-to-toe with him rather than back up. *This* woman he had no trouble identifying. Combative, curt, self-sufficient—

"How you ever got through the front door in the first place . . ." Her voice trailed off as her gaze swept past him to his portrait, paused, and snapped back. She had an exceptionally expressive face, ridiculously easy to read. Right now horror suffused every feature. Good.

He took up the pose he'd held for the months of the painting's creation. "A good likeness, don't you think?"

"Thorne." Her voice was flat.

"Yes."

"What are *you* doing here?"

"Now is that any way to greet your faithful correspondent after so many years?"

"Faithful?" she echoed tartly. "It seemed to me that I was the faithful one since I maintained the burden of discovering your whereabouts for five years. I felt like I was on some ridiculous scavenger hunt, what with the clues and hints you wrote me about your next location. If it hadn't been for the friends my parents had scattered about the globe I doubt I'd have succeeded in ever finding you. Sometimes I didn't. Not once did you inform me of where—last winter I was sure you were dead." She broke off and shook her head as though angry she'd been sidetracked. "*What* did you say you were doing here?"

"I didn't." He held up one hand. "I should think my presence here is self-explanatory. Your five years tenancy is nearly up, I had no pressing desire to further my travels and I thought I'd come here and scout out the terrain. See what sort of situation you're leaving me. One is always advised to do decent reconnaissance before heading into new territory."

"You're making an awfully large assumption," Lily Bede said stiffly. "What if Mill House is making a profit?"

He smiled. Presumably it looked gracious. It did not feel that way, however. "Well, then if I'm proved wrong, I shall simply use these weeks as a welcome respite from my travels. There's really no need to look so suspicious."

"I am naturally suspicious. God willing, I shall remain that way." She kept looking at his portrait and back again at him, as if by doing so she would discover some anomaly that would allow her to have him thrown out as an imposter. But with each glance her expression just grew bleaker. "Where will you be staying?"

"Why"—he looked around and opened his hands in an encompassing gesture—"here. At Mill House. It's still up for grabs, isn't it? I mean its ultimate ownership won't be decided until August, will it?"

"Correct." The word came out between stiff lips. Lips that looked much better soft and relaxed.

He looked away. *Not wise to think that way, Avery old son, he told himself. Not at all wise.*

"Good," he said. "I just wanted to make sure I understood the situation. Besides, Bernard invited me. As Mill House's *current* occupant you can, of course, refuse me." He tilted his head, mockingly recognizing her authority.

"I wouldn't dream of it. You're more than welcome to stay . . . as Bernard's *guest*."

"Thank you."

She scowled, her consternation evident in the tension of her face, the color staining the skin of her throat. The sight riveted him.

He'd had little experience with women. His parents had died when he was seven. Having lived already several years in the care of a boarding school, Avery's life hadn't changed appreciably. One absentee guardian had simply replaced another, his parents' for Horatio Thorne. It certainly hadn't brought him into any more contact with females.

He recognized his own deeply guarded susceptibility to beautiful women, just as he recognized the reasons for it. At the same time he realized how absurd the ugly looked yearning for the beautiful. Luckily, he had no masochistic tendencies.

So he'd traded clipped comments with a few young women at the fewer parties he attended and contented himself with admiring from afar. He'd never allowed himself to want. Never.

But on the passage to England a pretty blond heiress had sought his acquaintance. She'd been on the first leg of a world tour and had, he'd realized within an hour of their introduction, decided he would be her first stop.

She'd been warm and willing and she'd sighed dreamily that she'd never been with an adventurer before. If she hadn't wanted *him*, she'd apparently wanted something he'd represented—though God knew what that was—and he'd had no intention of questioning too carefully what. After they'd parted he'd thought of her only in a fond and remote way, as he well knew she thought of him, because the blond darling had never represented a danger to his heart. Or he to hers.

This, *her*, Lily Bede, was another matter entirely.

Lily Bede had read his words for over four years. He had for her a deep respect, one reserved for worthy opponents, and a certain bizarre appreciation for her undeniable wit. Dangerous enough without having her look like the distillation of his every carnal dream. And very dangerous—not to mention stupid—to give that sort of power to a woman who had stated quite openly that she intended to rob him of his inheritance. Clearly, she mustn't be allowed to know what weapons she had in her grasp.

For a long moment he traded speculative looks with the tall dark woman. For nearly five years she'd filled his imagination, been antagonist, irritant, and amusement. Why the hell did she have to be so achingly beautiful?

"How long are you staying?"

He came out of his reverie feeling angry. "Excuse me?"

"I said, how . . . long . . . are . . . you . . . staying?"

He stiffened. She smiled, a touch of triumph in her full lips. She might look as soft as summer passion, but she had a razor blade in place of a tongue. If given half a chance, he'd no doubt she'd use him as her strop.

Over the years he'd been in many perilous situations. On instinct alone, he'd made decisions that had meant life or death. Time and again those instincts had proven right. Right now they were screaming a warning.

God help him, he was attracted to Lily Bede.

Avery Thorne cleared his throat and replied, "Until I get what I came for—Mill House." Then he turned and walked away.

Chapter Six

Stunned speechless, Lily stared at his departing back. Even though he'd all but thrown down a gauntlet, practically threatening her with his intention, she found herself capable of only one thought: Francesca had been right. Avery Thorne had, indeed, filled out.

The seams of his tight, ill-fitting jacket strained to contain his shoulders. The top button on his shirt had to be left undone to accommodate his wide throat and the wrists stretching the white cuffs were broad and supple-looking.

She leaned sideways and watched him stride down the hall, tallying up his too long hair curling over his shirt collar, his too broad shoulders and his too long, too muscular legs. He disappeared around a corner.

Unaware she'd been holding her breath, she collapsed back against the window, her shoulders hitting it with a thud. She glared at the portrait across from her. The skinny, awkward-looking youth posing so self-consciously stared back. He'd grown into the oversized hands the painter had depicted. Strong hands: wide palms, long tensile fingers.

Her gaze traveled up to the painted face. Bold nose, gem-brilliant blue-green eyes, and a wide mouth. The right features were all accounted for but it didn't *look* like the man she'd envisioned writing those letters. She'd pictured him as being Ichabod Crane–like. He ought to be excitable, not confident. His movements ought be abrupt and nervy, not loose-limbed and self-assured.

And he hadn't sounded like Avery Thorne should have sounded: the type of nasal masculine voice that set her teeth on edge. Instead, his voice made her shiver. It was as rich as custard, as low as a courtier's bow, and its appeal went far deeper than simple hearing. His voice petted her psyche, stroked some deep auditory core. His voice made her feel all smoky.

With a sound of annoyance, she pushed herself upright. It wasn't fair. Avery Thorne shouldn't have the physique of an athlete, the jeweled eyes of some ancient tribal icon, and a voice like a big old tomcat after a successful night on the prowl. Avery Thorne was simply the most—

Her hands dropped. Her eyes widened in surprised recognition. She inhaled deeply. The most masculine creature she'd ever seen. And the most attractive. There.

She lifted her chin, congratulating herself on such dazzling honesty. At the very same time, she shivered.

She shook her head to clear her thoughts of Avery

Thorne. She had her future to protect. She couldn't afford to lose a single penny because of distraction. She'd barely managed to keep the books in the black since the wheat field had flooded.

Clearly Avery Thorne had arrived anticipating her failure. A bit premature for the vulture to be eyeing the corpse, she thought, and darn him, he wasn't a corpse yet. Nor did she intend to be.

This distraction would pass, she assured herself. After all, she'd experienced something like this before.

At fifteen she'd become enamored of one of her father's young protegees who had stayed at their apartments for the summer. She'd thought him the most gorgeous, fascinating man in the world. It had taken only one week in his constant company to discover that he felt exactly the same way about himself.

There was her answer! She halted again, smacking her fist into her open palm. She'd spend as many hours as possible with Avery and voila, this brain fever would disappear.

She headed for her room, satisfied with her prescription. The mood lasted while she washed her hands and re-pinned her hair and changed her blouse for something with a bit of lace at the throat. Half an hour later she went down to lunch.

The dining room was empty except for Kathy, one of the three maids currently employed by Mill House. Kathy was a very short brunette creature with a propensity for skirts too snug in the hips. At six months pregnant she still managed to squeeze into the one she'd arrived in. Much to Lily's consternation.

"What are you doing?" Lily asked.

Kathy placed a silver fork carefully beside the best china, her face taut with concentration. She nudged the demitasse spoon into alignment above the serving plate. "Have you seen 'im, then?" she finally asked.

"Seen who?"

"Mr. Avery Thorne. He come back from Africa or some such place and is 'ere, in this very 'ouse, at this very minute."

"Yes. I have," Lily said coolly.

"Coo! An ain't he every inch the bold adventurer? I've read every story written by 'im. Every one. He's committed feats of darin'-do that would curl your toes. Looks it, too, 'e does. All big and strong and—"

"That will do, Kathy." Lily had encouraged a peculiarly democratic household. Consequently, the maids often voiced opinions, sometimes unsolicited ones. "Now please explain to me why you are using the good china for lunch. Is Miss Francesca expecting company?"

Kathy positioned the last of the butter knives. "Not that I know. Missus Kettle told me to set best for Mr. Thorne. She said now that Mr. Thorne is home things is going to be run more in the way of a prop—er, con-ven-tion-al manor."

Now that Mr. Thorne was home? *Like a* proper *manor?* Lily felt a nerve seize up at the corner of her mouth.

Kathy took a step back. "I'm sure no 'arm was meant, miss. Missus Kettle says five years without no one to test her cul-in-ar-ee skills on 'as been right disheartenin' for a chef of 'er status. Least," she ended meekly, "that's what she always says when she's 'ad a nip of the port."

"Does she?" Lily asked, pleased her voice remained so calm and reasonable. "Well, in spite of Mrs. Kettle's alcohol-infused visions of Mill House's return to its former glory," she raised her voice a bit—simply to emphasize her point, "*I'm* running this house and shall do so for at least the next two months!"

Kathy gaped at her.

"Now." Lily smoothed her skirts. "There's no time to reset the table but henceforth we shall use the everyday ware. Also, since apparently Mr. Thorne will be staying on with us for a while, I need you to make up the corner bedroom for him. I'm sure he'd appreciate a place to wash before—"

"He asked for the blue bedroom up top, the one shaded by the cedar."

"No," Lily said decisively. "That entire floor has been put in sheets. I won't have extra work made because of a man's whim. He'll do just fine in—"

"He's already there," Kathy said sheepishly. "You wasn't about when he arrived so Missus Kettle asked 'is preference and Mr. Avery said 'as 'ow he always 'ad that room and might as well not change 'abits at this late date and so me and Merry turned it out."

Not two hours here and already Avery Thorne had

undermined her authority, appropriated her power, and upset her household.

"Didn't take much time, miss."

"No. It didn't, did it?" Lily agreed before realizing that Kathy was referring to the making up of the blue bedroom. "You can go now, Kathy."

Kathy bobbed a curtsey and fled. Lily stared at the array of silver, china, and crystal for a minute before realizing what she'd just seen: Kathy had *curtsied* to her.

No one curtsied at Mill House. Women did their work, they did it respectfully, and they were treated respectfully in return.

She'd thought her own attraction to Avery Thorne was her most pressing concern. It wasn't. He threatened every one of the advancements of women she'd worked so hard to install here at Mill House. He had only to arrive and the staff she'd so carefully transformed into emancipated, self-governing women became curtsey-bobbing, "yes, sir-ing," *family retainers*! Which was absurd since none of them had been here long enough to have a place to retain.

A few minutes later the hall clock chimed noon and Francesca entered the dining room, a half-emptied glass of sherry in her hand, cheerfully humming a little Gilbert and Sullivan ditty. She spied Lily.

"I think," Francesca said, "that there is something so aesthetically appealing about a man with bronzed skin and broad shoulders."

"You've seen Mr. Thorne."

"Yes. A short while back. Which reminds me, we shall certainly have to send word to Drummond to have a lamb butchered."

"Are you sure you wouldn't prefer a fatted calf?" Lily asked dryly.

Francesca carefully placed her glass above the china plate at her seat. "From the look of him, Avery will add substantially to the monthly grocer's bill."

"He won't be here that long."

"Won't he?" Avery challenged as he came through the doorway. "Good afternoon, Francesca. How pleasant to see you again so soon."

Lily turned. Avery Thorne had dressed for luncheon. He loomed in the doorway, all of his breadth and width contained by an immaculate, if outdated, jacket that looked a good two sizes too small. He'd taken the opportunity to wash his hair and it had not yet dried. It still coiled dark with moisture, dampening his white shirt collar, accenting his strong, bold features with a boyish air of haste. Lily strove to overcome her unwilling appreciation.

Avery kissed Francesca's cheek and then, like a sated lion unable to resist the allure of easy prey, his bright eyes drifted toward Lily and came to rest with unsettling purpose. A devastatingly attractive smile curved his wide mouth. The corners of his eyes fanned in deep laugh lines and his teeth gleamed white against his dark skin. "Miss Bede, we meet again."

"Good afternoon, Mr. Thorne." *Familiarity breeds contempt, familiarity breeds contempt,* she silently repeated. Then an evil suggestion occurred to her. But what if it bred something else entirely?

"I trust you found your chambers in order?" she said. "We generally keep that area shut off from the rest of the house, it being so remote and all, but we wouldn't want you to be unhappy in your room choice."

Avery, in the process of prowling toward her, stopped a few feet away. She forced herself not to back up. He was so damnably tall. She could almost feel him; his body sent out some sort of energy field, some—*thing* she could discern with a hitherto unused sense.

"I didn't mean to inconvenience you," he said, his smile fading. "It was the room I occupied when I stayed here as a child and thus the only one I remembered."

"No," Lily said hastily. "No trouble."

Avery's brows dipped as he studied Lily's stiff figure. Her smile was fixed, a subtle flavor of . . . fear in it? He frowned. What did Lily Bede have to fear from him? Except, of course, her imminent dispossession.

The idea gave him no satisfaction. He looked down into her dark, wary eyes, noting the way her honey-colored skin glowed with a sudden flush. Too appealing by half.

"Francesca, won't you have a seat?" he asked, turning away from Lily Bede.

Francesca smiled in startled delight. "Why Avery, how thoughtful. When did you acquire social graces?"

"I'm sure I don't know what you mean," Avery said, eyeing the heavy mahogany chair a second before lifting the entire thing out and away from the table. "I'm a gentleman. Of course, I'd hold a lady's chair."

He secured Francesca's arm, pulled her into the place vacated by the chair and slipped the chair under her. Perhaps a shade too forcefully. She dropped into the seat, blinking up at him.

"I may have spoken in haste—" Francesca said.

"Miss Bede?" He rounded the table, pulled Lily's chair out, and held it dangling from one hand while he waited for her.

Lily, also, blinked as if his actions surprised her. Was she such a stranger to etiquette that the simple act of being seated confounded her? Well, what could one expect of a household of women. "Miss Bede?" he urged.

She swallowed and gingerly moved into position. He slid the chair beneath her, pushing it forward. The edge of the seat hit her behind the knees and for a second she teetered. He grabbed her arm to steady her, and went still with shock.

Simple touch had never garnered from him such an intense physical reaction.

Suddenly he was completely aware of Lily Bede. He felt not merely the firm, lithe muscle of her upper arm, but the warmth of her skin, the smooth, velvety texture of it, suffused with her vitality. He wanted to rub his hand up and down her arm. He wanted to touch more of her. Lily Bede. His nemesis. He snatched his hand away.

Lily angled her head up. Her eyes looked brilliant. She'd felt it, too. She must have. She opened her mouth to speak as he bent nearer to her.

"I'm sorry Mrs. Thorne is not here to receive you," she said. Her words left Avery unsatisfied, vaguely disappointed. "Had she known you were arriving I am sure she would have postponed her trip. I hope you like mutton?"

He hated mutton. His distaste must have shown because Lily's expression became sharp. "Of course, it isn't exactly a Maori feast. But we do what we can."

"Maori feast?" Francesca quizzed.

"Mr. Thorne wrote Bernard a rather graphic account of a bushman feast he once attended, as guest of honor no doubt."

"No, not at all," Avery muttered uncomfortably. Drat, he'd forgotten all those overblown descriptions he'd written to his young cousin. "I was just passing through."

"And what did they have at this feast?" Francesca asked.

Lily smiled. "Bugs, was it?"

Francesca's mouth dropped open. "You ate *bugs*?"

"And snakes," Lily added, unable to control a mischievous impulse. He looked nonplussed for the first time since she'd met him. Almost shy. "Cuisine de rigueur for gods, I expect. Were they delicious?"

"Couldn't get enough of the little blighters," Avery said, meeting Lily's gaze and relaxing.

She was teasing him. He couldn't ever remember a woman actually teasing him. It was a novel experience. Not altogether unpleasant. He took his seat. "I strongly suspect that should Englishmen ever discover the culinary delights lurking beneath their dahlias the sheep industry shall forthwith collapse."

She laughed. A lovely sound, open and natural and inviting. And then, as if he'd caught her off-guard and tricked her into dangerous territory, her expression grew closed, her laughter faded. She turned toward Francesca, who was attending the conversation with an openly delighted expression. "Will you be going to the Derby again this year, Francesca?"

Still smiling, Francesca took a healthy swallow of sherry before answering. "I don't know. I'd thought to leave next Tuesday but there's really no reason to rush off. The Derby isn't for three weeks. Don't worry, Lil, I promise I'll find out the names of all the retirees for you."

"Retirees?" Avery cocked his head inquiringly.

"Lily collects retired race horses."

"Horses?" Startled, Avery glanced at Lily. She stared fixedly at her plate. Of course she would collect horses. What else would Lily Bede collect but his bête noir, the one remaining tie to the asthma that had molded and cursed his earliest years? Horses, to which he was amazingly, horribly, disastrously allergic. Of course, he would never allow *her* to know of this weakness.

"A few," Lily mumbled just as the hall door swung open, framing a woman sitting in a wheelchair. One leg stuck straight out before her, cotton batting co-cooning the limb. Her brown eyes gleamed with triumph beneath a broad, moist forehead fringed by gingery curls.

With a grunt she grasped the wheels, heaved her weight forward, and popped the chair over the threshold. Avery scrambled to his feet.

"If you would be so kind as to make room for me?" the newcomer asked. Her voice was deep and resonant with the lilt of the northern province.

"Allow me," Avery said.

"And who are you?" the woman asked as he went to her aid, her head falling back to take in all of him.

"Avery Thorne. Miss Thorne's cousin." He pushed her ahead of him toward the table.

"Avery Thorne?"

Lily, apparently recalled to her duty as hostess, pushed away from the table and scooted over to the woman's side. Carefully, but with the air of one who is unmuzzling a potentially dangerous dog, she helped to ease the woman's wheelchair into place.

"Miss Makepeace, I had no idea you would be joining us for lunch," she said. "However did you manage the stairs? *Should* you have managed the stairs?"

"A woman only does herself and her gender a gross disservice by pretending to be less than she is, or incapable of what she is not," Polly said, unfolding her napkin and arranging it on her lap. Her gaze, leveled on Francesca, said clearly that she considered Francesca to be guilty of at least one and probably both of these flaws.

Francesca yawned. "Excuse me, I was, er, up late last night."

"But how did you navigate the stairs?" Lily asked.

"Had the girls carry me down the stairs and I managed the flat parts myself."

"You must allow me to offer my services in the future," Avery said.

"Nope," Polly said. "A woman gets soft relying on men to do for her, and if there's one thing I can't abide it's a soft—"

"Well, it's lovely you can join us," Lily cut in, resettling herself as yet another short pregnant girl—Merry if Avery remembered correctly—bustled in and set another place. "Mr. Thorne, this is our guest, Miss Polly Makepeace. Miss Makepeace is one of the founding members of the Women's Coalition. We had our annual conference here not long ago. Unfortunately Miss Makepeace fell from her podium during the middle of her speech and broke her leg. She is convalescing here."

"I see," Avery said. Lily was using his home as a meeting house for suffragists? He disliked the idea. Intensely. Horses were one thing, political women were another. At least one could keep horses outside.

"She was in the midst of objecting to Lily's nomination as their little organization's secretary," Francesca said, helping herself to the decanter set in the middle of the table. "She became a shade enthusiastic in her denunciations."

Polly flushed plum colored and Lily's cheeks grew scarlet.

"I only had the best interests of the organization in mind. Nothing personal and Miss Bede knows that," Polly said and turned to him. "How'd you do? Heard of you. Adventurer chap. All 'into the jaws of death' and what not. Well, I tell you, sir, today there are more dire adventures awaiting London's poor women—"

The kitchen door opened, winning a look of relief from Francesca as Mrs. Kettle entered followed by Kathy bearing a huge porcelain dish from which a delicious aroma wafted.

Mrs. Kettle stopped before Avery and whisked the lid from the tureen. "Soupe a l'oignon, Mr. Avery, sir," she breathed.

"Very nice," Avery said, nodding.

"And after that coquilles Saint-Jacques au saumon, followed by the meat course, tendrons de gigot. For a salad we have d'epinards aux foies de gras and we finish with tarte au citron," Mrs. Kettle said.

"Thank you, Mrs. Kettle," Avery said. The elderly woman, Avery noted, kept her eyes strictly averted from Lily.

If Lily Bede spent money like this on every meal and hosted conventions for impecunious suffragists, and collected antique race horses as pets, she must be damn near running the estate into the ground. Which meant whatever niggling doubts he'd had regarding his anticipated ownership of Mill House could be put to rest.

He toyed with the silver demitasse spoon. The thought did not provide him the joy it should have.

Chapter Seven

The next evening, Avery exited his room, heading for the library where he intended to look over the household records. If he could find them. A pair of housemaids curtsied as he passed. They looked familiar. In fact, since his arrival yesterday he'd seen only three maids, all of them in various stages of gestation. He nodded. Their hands flew to cover their erupting giggles. Remarkable.

He'd little familiarity with female servants—none, actually—but suspected that in most households the maids didn't burst into laughter when a man walked by them. After spending a lifetime among men, he found the entirely feminine world of Mill House as exotic and foreign a country as any he'd explored. It fascinated him.

Female voices filled the halls from dawn to dusk with noisome music, trilling, warbling, croaking, laughter as light and incidental as a stone skipping on a mirrored pond, quarrelsome voices as harsh as a faulty brake. Or, sometimes, a murmur as fluid as a night bird's low call, like Lily Bede's—damn!

The woman sneaked into his thoughts, catching him unawares at the most improbable moments. He'd once seen a shaman employ a crude figurine likeness of a man to curse him. The shaman had sent demons to visit his enemy, demons only the cursed man could see. Drove the poor blighter stark raving mad. Avery was half tempted to search Lily Bede's room for his own waxen image because he could not get the blasted woman out of his mind.

Bloody hell. He was a gentleman, the penultimate example of self-control. God knew he'd spent his first two decades training himself in that discipline. He would *not* want her.

He rounded the corner and slowed, noting anew how the Mill House of his memory compared to the reality. He remembered acres of wainscoted hallways and cavernous rooms with cathedral height ceilings, a million esoteric tomes stocking the library shelves, and a battalion of footmen cleaning hundreds of glass windows.

In fact the rooms had two windows each; their ceilings were a uniform nine feet high; and the library was stocked with the overwrought sensations of forty years ago, not the lost Shakespearean folios he'd imagined. Mill House was simply a large country home with few pretensions and those it had, he found amusing. A stained glass oriel window, a Sevres vase; if he recalled correctly there was even a ballroom in one of the wings of the second floor. He liked the reality of Mill House, the uncluttered, relaxed atmosphere better even than he remembered.

"Mr. Thorne, sir?" A girl with red hair waddled up to him, her arms loaded with sheets, her face bright with her exertions.

"Yes, Merry?"

His query drew a burst of unwarranted hilarity. The housemaids' reactions to his simplest words were so universal that had he been in Africa he would have assumed this was some sort of ritual greeting.

"Oh, sir!" she gasped, pressing her hand to her belly. "Bless you, sir, you remembered my name!"

"Of course I did. You're the only redheaded preg— redheaded Merry employed here." This brought on a fresh onslaught of giggles.

Avery glanced worriedly at the girl's stomach. He'd once attended a birthing in an igloo. His only other choice had been to stand outside in –40 degree gale winds, an option he'd happily elected until he'd lost the feeling in his feet. The ensuing hours had been instructional. He'd no desire to ever repeat them again.

Avery scowled at her. "What do you want?"

"Miss Bede says I was to find you and ask what you wanted done with the invitations."

"What invitations?"

"The invitations from the local gentry," she explained, "for parties and soirees and fetes and balls and dances and musicales and picnics and such."

"I haven't any idea of what to do with the bloody invitations. Give them to Miss Bede." He started past her. She stepped in his way.

"I did," she said, "and she told me to give them to you, sir, so's you can decide which ones to accept. She said they're already piling up and 'as to be answered."

"She did, did she?"

What sort of game was Lily playing now? And where the blazes was she anyway?

Yesterday, she'd been his shadow. If she'd looked in the least bit happy about it he would have suspected her of nefarious purposes, but she wore an air of such pained resignation he could only guess she kept close to make sure he didn't nip off with the silver. She obviously disliked men—a fact made clear by her political associations and her letters.

"Merry—quiet girl," he growled as she started up that incessant giggling. "If I'm missaying your name just tell me. No? Fine, then listen. I am unacquainted with anyone within forty miles of Mill House. Therefore, in spite of Miss Bede's touching determination to include me in her entertainments, please inform her that I have no interest whatsoever in which parties she attends or does not attend. I certainly have no intention of accompanying her—what the bloody hell is that sound you're making?" he asked in horror.

"Ohmigawd!" The girl's eyes bulged and her knees buckled. She teetered over. Avery caught her and swung her up in his arms. Her stack of linens hit the ground with a thud. "Now I'll have to take 'em down to the laundry again!" she wailed.

"Good Lord, girl, are you daft? You ought to be with a midwife, not huffing around hallways. Has Miss Bede no decency? How can she force you to work in your condition?"

The girl blinked. "Miss Bede," she said in a solemn tone, "is a bleedin' saint. I wouldn't have no home at all if it weren't for her and neither would some of the other girls here."

And hires you cheaply, too. The cynical thought appeared.

The more he saw of Lily's economizing the less he liked it. They dined like kings yet Lily kept only three pregnant maids to do the work required by twice as many. Francesca dressed in the latest fashions and yet Lily dressed like an impecunious . . . squire. She should at least wear dresses. The once lovely rose gardens had gone wild through neglect yet twenty retired race horses ate oats in the stables.

Self-indulgence and parsimony abided hand in hand in Lily's management of Mill House, the estate getting the parsimony, Lily's favorites getting the indulgence. He had to admit that it had been a shrewd move to hire desperate girls. Each would do the work of two, happy to have any job at all.

He'd never doubted Lily's intelligence. Now he found himself suspecting her ethics. He didn't like it, particularly as his doubts didn't cool his ardor. What sort of gentleman had a preoccupation with such a woman? Yet he found himself unwilling to believe the worst of her.

Grimly, Avery hefted Merry higher against his chest, as he looked around for someplace to set her. Not a chair or bench in sight.

"Coo!" The girl's eyes went as round as her mouth. "Teresa said you'd be as strong as a young bullock."

Young bullock? He was being compared in the servants quarters to a young *bullock*? His mouth flattened. "Do you think you can stand—"

Before he could finish his question her arms wound around his neck in a stranglehold. Another groan escaped her lips. Dear Lord, she couldn't be—

"Is it happening?" he demanded. Where the hell was Lily? He needed to get Merry down to her room.

"It?" Merry asked blankly. "Oh! *It.* No, sir. Bless you, sir. The little bugger just rammed his foot into me bladder is all. *It* isn't going to happen for a while yet."

Avery stared at the enormous belly so close to his nose. Ridiculous. No one could go about like that for "a while yet." There were certain laws of physics that demanded obedience and gravity was one of them.

"Just give me a moment more to catch me breath, sir. Now let me see, what was it I was sent to tell you . . . ?"

"Something about invitations," he prompted.

"Right you are, sir!" Merry beamed up at him. "I was just about to say as how the invitations is all for you, sir."

"Impossible," he said impatiently. "I just told you. I don't know anyone."

"But Mr. Thorne, you're *Mr. Thorne*. That's all you'd need be, but you're also Mr. Thorne what folks round here is been reading about for years. The gentry is mad with curiosity." Merry's head bobbed up and down. "Every last card is addressed to you. Miss Bede never gets invitations. Occasionally Miss and Mrs. Thorne do, but not Miss Bede. Not from the locals."

For some reason this set fire to his already exacerbated temper.

"I'm not surprised," he ground out. "Given time that woman could alienate an entire nation what with striding all over the countryside in those ridiculous bloomers and her arms swinging like a navy's. Did you see her yesterday morning?" he demanded. Merry's eyes grew round. "She was outside. Walking down the drive. And her hair was down. *Down*. For the whole bloody world to see!"

"Yes, sir," Merry said meekly.

"For God's sake don't cringe, girl. Do you see Miss Bede cringing? You do not. And why should she? I'm the gentlest of men!"

"Yes, sir," Merry agreed.

"A *gentleman*," he went on forcefully, "a breed I'm sure you're unfamiliar with living under Miss Bede's regime, you poor creature."

The girl glanced down at the huge mound of her

stomach. "Oh, I assure you," she muttered, "I've known my share of gentlemen."

"And as for the damned gentry around here not inviting her to their little parties," Avery shouted, "we'll bloody well see about that!"

"Really, Thorne," a familiar female voice rose from the stairwell, its clarion challenge as easily ignored as a train whistle, "you must learn to control the volume of your bellows. I could hear you from all the way upstairs."

Lily Bede appeared at the top of the stairs. Her gorgeous black eyes widened a second.

"Miss Bede," Avery said, facing off with her, "I do not bellow. I speak in a clear, easily heard voice. I was speaking to this young woman"—he bent his head at Merry—"*trying* to make a point."

Lily paid no attention to the little maid. She strode toward him, her chin held up in that entirely provocative way. "Some people make their point without shouting down the rafters. Were your travel companions by any chance deaf or is it you who have a hearing impairment?" she asked serenely.

"My hearing is perfect," he said, "as was my companions'. Indeed, I do not remember ever having raised my voice during the nearly five years I spent in their company."

She lifted one eyebrow in patent disbelief.

"And," he went on, determined not to increase his volume by so much as a decibel, "*if* my voice is raised it is only because I am sorely tested."

Primarily by Lily. Her hair was down again, and her collar was open, as though she'd forgotten to button it and he could see the fragile, shallow indentation that delineated her collarbone and the end of her lovely, long throat.

"Do I dare ask what so sorely tested you *this* morning?" she asked sweetly. "Last evening it was your wardrobe."

"None of my clothes fit," he replied, pleased with his calm tone. "I was merely expressing my exasperation with the situation."

"You were shouting," she said flatly. "This morning you were 'sorely tested' by my request that you limit smoking those filthy weeds to the outside."

He glowered at her. Perhaps he had protested her unreasonable request a shade more strenuously than a gentleman ought.

"And after luncheon you were 'sorely tested' because you misplaced some book—"

"My journal," he growled. "And I did *not* misplace it. One of the servants secreted it away!"

"*She put it on the bookshelf,*" Lily shouted back. "I'm sure she thought putting your book on your bookshelf wouldn't pose too great a challenge to your deductive capabilities."

"I didn't *leave* it on the bookshelf," he shot back. "I left it on the desk, which is where I wanted it. And I'd thank you to relay this information to the woman who does my room."

"Do it yourself." Her eyes flashed. "You're holding her."

Throughout this entire exchange Merry, cradled in Avery's arms, had maintained absolute silence. Now she produced a sickly smile. "Won't happen again, sir. I'll just leave everything right where you puts it." She looked so miserable, he couldn't remain angry with her.

"Fine then," he said kindly. "I'm sure you meant no harm."

"Is there anything else you wish to tell Merry?" Lily asked.

Avery glanced down at the girl. "No."

"Then why don't you put her down? Unless, of course," she said turning her gaze on Merry, "you object, Merry dear."

Merry squirmed. "No. Not at all. Not me," she said. "You can put me down now, sir."

Avery lowered her to the ground and stepped back, keeping one hand at ready in case she lost her balance.

"I feel much better. Thank you for your kindness." With amazing agility, Merry squatted, gathered up the pile of linens and scuttled away.

Lily watched Merry go with a sense of amusement mixed with relief. Merry was, to put it bluntly, incorrigible. But for one horrible instant, coming upon them, she'd thought she'd interrupted a tryst. Until she'd seen Avery's face. He'd been completely oblivious to any impropriety. Even in Lily's admittedly limited experience men did not look blankly oblivious unless they were.

No, Avery was simply doing what the situation demanded. The fact that others might not think well of him standing about a hallway holding a pregnant maid would never have occurred to him. Avery Thorne, for all his insistence on being a gentleman, was about as conversant with social niceties—and social prejudices—as a magpie was with Latin. And God help her, it only made her like him.

She couldn't afford to *like* Avery Thorne. He'd come to claim the home she'd worked five years to obtain.

She turned around. Bad idea. He was standing right beside her, so close her shoulder brushed his chest, sending tendrils of electricity coursing through her.

Luckily, he was scowling at Merry's departing back and did not notice her interest. She studied him.

He still hadn't acquired any new shirts and this one pulled tightly, clearly revealing the muscles of his chest. He'd dispensed with collars altogether—none came close to closing around his neck. He wore a pair of loose, much-laundered khaki trousers that did absolutely nothing to dampen her intrigue. They draped low around his hips and hung from his legs, hinting at the powerful muscles.

Lily bit her lip in frustration. This proximity thing was not working. She'd spent all of yesterday following him around waiting for the brain fever to break.

Her infatuation hadn't dimmed; it had grown. She had to do something about it.

"Should she be working this close to her . . . to her . . . now?" Avery suddenly turned, leveling an accusatory gaze upon her.

"Now?" Lily echoed, lost in contemplation of his newly shaved skin.

"Yes. *Now*." He lowered his head, peering into her face. "What the devil is wrong with you? Are you un-well?"

Too close. She backpedaled, stumbling toward the stairs. Her heels caught on the first riser and she be-gan to fall—Avery's hands shot out. He grabbed her shoulders and pulled her into his arms, away from the stairs.

For a second they stood, her breasts molded to his chest, his big hands tangled in her hair, the air static with the same attraction that had left her dry-mouthed and incoherent at the lunch table yesterday.

"Thank you." Her voice was high, superficial. "Ex-cuse me. I have things to do."

She pulled away and fled, pursued by the knowl-edge that Avery Thorne, the one man she'd ever felt so much affinity, oh damn, so much *attraction toward*, was her competition, her adversary, and thus, her dearest enemy.

Chapter Eight

"I don't care what you do with the invitations but I will certainly not be answering them. I am not your secretary."

Hearing Lily in the sitting room, Evelyn tossed her gloves on the hall table and, smiling at her son, motioned him to follow her.

She cracked the door and peeked inside. Her family was there. Lily sat on the window seat and Francesca on the sofa. Even the presense of that prickly Polly Makepeace sitting in a chair pulled next to the sofa couldn't dim her pleasure.

With a smile, she threw open the door, announcing to the startled inhabitants, "Look who I've brought home."

She took hold of Bernard's hand and tugged him into the room beside her. "You would have been proud of me, Lily. I was really quite firm—" She turned to shut the door and saw him.

Gerald.

The air left her lungs in a sharp gasp. She clutched Bernard's arm. *He* rose to his feet and came toward her, his features swimming out of focus.

"Evelyn?" She heard the concern in Lily's voice but could not tear her gaze from the approaching man.

"I'm delighted to meet you again," he said, "Cousin Evelyn."

Cousin Evelyn? He made as though to take her hand. Tremors of revulsion danced through her and she jerked away.

For a second he froze and then said smoothly, "How trying it must be to arrive home only to find it infiltrated by guests. Avery Thorne, ma'am. It's been a long time."

"Mr. Thorne!" Bernard said with surprised delight. He cleared his throat, reaching past her and holding out his hand. Avery shook it. "I'm pleased to make your acquaintance, sir."

"And I yours."

Avery Thorne, Evelyn thought faintly. *Yes, that would explain the resemblance.*

"Though," Avery went on, "I must point out that we have met before. You were in nappies and I was in knickers." He inclined his head. "But I am remiss. Won't you be seated, Cousin Evelyn?"

"Of course." She tried to smile, knew it to be a failure. "You've caught me unawares, I'm afraid. Forgive me for not properly greeting you . . . Cousin Avery."

"I believe I've taken everyone unawares, ma'am."

His gaze flickered toward where Lily sat watching intently. Poor Lily. Unused to men as she was, this great huge creature must terrify her.

Evelyn, using his momentary distraction to skirt by him, seated herself next to Polly Makepeace.

"It's a pleasure to see you again, Aunt Francesca." Bernard, displaying his newfound maturity, bent over his aunt's hand.

"And it's a pleasure to see you again, Bernard," Francesca said. "Since no one else seems likely to do so, let me introduce you to our houseguest, Miss Polly Makepeace. Miss Makepeace is recovering from an accident."

Evelyn flushed guiltily. She'd so focused on Avery that she'd failed to extend the simple courtesy of concern to their guest—however that guest had come by that status. Miss Makepeace hadn't meant to fall off the podium.

"I'm so glad you feel well enough to join the family, Miss Makepeace," she said.

"I know what you're thinking," Polly said gruffly. "Believe me, I wouldn't still be here but Miss Bede insisted I stay until I am able to walk unaided."

"Lily is absolutely right," Evelyn murmured. "We are only too pleased to have you."

"Hmph." Polly sank back in her chair as Bernard executed a polite bow in her direction.

Mindful of Lily's unusual silence, Evelyn studied the girl, noting worriedly that Lily was dressed in what she called her "rationals." Her color was high;

her eyes glittered dangerously. Men disliked women in masculine garb. Particularly men like Avery Thorne. And Evelyn knew all too well how important it was to curry favor with men.

Right now Lily's garment didn't seem rational so much as rash. The trouser-like things drew attention to hips and lower curves that were far from masculine and her man's shirt only accented her exotic femininity. Only her hair, pulled into a nice neat chignon, looked unexceptional.

Evelyn turned her attention to Avery. Soon he would be Bernard's guardian. The thought brought a wave of despair.

For nearly five years they'd rattled happily along at Mill House, their occasional crisis put to rights by Lily's skillful management, their wants gratified by Lily's generous nature, their rare instances of friction soothed by Lily's diplomacy. Their lives had flowed on like a feather drifting down a slow river.

They rarely socialized, Francesca because she was nearly as notorious as Lily was unacceptable and Evelyn because she would not associate with those who snubbed Lily. Not that she missed country society, not at all.

Others might consider their lives dull. Evelyn liked it that way. She'd had quite enough excitement in her eight years of marriage. Here with Lily, for the first time in her life, a man was not ordering her world; she didn't need to flatter a man to ensure domestic harmony or trade her body for his goodwill or pacify him in order to win some small liberty. And yet now, suddenly, Avery Thorne appeared, resurrecting memories. Unpleasant memories.

He looked so very much like Gerald. The same bold features, the same startlingly colored eyes, the large hands capable of such punishing strength. Only his expression was different, but then, the candor and integrity in his face could be a trick of light. . . .

Avery looked up, catching Evelyn's eye. He smiled slightly, an ironic twist of the lips that sent Evelyn's gaze plummeting to her lap. She cursed herself as a coward.

How could she give up all the privileges and freedoms she'd discovered? Indeed, how could she ask this man for anything when she couldn't even meet his gaze?

"Miss Bede." Having done his duty by his aunt and Polly, Bernard was approaching Lily. "I trust you are keeping well."

"Very well, thank you," Lily said. "You've certainly, grown, haven't you?"

At nearly six feet, Bernard towered over his next tallest classmate by a good six inches. He would even top Lily by some inches.

"Yes, Miss Bede. So they say."

"Aren't you going to offer him some of Francesca's chocolate?" Avery asked. The innocuous question brought a flush to Lily's cheeks. Her head snapped up and she pierced Avery with a glare.

Evelyn stared at Lily, amazed at her boldness, until

she remembered that Lily had spent four years trading written volleys point for point with this man. Never once had she backed down. Evelyn watched with wistful admiration as Lily rose to her full height—and no one could call it any less than impressive—battle lights gleaming in her sloe black eyes. A man would never cow Lily.

With a sigh of resignation, Avery followed suit. "You pop up and down more often than a child's Jack-in-the-box," he said.

"No one forced you to your feet," Lily said.

"Only manners," Avery replied. Apparently the conversation had occurred before and with no satisfactory outcome since neither of them bothered to pursue it.

"And as for chocolate, I'd sooner give Bernard a kiss," she said and, suiting the act to the words, bussed Bernard gently on his smooth cheek. "Welcome home, Bernard."

Bernard suffered this assault on his teenage dignity without flinching. But Lily, ever sensitive to those she loved, saw the embarrassment her kiss caused.

"Stand still, lad," Avery murmured lazily. "Miss Bede is simply demonstrating her affectionate nature."

Bernard colored. In concern Evelyn leaned forward. Highly emotional episodes sometimes precipitated Bernard's bouts with breathlessness.

"He's fine," Polly whispered comfortingly. "Listen. You can't hear a thing untoward." At Evelyn's startled glance she went on. "Miss Bede told me about his lungs."

"I didn't mean to offend you, Bernard," Lily said.

"Not at all," Bernard replied. He did sound fine. Evelyn relaxed. "As Cousin Avery pointed out, you are blessed with a warm heart. Your welcome simply surprised me. Harrow's deans are seldom so affectionate."

"Well said, lad," Avery said approvingly. "Your Latin might stand improving, but I see Harrow has succeeded in making a gentleman of you."

Bernard acknowledged this accolade by beaming with pleasure.

"That's all they need do at his school to meet your approval?" Lily asked Avery. "Teach him the right manners, the right way to act, give him a list of the right things to say?"

"Right," Avery said, watching Lily with the same lazy attentiveness the barn cat might watch newborn chicks.

As if she couldn't believe her ears, she moved closer to him. "Does that not strike you as a trifle elitist?"

"Gentlemanly behavior *is* elitism of the most welcome variety," Avery said. "I hope Bernard aspires to codes of conduct which will serve him well throughout his life."

"As it has served you."

"I can only hope so, yes." They glared at each other.

Evelyn's stomach fluttered unpleasantly. Lily, apparently oblivious to any danger, moved within a few feet of Avery. In distress Evelyn realized how exceptionally tall he was; he topped Lily by at least five inches. He banked his brilliant gaze behind bronze lashes. Evelyn mistrusted that unfathomable expression. He could reach out and strike—

"Mr. Thorne," Lily said, "you may pine for the days when one could demand pistols at dawn simply because someone declared your gloves an imperfect fit, but I assure you that the modern world doesn't give this for such things."

She snapped her fingers under his chin. Evelyn's breath caught in her throat.

Avery simply looked down in telling silence upon the slender fingers beneath his chin and with even more telling silence up again into Lily's eyes.

Lily arched one black brow. "*I* consider it far more important that Bernard learn mathematics, economics, and history. Someday he will have the responsibility of an enormous inheritance. That word, in case you aren't familiar with it, is spelled r-e—"

"I seem to recall having heard it once or twice," Avery broke in.

"Good. Then perhaps you'll understand that Bernard has better ways to occupy his time than committing to memory an antiquated list of gentlemanly do's and don'ts."

"If you really believe that academic gymnastics are more important than one's conduct," Avery said clearly, "it's fortunate Bernard's education shall soon be in my hands, isn't it?"

"Of all the—"

"Excuse me for interrupting," Bernard's voice cut across Lily's sputtering, "but may I ask how you knew about the Latin, sir?"

His eyes never leaving Lily's face, Avery answered. "Oh, I haven't taken my *responsibilities* quite as lightly as Miss Bede assumes. I've had an ongoing correspondence with your deans for the last five years."

"You mean you told Bernard's tutors where to write you and you never told me?" Lily asked, her voice rising.

"I thought you rather enjoyed the challenge of finding me," Avery replied.

Evelyn could practically see the sparks leaping between their locked gazes.

"Something is definitely up between them," Polly Makepeace whispered as Lily struggled for her composure. "My old mum's corset laces had less strain on them than there is between those two. And she weighed near thirty stone."

Evelyn caught back a burst of laughter, her anxiety fleeing before the absurd image. She had never spent more time than necessary in Polly's company simply because the woman not only had the bad manners to think Lily unfit to lead her precious Coalition but worse, said so at every opportunity. She'd no idea Polly had a sense of humor.

"Why does she purposely antagonize him?" Evelyn

asked in a low voice. "Doesn't she realize he's getting angry?"

"Mrs. Thorne," Polly said, "whatever I think about Miss Bede's qualifications to lead the Coalition, I have never doubted her courage. She and that fellow have been at it since he arrived and she's not yet come out of one of these verbal scrimmages the loser—though honesty compels me to admit she's not been the winner, either."

Fascinated by the notion that Lily had continually held her own against this huge male, Evelyn grew pensive.

"Why the long face, Mrs. Thorne?" Polly asked as Lily launched into another diatribe, still standing toe to toe with the tall, muscular young man in the ill-fitting coat.

"Lily," she murmured. "She is so much better suited to dealing with men. Avery Thorne doesn't intimidate her in the least. I envy that."

"Oh come," Polly said, but not unkindly, "Mr. Thorne doesn't appear to be an unreasonable fellow. Loud and a bit brusque, barely any manners. But a good heart. An honorable sort. In short not unlike Miss Bede herself. Personally, I rather appreciate such straightforwardness in a man."

For the life of her Evelyn could not have said what made her confide in Polly Makepeace. Perhaps her unexpected sympathy, perhaps the suddenness with which the situation had been thrust upon her made it hard to keep her anxiety contained. Whatever the reason, she found the words coming from her lips.

"I would appreciate never having to deal with such a man again," she said. "I cannot imagine what it will be like living under his aegis without Lily to act as our voice."

"Why would you need another woman to speak for you, Mrs. Thorne?" Polly cocked her head inquiringly.

"Come, Miss Makepeace," Evelyn said without rancor, "surely you do not assume that the lower classes have monopoly on matrimonial . . . discord. My own experience has rendered me quite unwilling, perhaps even incapable, of dealing adequately with 'brusque, loud men.'"

"I see."

Evelyn smiled wanly. "Do you?"

"And you think Miss Bede better suited to dealing with Mr. Thorne and his ilk?"

"How can you doubt it?" Evelyn asked. "Look at her. Even if she doesn't win these confrontations, she's fully in the fray. She's magnificent."

"Yes," Polly said thoughtfully. "She certainly seems to be enjoying herself. And he is nearly as exhilarated. Look at how he devours her with his gaze. Look how she glares back."

Evelyn nodded her head miserably. "Yes. I would never be able to stand up to him like that."

Images of a bleak, anxious future wrung tears from her eyes. She groped in her pocket, glad Bernard's attention was still centered on Lily and Avery Thorne. Amazingly, it was Polly's small, rough hand that tucked a handkerchief into hers, patting her fist awkwardly. The kindness was nearly her undoing. She sniffed softly. "Dear God, how am I going to—how can I ever hope—"

"Hush, now," Polly advised softly. "If you would do me the favor of wheeling me into the hall, Mrs. Thorne, I think I may have a solution to all our problems."

Chapter Nine

"I enjoyed your letters, Cousin Avery," the boy said.

"Good," Avery replied, eyes fixed on the straight figure of Lily Bede eating up the ground in long graceful strides fifty yards ahead. In spite of her speed, her hips swayed gently, her arms, relaxed at her sides, moved in fluid rhythm matching her pace. She moved with an elemental sort of comeliness, like a dancer in a dream, unself-conscious and stirringly natural.

The sun beat down upon them with unseasonable virulence. Dragonflies with slender, iridescent blue bodies rose from the edges of the path in silent battalions as they passed. The field grasses hissed sotto voce with a dry, warm wind.

Lily had decided they would eat alfresco.

One minute she'd been locked in battle with him, her whole body shivering with contention, the next she'd announced they would eat outside to celebrate Bernard's homecoming.

"The other lads did, too."

"Come again?" Avery said, pushing the sleeves of his coat up. Too hot for wool. Too hot for a jacket, for that matter. He yanked it off.

"The lads at school. They enjoyed your stories, too."

"Oh. Good." *She* didn't look overheated.

"Particularly the ones about Africa." The lad sounded a bit winded.

"Africa is an interesting place," he said falling back and slowing his pace to accommodate Bernard's. Lily opened the distance between them, her bloomers cutting a swathe through the grass as she led Francesca and Evelyn across the back lawn toward a magnificent beech tree. A short distance behind plodded Hob, loaded down like a pack mule.

Francesca, her expertly painted face suffering under a combination of heat and sweat, struggled along in her lacey skirts to keep up. Evelyn, looking bewildered, was actually trotting.

Not that Lily noticed. To notice she would have needed to turn around and risk seeing him, something she suddenly seemed loathe to do. Exasperating woman.

"—Miss Bede's future."

"What?"

Avery stopped. Bernard stopped.

"I was saying how sometime soon, at your convenience, I would appreciate the opportunity to discuss Miss Bede's future."

"What about Miss Bede's future?" Avery demanded.

Bernard's dark blond hair clung damply to his temples and his pallor was waxen. His wrists, sticking out from the ends of his snug tweed jacket, were chaffed and his collar points wilted.

"Take the blasted thing off, Bernard. You'll pass out. Now what about Miss Bede's future?"

"Sir,"—the boy shrugged off his jacket—"do you really think this is the place? I mean, as gentlemen ought we to be discussing Miss Bede so publicly?"

"Bernard," Avery said with exasperated patience, "I am entirely conversant with gentlemanly behavior. This is as good a place as any for a discussion."

"Yes, sir." Bernard didn't sound convinced.

"Out with it."

"Well, sir, I was wondering what you proposed to do about it. Her future, that is."

"I wasn't aware I needed to do anything about it," Avery answered. "In fact I have learned only this morning that I may be entirely—and I do not hesitate to add happily—excluded from any involvement in Miss Bede's future whatsoever."

"Sir?"

"I've had contact with Horatio's bank and, er, glanced over the household records," Avery explained. "It is not too far beyond the realms of possibility that Lily Bede might actually end her five years as manager here with a small profit to show. If she does, she'll inherit Mill House."

The boy met his gaze directly. "And then what?"

"What do you mean, then what?" Avery said irritably. Lily inheriting Mill House wasn't the best possible situation but the end result would be the same. "She'll sell the place—to me—and go off and do whatever it is she wants to do. Buy herself a closet full of menswear, I should imagine." His gaze flickered toward the enticing swell filling out the backside of Lily's bloomers.

"I doubt she'll sell Mill House to you."

"Whyever not?" Avery asked in amazement.

He'd designed solutions to meet every possible contingency that might interfere with his acquisition of Mill House, even the unlikely one where Lily inherited it. In that case, he'd planned on paying Lily a generous price for the estate, which she would then gratefully accept and go away. The boy's doubts disrupted that neat little bit of scripting.

"Who else would she sell it to?" he asked.

"I think it likely she'd sell it to Mr. Camfield."

"And who the bloody hell is Mr. Camfield?"

"Please, lower your voice, Cousin Avery. Mr. Camfield is our neighbor. He bought Parkwood last spring. He's ever so rich, at least mother says he is, and he wants to expand his holdings. Miss Bede says he's a progressive thinker, very supportive of women."

"I'll bet he is. And I'll bet he joined the progressive thinker ranks the day he met Lil—Miss Bede," Avery muttered darkly.

"Well, she did say as how she had aided at least one male in seeing reason."

Avery made a disparaging sound. "Mr. Camfield is doomed to disappointment if he is counting on acquiring Mill House. It's mine. If by some miracle Miss Bede inherits it, she'll deal with *me* and none other."

"Perhaps, in spite of what mother thinks, she won't want to sell at all," Bernard suggested. "Perhaps she'll try to run the estate herself."

Avery snorted. "Unlikely. Whatever else Miss Bede is, she is no fool and only a fool would choose a risky venture over a comfortable future."

"Where would this comfortable future be?" Bernard asked.

Avery shrugged. "Wherever she wants it to be."

The boy ran his hand through his hair, setting it on end. "I can't accept that. You can't just leave her to her own devices. It won't do."

Can't accept that? Won't do? Now, Avery appreciated a strong-willed lad as much as the next man—he'd been one himself—but this bordered on insolence. "Would you care to elaborate?" he asked in a careful voice.

The boy rounded on Avery. "I know she'll have money, but if she sells the estate she won't have anywhere to go. Mill House is her *home;* my mother and my aunt are her family. She'll be torn from those who love her."

Bernard flung out his arm in passionate appeal. Avery gazed at it, touched in spite of himself. He could imagine what a home could mean . . . and the loss of it.

"No one's tearing Miss Bede from anywhere and while your concern for her is noble, remember, even if she does inherit, your mother and aunt would still leave."

The boy scowled at him in confusion.

"You wouldn't expect them to stay here as Miss Bede's boarders, would you?"

Bernard shook his head.

"But," he said consolingly, "once I acquire it, your mother can continue to make her home here with me. Don't worry. I wouldn't bar Miss Bede from the door when she comes visiting, if that's what you fear."

"You don't understand. Miss Bede won't come visiting."

He didn't like that. He'd developed a rather nice image of Lily Bede knocking on his door. He would invite her in and treat her with all the courtesies and geniality she'd lacked in her reception of him. It would irk her no end. "Whyever not?" he demanded.

"Because of society!"

The meaning of the boy's words hit Avery with unnerving force. Bernard hurried on, taking advantage of the splinter of pain revealed for a second on Avery's face.

"Miss Bede is proud," Bernard said earnestly. "Very proud. Once she's left this house, I can all but assure you she'll never call on mother and Aunt Francesca again. She'd never risk bringing censure down upon them by presuming on an acquaintance."

"That's absurd," Avery bit out.

"Is it?" The boy's blue-green eyes, which were the same color as his own, begged for assurance.

"Of course. Money buys expiation for a multitude of sins. The small matter of her illegitimacy will soon be forgotten."

"Maybe amongst the aristocracy but country society is a far more unforgiving lot."

"Then she'll move to London," Avery said, feeling more and more that he was being backed into a corner.

"Away from mother and Aunt Francesca? Away from her horses? She *hates* London."

"Drat it all, Bernard," Avery said, "you're borrowing trouble. The chance of Lily Bede succeeding, though greater than I'd ever anticipated, is still damn nigh nonexistent. All it would take would be a worm infestation in the orchard or a bit of dry rot discovered in the barn to eat up that pitiful profit she's managed to scrape together."

For a long minute, Bernard stood silent, his brow furrowed in imitation of a much older man's concern.

Avery laid his hand on Bernard's shoulder. "I promise you," he said, "that I am, and will remain, mindful of my obligations to Miss Bede."

Whatever the boy read in Avery's eyes seemed to satisfy him, at least for the time being, for he let go a

small sigh of pent-up anxiety. With the uneasy sense
that he'd just promised far more than he'd intended,
Avery dropped his hand and started toward the beech
tree. Beneath it the three women were spreading blankets while Hob drove stakes into the ground to secure
the small striped pavilion Francesca had insisted on
bringing.

"And if she doesn't succeed in winning Mill House
what will you do then?"

With a growl, Avery swung around. Bernard
blinked at him. The lad was like some terrier with a
rat. He just didn't give up. *Just like myself at that age*,
Avery thought. He, too, had never lacked courage—
though some would call it suicidal impertinence, he
amended with an inner smile. Obviously a family trait.
"I'll take care of her." He turned around again.

"Really?"

He stopped. "Really."

"You swear?"

Family traits aside, there was such a thing as knowing when to quit. "Bernard—" he began warningly.

"What if she doesn't want to be taken care of?" the
boy pressed.

Avery spun around. "I don't give a bloody damn
what she wants!" he thundered. "I'm a *gentleman*,
damn it all. As long as she's my responsibility, I'll do
whatever is necessary to see she's provided for. If that
means keeping her at Mill House, that's what I'll do,
even if I have to chain her to the bloody wall!"

"Could you really do that?" Bernard asked, wide-eyed.

Avery shot him a sardonic glance and stalked away, flinging over his shoulder as he went, "Do you doubt it?"

Lily flipped open the lid of the woven basket and surveyed the contents. Cheese, ham, a potted quail, a half dozen loaves of crusty bread, ceramic jars of butter, and an oiled paper wrapper containing a heavy butter cake saturated in rum. She sighed.

She was going to have to speak to Mrs. Kettle about her current flights into the exalted—and blasted expensive—heights of haute cuisine. They simply couldn't afford it.

Each morning Lily found the small, wizened cook bent over scraps of paper scrawled in an unintelligible hand, her lips moving silently as she read to herself the magic ingredients inscribed thereon. And she did it all for *him*. In fact the entire household seemed in thrall to the dratted creature.

Including me, she thought. She kept her head averted, but could not help seeing him out of the corner of her eye. He'd flung his jacket over his shoulder and his shirt was open at the throat. The sun flared off his rumpled, unkempt locks with a buttery gleam.

Lily stopped unpacking, sitting back on her heels and listening. For a second there she could have sworn she heard him shouting her name.

Nonsense. They were enemies, for God's sake. Two

dogs on opposite ends of a juicy bone. She should be worrying about the *bone*, not the color of the other hound's eyes!

Lily could have pinched herself in frustration. Not only was her plan to rid herself of her infatuation through familiarity not working, it was ricocheting.

Arguing with him in the sitting room a while ago, her eye on a level with his strong, tanned throat she'd been seized by the most amazing impulse and she knew, not feared, she *knew* that if she remained within arm's reach of him she would act upon it. She'd touch him.

She'd practically run from the house. And she'd planned this picnic in order to blow some of the cobwebs from her thoughts, but her thoughts remained stubbornly entangled with him.

A kiss would do the trick, Lily thought. Just one kiss and she would realize that she'd invested the experience with a momentousness that in reality it simply didn't own. She'd be cured. She'd stop waking up in the middle of the night to vague, disturbing images of Avery Thorne and far less vague, but decidedly more disturbing, sensations involving the same man. And his mouth. And his chest. And his hands.

Unfortunately, the likelihood of Avery kissing her and putting an end to this nonsense was about the same as her farm manager Drummond being civil. In other words, none.

It wasn't fair. Men went about deciding whom

they'd like to kiss and acting on it. Why shouldn't women be allowed to take a like initiative?

She glanced over her shoulder. Avery and Bernard were still deep in conversation. Avery turned so he was facing her. Against his skin, burnished beneath tropical suns, his shirt looked dazzling white. His Mediterranean-colored eyes were narrowed against the midday glare of the sun. That must have been where he'd gotten that fine fanning of pale lines at their corners.

"Gorgeous, isn't he?" Francesca whispered.

"I'm sure I don't know what you mean." Lily returned to rummaging in the bottom of the basket for the oranges she'd seen Mrs. Kettle pack.

"And so shy," Francesca murmured.

"Shy?" Lily asked increduously, ignoring the fact that she'd had the same impression. Francesca nodded. "He is the most domineering, arrogant, autocratic man I have ever met."

"You obviously haven't met many men."

"You're teasing me," Lily said flatly. "You must be."

"No," Francesca denied. "I'm quite sincere. Avery Thorne is a very shy man. I will admit that something about you seems to draw out his finer qualities—"

"Finer qualities?" Lily sputtered.

"Yes. He's quite quick-witted when engaged in a conversation with you. When he's with me, or even Evelyn, he's painfully reticent."

"Ha, you mistake him. He doesn't speak to you because he's a misogynist. As a woman you are beneath his notice."

"Don't be obtuse," Francesca said flatly. "He's a man. If he was as haughty and full of himself as you think, don't you imagine he'd spend his time regaling us with tales of his adventures? He'd constantly be driving home his superiority with tales of his fearlessness."

Lily was unconvinced.

"Lily," Francesca sighed, "the man has been around the world. He has seen things no European has ever witnessed. If anyone has cause to be proud, it would be him. Yet he never speaks of himself at all. I tell you, he's shy, at least around women, and who would expect different? He was raised in the company of males."

"He doesn't seem to have any trouble voicing his opinions around me," Lily said gruffly. Apparently he considered her so far removed from being a regular woman that he felt none of the discomfort around her that he did around feminine creatures. She glanced down at her bloomers.

"Yes." Francesca grinned. "I've noticed that."

"Not that I care," Lily said.

Francesca chuckled, tapping her lightly on the cheek. "You're a terrible liar, Lil, not to mention sincere and valiant and worthy. I swear you'd bore me to tears if it weren't for that delicious little hedonist you keep so carefully hidden."

"I'm delighted I amuse you," Lily said. She found an orange.

"Oh, you do," Francesca said. "But even more than amuse, you intrigue me. Such middle-class constraints choking that bohemian heart of yours. You look like a refugee from a seraglio and act like a prioress."

"I'm sure I don't know what you mean," Lily said, lying back against the tree trunk and digging her nails into an orange rind. She pared it away, careful to avoid looking in the direction of the approaching males.

Francesca spread her skirts with an elegant flip of her wrists and settled like a butterfly on the lawn beside her. She reached into the basket and withdrew her own orange. "I mean that if I were you I would never allow a man to get me into such a state."

"I'm not in a state."

"Oh, darling." Francesca shook her head, her mouth tipping with amusement. "You are in *such* a state."

"I don't like this!" Lily burst out.

"That's obvious."

"For me to be so preoccupied with . . . it is *stupid*!"

"Well now—"

"It's unfair!"

"Decidedly."

"It's such a waste of time!"

"Don't blaspheme, dear."

"What am I going to do?" she finally asked. Francesca dropped the orange she'd been inspecting and with a delighted smile that seemed to say she'd been waiting for Lily to ask just that question, moved nearer—and told her.

Chapter Ten

Resting on his elbows, one leg crooked and the other stretched out before him, his vest unbuttoned and his collar agape, Avery tilted his head back and blew out a fragrant cloud of cigar smoke. Through the bluish haze, he saw Lily, seated at least a dozen feet away and upwind, wrinkle her nose and cough. Nearby Polly Makepeace grilled poor Bernard about his "life at an institution." Hob had managed to shove her here in her wheelchair.

Perhaps it was because he'd never had the opportunity to enjoy the company of women when they were at ease and relaxed, but he found he rather enjoyed listening to them. He discovered they were much more complex than he'd have guessed. Except for Lily Bede—whom he'd never made the mistake of underestimating.

He turned his head to see her better. In profile her lashes were extravagantly long, her nose patrician, her nostrils wide, her lips full.

Impossible creature. Argumentative. Pinch-penny. Incisive. Tender. She probably laid abed at night plotting ways to provoke him. Her determination to have Mill House was nearly as great as his own. Finding such resolution and intensity in one of the creatures he'd been taught were pliant and tractable confounded him and must account for his utterly inexplicable fascination with her.

"What are your plans for tomorrow, Lily?" Evelyn was asking.

"Not much," Lily responded. "I have an appointment to speak to Mr. Drummond, the same as I do every third Monday of the month."

"You should tell your overseer to wash the raddle off your sheep soon," Polly spoke up, drawing the amazed looks of the entire party. "Saw the beasts standing about in the stuff. It's going to be a nasty hot summer. You don't want the sheep sickening while their wool dries."

"I will mention it," Lily said.

"Miss Makepeace's father oversaw one of the Earl of Hinton's farms," Evelyn confided.

"Sounds tedious," Francesca said and then, at Evelyn's gasp, added, "Oh, not your father's occupation, Miss Makepeace. Lily's plans for the morrow. Drummond and she have never gotten along."

Lily wished Francesca hadn't brought up her problems with the farm manager. Avery would see her inability to handle Drummond as evidence of her ineffectiveness. Though why that should matter to her was beyond her understanding. "We deal reasonably well together."

"But Lily!" Evelyn exclaimed. "You are always saying that the man has no respect for you. Last time you had an appointment, he locked you out of his office."

Lily produced a nervous laugh. "Oh, that was just his little joke."

"I suspect he'd listen to you if Avery stood at your side," Evelyn said sagely. Lily glared at her.

"That won't be necessary." She glanced at Avery, who lay spread out like a potentate amidst his concubines.

"I remember old Drummond," he said lazily. An idea was taking form. He wanted to discover what Lily had done to the farm. The record from the household had only told of expenditures on soap, dry goods, and groceries. The bank's officers had not known how she'd managed to accrue a positive balance, only that she had. Perhaps she'd made her profits by selling off equipment, or by overgrazing the pastures. Drummond could tell him. "Taught me to snare rabbits."

"Such a font of knowledge," Lily said.

"Oh, you'd be amazed," Avery told her. "Drummond's really rather a dear."

Lily's mouth dropped open. "Drummond? *Dear*?"

"Well, maybe 'dear' is overstating his appeal a bit." Avery couldn't help but grin.

Lily's dark eyes widened, her brows rose, the corners of her mouth tipped up, and she laughed.

Throaty, deep, delicious laughter that vibrated through his heart.

"Drummond's allure is rather elusive," she said with that throaty chuckle.

His own smile widened. She leaned forward, as though to say something more. He tossed his cigar away and sat up to hear her better. Her lips still held the shadow of her smile. Her expression was genial and unguarded. A wisp of raven hair that had escaped captivity danced across her smooth brow.

With the slightest effort he could bridge the distance between them, curl his fingers around her slender throat, and pull her mouth down to his and—

What the hell was he thinking? Abruptly he recognized the silence surrounding them. He looked around. All eyes were turned in their direction. Expectancy vibrated in the air. Lily, shaking her head like a swimmer coming up from too long underwater, sank back against the tree.

Evelyn sighed, Francesca closed her eyes with an air of disgust, Polly Makepeace snorted, and Bernard divided anxious glances amongst them all.

Avery's instincts were clamoring again. Something was going on. Well, he had a few plans of his own. "Drummond's probably the last person still here who worked on the estate when I was a boy. I wonder if he remembers me." He paused. "Mind if I tag along after you tomorrow?"

Lily eyed him warily. "You'd be bored."

"That's right. She does have an estate to run, you

know," Polly said with grudging pride. "She can't play hostess all the time. Besides, I'm sure you wouldn't understand half of what they'll be discussing."

"I'm confident I would cull the essentials from their discussion," he replied with forced calm. The truth was he knew next to nothing about farming. The realization that Polly Makepeace did was irksome in the extreme.

"You'd be better off visiting this man later when they have finished their business," Polly went on in that off-putting tone. "Then you and this Drummond can reminisce about rabbits to your heart's content. No need to interfere with important work. Don't you agree, Mrs. Thorne?"

Evelyn gulped and nodded.

Stonily, Avery regarded Polly Makepeace. Now she'd crossed the line from advising to patronizing—which was intolerable.

Evelyn took a deep breath. "If you're bored, Mr. Thorne, perhaps Mrs. Kettle will pack you a nice lunch. You could eat by the river. Perhaps even fish. I'm sure Bernard would be happy to help you dig worms in the morning." She finished her little speech in a breathless rush and slumped down in her chair as if near fainting.

"Ah." Bernard's head snapped back and forth between his mother and Polly Makepeace. "Of course. My pleasure."

Fishing. Picnics. Digging for worms. They even thought they'd found the useless male a playmate in old Drummond. Next they'd be suggesting a rousing game of badminton so he'd sleep well tonight.

"That's settled then," Lily said, clapping her hands together and rummaging into one of the oversized wicker baskets. "Now, how about a nice game of badminton?"

Francesca shrugged. Bernard nodded eagerly. Even Evelyn's wan face lit up as she rose to her feet.

"No."

The women, in the process of handing out rackets, stopped and blinked at him.

"It's quite an enjoyable game, Mr. Thorne," Polly said. "You shouldn't have any trouble learning the rules."

He struggled to keep his voice level. "I meant 'no' it's not settled. Not 'no' to your game."

"What's not settled?" Lily asked.

"Whether or not I accompany you to Drummond's office tomorrow. Unless there is something you specifically wish me not to know, I see no reason why I shouldn't go along with you."

Lily drew a hissing breath. "Are you suggesting I—"

"I'm *suggesting* that there is no reason at all why I shouldn't hear what you and Drummond discuss. I already have plans to leave for London the following day."

"Oh? Why?" she asked.

"To order some"—he glanced down—"clothes."

Triumphantly he indicated where his shirt stretched tightly across his chest. "Unless you object?"

Point to him. Lily regarded him with an unreadable expression. Rather like a desert rat held in the mesmerizing sway of a cobra, though the reason why she should suddenly look so threatened eluded him.

"No," she said in an odd, stilted voice, "no objections. Suit yourself."

Francesca, who'd been uncharacteristically silent during the entire exchange, laughed. "I may have to foreswear the Derby entirely this year. The entertainment at Mill House promises to be far more diverting."

"Yoo-hoo!" A girlish voice trumpeted from somewhere between them and the house. A second later Teresa, the most pregnant of Mill House's three maids, trudged into view. Spying them, she stopped dead, clutched her chest, and fell over flat on her back, stiff legs poking dramatically above the grass before dropping out of sight.

"My God!" Bernard exclaimed. Before Avery could act, Bernard took off across the field, his long legs and flapping coat conspiring to give him the appearance of a giant stork attacking a mollusk.

"Oh, my," Evelyn murmured.

Without a word, Avery headed for where he could see Bernard attempting to hoist Teresa. It didn't look to be going too well. Bernard had Teresa under her knees and around her shoulders. If she hadn't been swollen like an October pumpkin she would have folded in the middle. As it was, she looked like a fat octopus perched on a piece of coral. Legs and arms wheeled madly as the boy struggled to carry her.

Avery tapped the struggling Bernard on the shoulder. The boy's head swung around. "I'm . . . fine . . . sir."

"No, he ain't," complained Teresa, apparently quite conscious. "He's gonna drop me!"

"Maybe I should carry—" Avery started to say, but the wounded expression on Bernard's face stopped him.

Teresa, however, was not quite so sensitive to Bernard's role as her knight-errant. "Yes, sir," she said eagerly. "I think you should. Wouldn't do to injure the poor boy's back now, would it? Not when a strapping fellow like you could carry poor wee me without raising a sweat."

"Hmm," Avery said. Sweat was indeed beading up on Bernard's forehead, and his breathing had developed a familiar rattling quality. Much more of his present exertion and Bernard would succumb to a full-blown attack. And yet, Avery all too well remembered the humiliation of being physically inadequate. Of feeling ineffectual, powerless . . . less than a man.

"Perhaps she might proceed under her own power?" Lily suggested.

He hadn't heard her approach. She stood very tall, eyes as piercing as a member of the Spanish Inquisition about to begin an examination. Behind her came

Francesca, Evelyn, and Polly Makepeace being shoved along by a grumbling Hobs.

Teresa smiled weakly. "I swear I don't know what come over me, Miss Bede."

"Really?" Lily's cool gaze encompassed them. "I wonder if I could guess? Bernard, put her down. And, no, Mr. Thorne, your services won't be needed. The girl is fine. Aren't you, Teresa?"

Bernard lowered Teresa awkwardly to her feet. She gave a sickly grin and nervously wiped her hands on her apron. "Yes, ma'am. I'm fine now. I think it was the heat, ma'am."

"Heat? Pshaw! Women are far too frail these days," Polly declared. "I think it is because of those unnatural contraptions they wear beneath their clothing. Corsets and bustles and such. What do you think, Mr. Thorne?"

"I?" Thorne echoed, confounded by the turn of the conversation. He'd never given any thought to women's undergarments. Well, actually, as a boy he'd given it quite a lot of thought, but never in concert with health considerations. "I don't think anything."

"As suspected," Lily muttered.

"I meant," he said with formidable calm, "that I do not have an opinion."

"Well, I do," Miss Makepeace said. "If women stopped wearing all that rubbish they'd find themselves capable of much more. In fact, I suspect corsets were created by men to keep women from discovering that except for certain unavoidable procreative functions men are by and large unnecessary."

"That," Avery said, "is the most ridiculous piece of bull—of vanity I have ever heard."

"I think Miss Makepeace makes an excellent point," Lily said. "Except for cruder matters requiring bulk and brawn, a woman can do anything a man can."

"Please," Avery said, "don't embarrass yourself."

"Would you like me to prove it?"

"This is not worth discussing."

She tossed her head. "Ha! Men always say that when they are about to lose an argument."

He'd had enough. "How would *you* know what men always say, Miss Bede? I'd thought that hitherto you'd dedicated yourself to living as independently of men as possible."

"Oh!"

"Women always say that when they're about to lose an argument," he purred.

Arriving last, Francesca flopped down on the grass and cradled her chin in her palm. Evelyn, after a confused glance around, sank down next to her and folded her hands. Teresa, forgotten, shuffled uncomfortably.

"Are you afraid to accept such a challenge?"

For ten long heartbeats, they faced each other, energy, frustration, and pure, unadulterated heat burning up the space between them.

"No," he finally said, "I am a gentleman. I will not accept a spurious dare that would only make us both look foolish." He turned.

"Coward."

His head snapped back a fraction of an inch, but he did not retaliate. He *would* be a gentleman.

"Why did you come out here?" he addressed Teresa.

"Huh? Oh. I came out to tell you there's guests arrived. A gentleman and two ladies. Quality. For Mr. Thorne."

"A *gentleman*, Teresa?" Lily asked in a patently false tone of awe. "And Quality to boot? For Mr. Thorne? My, we are blessed!"

With her chin high, she whirled and headed for the house, leaving Avery to pull Francesca to her feet while Bernard performed a similar gallantry for his mother and Hob resumed shoving Polly's wheelchair.

They arrived to find Lily in the sitting room greeting a dark-haired, mustachioed young man and two pretty, fresh-faced blond girls.

"Excuse us, Miss Bede, for being so presumptuous but my sisters and I were driving by and decided to chance you would be at home and willing to receive us," the man was saying.

Well-fed, well-groomed looking chap, thought Avery. Silly mustachio. Nice boots.

"Your sisters?" A hollowness in Lily's simple query struck Avery. "But how kind, how very delightful that you would think of us," she went on, tripping over her words. "I wasn't even aware you had—I mean, your sisters! My. This seems to be a week for unantici-

pated—albeit happy—arrivals. Bernard has been restored to us for the summer."

He'd never heard a false tone from her before and
it irritated him to hear the supercilious accents now.

" 'Restored?' " Avery muttered. "You make it sound
as if you found the lad packed in mothballs in the
attic."

The two pretty girls snickered behind their gloved
fingertips. Lily's back stiffened.

"Allow me to introduce Avery Thorne." Without a
glance his way, she wiggled her fingers in his general
direction. "He's visiting. Mr. Thorne, our neighbor,
Mr. Martin Camfield."

The two men nodded at each other.

Camfield? The man who wants to expand his farm,
Avery thought, by acquiring mine.

Avery studied him more closely. His jacket was tai-
lor-made, his eyes light colored, his hair thick, and his
mustachio too extravagant. He'd never noticed how
facial hair made a man look fatuous, though from the
way certain ladies were oggling him, his opinion was
in the minority.

Camfield smiled; at least Avery assumed he was
smiling since his teeth appeared briefly beneath that
brush. "Miss Bede," he said, "you are looking in extremely fine health."

Health? Lily looked stunning, not healthy. A dimple
appeared in her cheek. He'd not known she had a
dimple. Damn it.

"Thank you, sir."

The man simply stood smiling. Lily smiled back. During all this inane grimacing Avery noted Bernard's expression. Really, it was unfeeling of Lily not to notice how difficult a time the lad was having being forced to watch her make cow's eyes at this Camfield fellow.

"Who are those girls?" Avery asked, coming to Bernard's aid since Lily obviously was too smitten to note the lad's discomfort.

"Hmm?" Camfield echoed dumbly. "Girls?"

"Yes. The girls that followed you in. I assume you didn't simply find them on the front doorstep?" Avery said.

"Oh!" With an abashed air, Camfield gestured toward the two younger women. "Pray forgive me. Miss Bede, may I introduce my sisters, Molly and Mary?" he said pleasantly.

The young women exchanged cool pleasantries with Lily before Camfield ushered them off to be introduced to the rest, finally finding their way back to Avery. As soon as he'd made the necessary introductions, Camfield abandoned his sisters to Avery and headed once more for Lily.

"Oh, Mr. Thorne," one of them said, "we must own, we are so delighted to meet you."

"Hmm." Avery's gaze drifted toward the corner where Camfield was monopolizing Lily's attention. Poor Bernard stood nearby looking as glum as a puppy who'd been shouldered from the teat.

"Do say you'll come to our little ball next Monday," the other said.

"Yes, do!"

Lily leaned closer to Camfield, as though listening. Really, there was no reason for the man to speak so softly Lily needed to strain to hear him.

"Please?" the blondest of the girlish pair implored.

"Please, what?"

"The party!" Her sister shook a little pink-nailed finger at him. "Naughty fellow. Say you'll come."

Camfield had moved even closer to Lily now. Bloody impertinence.

"If you come we'll be quite the envy of our little society." This one's yellow ringlets bobbed with enthusiasm.

"Whatever for?"

They giggled in unison. "Fie on you, sir," one of the pair said.

Confound it, he thought, pretty they might be but he wished they'd make some sense. "Pray enlighten me, Miss, er, . . . Miss?"

"Well, sir, you are quite the last word in exclusivity, aren't you?"

"Miss Camfield," he said in exasperation, "whatever are you nattering about?"

More giggles. He cast about for some way to extradite himself. Lily wouldn't help. She was too busy simpering over the hairy-faced, would-be owner of Mill House.

"You haven't accepted *any* invitations!" one said.

"Not even the one from Lord Jessup!" the other added.

"Oh. Those. I don't answer invitations. Miss Bede does. If she's been remiss, I suggest you take it up with her. In fact, that's not a bad idea. Come along, I'll—" He stopped. The two little blond bits of indiscretion were staring at each other in dismay. "What is it?"

"Well"—the younger Miss Camfield tried on a smile—"it's just that, well, you see, I'm not sure Miss Bede would *have* the opportunity to be remiss."

"Say again?"

The other one winced. "The invitations may not, specifically that is, have included her."

His expression hardened immediately into forbidding smoothness. The two sheltered young women stepped back, driven by some instinct that though buried under generations of privilege and pampering was still alert enough to recognize danger.

He forced himself to smile. "I see. That wouldn't be the case with *your* invitation though, would it?"

"Oh, well," the blondest said breathlessly, "we were discussing that very matter on our drive over, I mean *by*, our drive *by*. You must understand that Miss Bede's circumstances, aside from the misfortune of her bir—"

"I wouldn't continue," Avery advised.

She gulped, looking around for their brother, uncomfortable yet unwilling, even after he'd frightened her, to forfeit the coup he represented. At least they'd stopped giggling.

"I should very much like to attend your ball." Their

faces lit up. He didn't give a damn if they saw him as a feather in their social caps. He'd only cared that they paid his price. "Of course, I could not attend without my cousins."

"Of course not," one of them immediately agreed.

"Or Miss Bede."

Not a second's hesitation this time. "Oh, yes. Of course. We wouldn't have it any other way."

"Good," he said, "because neither would I."

Chapter Eleven

"What have you done to your cheek?" Lily lifted Bernard's chin with her fingertips, peering at the nasty red abrasion.

Standing in the hall in the light of the front door window, Lily watched Bernard's tallow-colored skin turn pink.

"Nothing," he said. "I mean, we were climbing the cedar tree last night and I lost my grip for a second and scraped my face against the bark."

"We?" She released her hold.

"Cousin Avery and I."

"And why were you and Mr. Thorne in the cedar tree?"

His blush became more pronounced. "He was showing me how he used to get out of the house after the rest of the household was asleep."

"Hm. Sneak out, you mean."

Bernard's abashment suddenly dissolved and the grin he gave her was one hundred percent roguish boy. "Yes," he said with a cheeky self-assurance she'd have thought impossible, "I guess we did."

For Bernard's one moment of unfettered roguishness Lily silently thanked Avery Thorne.

Avery treated Bernard not as an equal, but yet not like some empty vessel waiting to be filled with manly wisdom. Yesterday, several times, Lily had seen Avery listening intently to Bernard as well as talking to him. The boy was expanding under the attention.

She'd always thought men were little use in childrearing. Though her father had been loving, he'd not spent much time alone with her, discussing his interests or discovering hers. It was always her mother she'd turned to for comfort and conversation and guidance. But seeing Bernard with Avery she could begin to imagine the benefit a father might represent.

Had her siblings' father cared for them? So much so that he couldn't bear to be parted from them?

It was the first time she'd ever wondered such a thing. It felt horrible, blasphemous. Her unknown half-brother and sister's father had taken them away from her mother to torture her. How well he'd succeeded only Lily knew.

"Miss Bede?" Bernard sounded concerned. "Is anything wrong? You look quite unhappy. If my climbing about the cedar tree upsets you so, I won't do it again."

"No!" Lily exclaimed. "No. Clamber about as much as you like, just be careful and may I suggest you, er, omit telling your mother about your new hobby? Unless of course she asks. Specifically."

Bernard's mouth stretched into that delightful grin again and he nodded. "Are you doing anything today?"

"Today?" she asked, her eyes falling on the large stack of mail lying on the front hall table. "Yes. Mr. Thorne and I are going to see Drummond."

"Oh."

Lily picked up the stack of envelopes. Bernard, apparently with no pressing engagements, looked over her shoulder. She heard him inhale deeply. "You smell wonderful."

Little alarms went off in her head. "Thank you, Bernard." She sidestepped, careful to make the movement casual.

He followed her, sniffing deeply again. "What type of perfume is it?"

"Soap." She took another step away, her head determinedly bent over the letters.

"Anything interesting?" he asked over her shoulder.

"No. Just more invitations for your cousin. Mr. Avery Thorne, Mr. Thorne, Mr. Avery Thorne, Avery Thorne, Miss Bede—"

She stopped, staring at the thick vellum envelope addressed to her. Calmly, as if getting invitations was an everyday occurrence, she slipped the letter opener under the flap and sliced it open, casually withdrawing the embossed card.

"It's from the Camfields."

"Camfields?" Bernard's voice sounded all drifty and muzzy and far too close behind. If she turned they'd be cheek to jowl.

"The people who were here yesterday."

"Oh! The mustachioed fellow and the two pretty girls."

Bernard thought the young Miss Camfields pretty? Lily thought gleefully, envisioning a likely place for him to transfer his adolescent fantasies. It would be worth encouraging this. "Yes. They're having a party at the end of the month."

"Will you go?" Bernard asked.

Go? And be confronted with her social undesirability? "I doubt it."

"Then neither shall I," Bernard declared staunchly.

"Oh, come, Bernard. You're their social equal. Your family has owned Mill House for years. It's only right that you should go." She realized the admission in those words as she said them. Mill House by all rights belonged to the Thornes. All rights but one, she amended desperately, a legal one that had given her the opportunity to take it. "Besides, you'll have fun. All those pretty girls. Delicious food. They'll have dancing and charades and wonderful music—"

"Not if you're not there," he said stubbornly.

There was no way out of it. If she wanted to promote Bernard's interest in the Camfield girls, she needed to go to that party.

"You know, Bernard?" she said brightly, taking a

quick step back and to the side, holding the mail at arm's length between them, "I believe I've talked myself into attending. I'll reply in the affirmative this very day."

"There they go." Polly Makepeace released the brocade drapery on the sight of Lily and Avery striding purposefully off down the lane. "I must say, I think it was a stroke of genius having that pregnant gel drop all of Miss Bede's 'rationals' in the mud beneath the clothesline." She gave Evelyn an admiring glance. "And hiding her only remaining pair away so she'd be forced to don that fribbly skirt."

"Lily does look rather nice," Evelyn allowed in a cautious tone but with a soft smile as she glanced out the window at the receding couple. "She looks so well in pink. But then, so many women do."

"Hmm," Polly murmured, her interest in fashion rapidly waning. She brightened. "And I think our little playacting yesterday at the picnic went jolly well."

"Do you?" Evelyn selected a fine ecru strand of lisle from amongst those arrayed across the arm of her chair and began working an intricate series of knots, her fingers flying with nervous energy. "Do you think the best way to promote their, uh, regard for each other is to encourage their fighting?"

Polly, after another glance out the window, rolled her wheelchair closer to where Evelyn sat. "Oh, yes," she stated. "They adore sparring with each other. Passionate sorts, both of them. If they pussyfooted around each other they'd never admit to what is quite obvious."

"And that is?" Evelyn asked. What would this plain, pugnacious woman know of passionate types?

"Sex."

Evelyn blinked.

"They hum with it whenever they're within a half dozen feet of each other. If I were a genteel lady like you, Mrs. Thorne, I should be thoroughly scandalized by such extravagant goings-on. I must own your broad-mindedness surprises me. You can pratically feel the air crackle, haven't you noticed?"

"She will now that you've alerted her to the matter," Francesca said, entering the room amidst a whisper of orchid-colored chiffon. She looked a bit muzzy. Strands of hair flew out from her temple and the ruffles bordering her low décolletage were askew.

"May I give you some advice from a master?" she asked.

Evelyn glanced guiltily at Polly. It was one thing to agree to try to maneuver a person she was very fond of into an involvement with a man who frankly scared her—her maternal concern for her son's future demanded such extraordinary measures—but it was another to be found out.

"I don't know what you mean, Francesca," she mumbled.

Polly, rather than looking abashed, simply eyed Francesca assessingly.

Francesca paused before the enormous Sevres vase

overflowing with fat cabbage roses and delphiniums that squatted in the center of the sideboard. "This vase is one of the loveliest things Mill House owns," she murmured half to herself. "I'm amazed old Horatio allowed something so valuable to reside here."

"What advice would you give us, Miss Thorne?" Polly asked.

Francesca snapped a faded bloom from the bouquet and dropped it on the table. "You ought to be more subtle. Luckily, Miss Makepeace is correct in her appraisal of your two victims. All right, Evie, if you object to 'victims' how about 'subjects'?

"Whatever you want to call them, if they weren't so completely absorbed in each other, they'd realize immediately they're being manipulated. Neither of them is dull-witted." She abandoned the vase and went to fill a crystal glass with port.

"Good point," Polly said.

"Polly!" Evelyn exclaimed.

"I'm sorry, Mrs. Thorne, but why deny it? Miss Thorne here wouldn't be making helpful suggestions if she were going to blow the whistle on us would she? The only question remains is why she would help us?"

Francesca gave them her most enigmatic smile. "Oh, I still might 'blow the whistle' on you, Miss Makepeace. I'm very fond of Lily. Very fond."

"So am I!" Evelyn exclaimed guiltily.

"Of course you are, Mrs. Thorne," Polly soothed. She faced Francesca. "Let's lay our cards on the table, Miss Thorne. Though Mrs. Thorne and I have a common interest in seeing that Mr. Thorne and Miss Bede become involved our reasons are quite dissimilar."

"So I gathered," Francesca said, tipping her glass in Polly's direction. "I'd like to hear them."

Polly drew herself up in her chair. "I believe Miss Bede lacks the necessary commitment and resolve to become the next chairwoman of the Women's Emancipation Coalition. Now before you fly into fits, please hear me out."

Evelyn scowled. Though she knew Polly's arguments were self-serving, she could not fault her honesty.

"Without a doubt Miss Bede has qualities that recommend her," Polly said. "Charm, smarts, her father's blue blood and her mother's not-so-blue blood . . . even her illegitimacy is an advantage since it extends her appeal to the lowest classes. But most important of all is how Miss Bede, a very pretty girl, has lived without a man, completely independent of men, and swears she'll continue to do so."

Francesca listened. "Go on, Miss Makepeace."

"There are certain people in the Coalition who feel we need a popular, charismatic leader like Miss Bede." Polly leaned forward in her chair. "They'd like to raise her up as a sort of Virgin Queen: strong, independent, above physical urges."

Francesca laughed. Polly waited until Francesca's chuckles had subsided. One would almost think she regarded the older woman with something like pity.

"Forgive me, Miss Makepeace," Francesca said,

dabbing at her eyes with the edge of her sleeve. "I'm simply stunned that anyone would—pray, continue."

"Miss Bede is not above such impulses. Her reactions to Mr. Thorne are proof enough of that," Polly said. "Now, if Lily Bede forms a relationship with Mr. Thorne, legal or otherwise, she's not going to be eligible to be anyone's Virgin Queen. The Coalition can then elect a leader, not a figurehead." She slapped her hands on her knees. "And that's my reason for doing what I'm doing."

Francesca tapped her fingertips thoughtfully against her lips. "All right, Miss Makepeace's motives for playing matchmaker are clear," she said, turning her cynical gaze on Evelyn, "but I confess I am at a loss to understand what you hope to achieve, Evie."

The short band of narrow lace forming beneath Evelyn's fingers dropped off. "Oh, my. How clumsy of me!"

"Evie?" Francesca repeated softly.

Her head bent, Evelyn fumbled to pick up the lost knots. "I do it for my life," she whispered to her lap. "Bernard's life."

"Excuse me?" Francesca said blankly.

"Francesca." Evelyn's gaze pierced Francesca with its impact. "You know. You saw what things were like when Gerald was alive. You lived with him," she murmured. "You know how he . . . I couldn't ever . . ."

She almost stopped then. But Francesca was demanding answers and Polly's face had aged with sad wisdom and she might as well admit, to them and herself, the reason she was willing to surrender Lily to a man. "I am a coward."

"No, you aren't, Mrs. Thorne," Polly said. "You are a survivor."

Evelyn shook her head. "No. I'm a coward. I spent a decade cow—" Marriage was a private matter, sacrosanct. She spent her entire life believing that, living by that. The dignity of the family name, Bernard's name, must remain unassailable, no matter what.

Polly's head was averted, her gaze fixed outside the window, allowing Evelyn time to collect herself. The simple innate sensitivity of that gesture touched Evelyn, allowed her to gather her dignity and go on.

"I cannot deal with Avery Thorne," she said. "I cannot. If I cannot make the simplest request of him for my sake, I can scarcely make petitions on my son's behalf. And," her voice trembled with self-loathing, "should it be necessary, even for Bernard's safety, to make demands on Avery Thorne, I doubt whether I should be able to do so."

"Surely, Evie," Francesca said, "if Bernard's safety were at stake you would—"

Evelyn lifted a stricken face. "Would I, Francesca? I would like to think so, but I am unwilling to entrust Bernard's future to something so uncertain as my courage. The fact is that I am afraid and Lily is not.

"She'll never be afraid," Evelyn said. "If she stays— and one way or the other she must stay, she'll have nowhere else to go if she loses and Avery cannot throw her out—she'll act on Bernard's behalf where I cannot. She'll never betray her conscience to save her flesh; she'll never run instead of stand. And if he should abuse her, she'll have the courage to leave."

"Oh, Evie," Francesca said, her voice weary. "I wish you could have known something different. It can be so wonderful."

"Can it?" The brittle, cynical tone coming from Evelyn sounded as unnatural as a cat's cry coming from a dog's maw.

"Oh. Yes," Francesca whispered and in that moment revealed her frailty. Tissue-thin skin pouched beneath her lovely eyes, the wavering line of too-red salve on narrowing lips, the delicate mauve veins that lay like tracery beneath marble smooth temples were signs of age that her vivacity alone usually kept at bay. "Oh, yes.

"It can be so wonderful," she went on. "You think for one brilliant instant, that it is all worth it, that you have found your heart's desire, your Nirvana . . . your Eden, and you are as pure and innocent in taking your pleasure as you were wicked in seeking it."

Her eyelids fluttered shut and her head fell back against the cushions and she laughed, a gruff sound: a little lost, a shade betrayed. "Of course, it's not Eden. It's not even the Promised Land. But just the echoes of the illusion keep you searching, looking . . . bargaining."

She opened her eyes and for a second Evelyn could see the hunger in her, the desperate hunger, before the old self-mockery overtook it and disguised it in insouciance. She took a long draught of port.

"Some people swear it exists," she continued. "That it can grow with each encounter, not fade. And that it freshens the spirit not sickens the soul. And that it lasts forever. Of course," she sniffed, "I have my suspicions about those people's drinking habits, but still, as a romantic, I am willing to suspend my disbelief.

"But whether or not it exists, I am at least absolutely certain that no one should end their life without experiencing even that dim echo of it with which I am so well-acquainted. There. Haven't I couched that in the most delicate terms, Evie? I swear father would be proud."

"Francesca—"

Francesca rose to her feet, ignoring Evelyn's outstretched hand. "And that, Miss Makepeace, is your answer."

"My answer, Miss Thorne?" Polly said, her usually strident voice subdued.

"As to why I would help you throw Avery and Lily together." Francesca adjusted her neckline. "As I said, I am very fond of Lily. I'd like to think she is one of those who can find . . . Eden."

Chapter Twelve

Normally Lily would have enjoyed the mile long walk to Drummond's office, if not the destination. Especially on a fine day like this, with the warm sun shining, the dog roses blooming red in the hedgerows and green leaves scenting the air. But today she was too conscious of the reception Drummond was likely to give her and far too conscious of Avery Thorne walking beside her.

She kept recalling her childish insistence that women could do anything men could do and Avery's efforts to ignore her more provocative statements which, rather than offer her a way out, had only provoked her more.

Avery was the sort of man who had all the answers, who would take control of any situation no matter how distasteful or dire and make it work, who simply did not allow things to go wrong. Capable, bold, dauntless, and supremely confident, he was the quintessential male.

And the very strength that she resented made him undeniably attractive. Like a mesmerist's suggestions, Francesca's words from their tête-à-tête whispered irrepressibly in her mind. *Act. Take what you want. Why be passive—are you some inanimate thing?*

Her tone had been so amused, so sanguine. *Are your desires any less real for being female, Lily? I assure you they are quite as real as any man's.*

Lily lengthened her stride but it was impossible to outdistance Francesca's voice. *Why wonder what it would be like when the smallest effort could so easily yield the knowledge you want?*

"Are you late for your appointment?"

Lily, by now trotting along the footpath bordering the pond, forced herself to slow down. "No. Not at all. Sorry."

Avery paused by the mill pond and measured the berms with his gaze, probably wondering why she hadn't had them built up in order to prevent the flooding that had ruined the wheat field this spring. The answer was simple: she hadn't had the money to build them up and she'd refused to ask for credit.

While he stood surveying the land, she moved on toward the stable. The door stood open and the soft dusty-warm fragrance of horse drifted out. Her footsteps slowed. A soft whicker greeted them. Lily smiled. It sounded like India.

Unable to resist, she went inside, inhaling the earthy scent of manure and sweet hay—hay she'd been obliged to buy with a portion of her small, precious cash reserves.

Quietly, she moved down the long line of box stalls, her feet sinking noiselessly into the soft, freshly raked sand alley. From overhead the filtered sun created puddles of light on the alley. The cloistered sound of shifting hooves rose like a mummer's chant as she passed the stalls.

This was her favorite place. It housed twenty horses, most never even ridden. Avery must think her daft to keep so many.

A small delicately shaped muzzle pushed its way between the bars of the box stall nearest her. Lily stopped and rubbed the soft, velvety nose. " 'Allo, India, my love."

She glanced over her shoulder. Avery hadn't followed her. Instead, he stood outside his tall, broad-shouldered frame silhouetted against the bright May sky. He couldn't dislike horses. No one disliked horses. Regretfully leaving India's stall, she joined him outside.

"They didn't cost much. Hardly anything."

"What didn't?" he asked.

"The horses. They were nearly gifts."

He sniffed. "I see."

He turned, but she snagged his sleeve. Startled he looked down at her, his expression wary. Normally she would have taken umbrage at that sniff but this was too important. If she failed to inherit Mill House, *he* would have to take care of her horses.

"I don't think you do," she said. "If I didn't buy
them they'd have been slaughtered outright or sold
cheap to drag plows or overloaded carts in the city.
They're race horses. They're built differently. Delicate. They'd be broken and dead within a month."

He sniffed again.

"That's not fair. They gave their hearts and souls.
It isn't their fault if they didn't win the bloody races."

His gaze remained fixed on her fingers still clutching his jacket. Flushing she removed them, patting the
wrinkles her clasp had left behind.

"You keep failed race horses." His voice sounded
odd, rough.

"Not all failed," she said. "India placed in any
number of county races and there's a gelding in there
that showed against Gladiateur himself."

"Congratulations."

"Don't patronize me," she said. "I know full well
the drain these horses are on my finances. But at least
as of now they're *my* finances."

"I didn't suggest otherwise." He cleared his throat.

She tried to read any hint of mockery in his extraordinary blue-green eyes. She couldn't. They were
suspiciously reddened around the edge and the sheen
of moisture dazzled their blue-green color to brilliance. Realization hit her with the force of a blow.
Avery Thorne was struggling to keep his emotions in
check. He'd been touched . . . no deeply moved by
these horses' story. She stared at him in mute amazement.

"Can we get away from here?" he asked gruffly.

He must deem the expense of keeping the horses a nearly cretinous mismanagement of money. Yet he didn't argue at all, he simply looked miserable, his wide mouth pulled down.

"Would you—" she hesitated "—would you like to see them?"

His brows drew together, as if he suspected her of some nefarious purpose.

"No," he answered, clearing his throat again. "No, I think we'd better press on."

He motioned her to precede him, falling into step beside her as they followed the footpath into the orchard. Ancient, gnarled arms of apple trees bowed beneath the weight of blossoms. Bees, like diminutive courtiers bedecked in gold pantaloons, complained drowsily as they went about their errands in the pink shadowed warmth, and an occasional breeze sent handfuls of thin petal confetti swirling down upon their heads.

"I thought the orchard larger than this," Avery said.

"It's exactly the same size it was five years ago," Lily said quickly. In here, his eyes appeared darker, deeper, like smoky blue-green jade.

"I only meant," he said, picking up a slender stick, "that when I was a child I thought this orchard stretched to the sea. It was a vast wilderness and the potential for adventure just as far as the next hillock. A dragon, Robin Hood, Lancelot, they all lived here. I met them all."

He lunged forward as if he wielded a rapier. A quick parry and he saluted her. Without thinking, she scooped up a slender branch, the end still tufted with leaves and raised it before her face.

"En garde!"

For a second his eyes widened in surprise. She took advantage, lunging forward and plunging the leafy tip into his mid-section.

"Point!"

His eyes narrowed, with delight or promise of retribution? she wondered. Probably both.

"Thornes don't die so easily, m'dear," he said and with that whacked her branch away with his stick before swirling it in a series of dizzying feints and parries that had her stumbling backward.

"No fair," she panted. "You're mortally wounded."

"A mere scratch," he contradicted, knocking away leaf after leaf from the tip of her woodland épée. "Never underestimate the power of sheer determination."

"Or sheer perverseness?" she asked darting behind a gnarled ancient apple's trunk and giving him a cheeky grin.

"That, too," he allowed and disappeared behind another tree.

She withdrew behind the trunk to catch her breath before peeking out and looking for him. He hadn't yet emerged. With a small, triumphant smile she stole from where she stood, moving behind a tree directly to his left. She could see the edge of his jacket. She had him.

With a triumphant cry she jumped forth, branch at the ready, arm curled behind her head in the prescribed manner, eyes gleaming and cried, "Throw down!"

His jacket hung from a broken limb.

"That would be my suggestion, yes."

She whirled. Avery stood behind her, one shoulder jammed nonchalantly against a tree trunk, legs crossed, twirling his stick like a baton. He raised a dark, winged brow. "In the parlance of popular melodrama, I believe I have you in my power."

A deeper meaning seemed to suffuse his words and for a second his extraordinary eyes were dark with speculation . . . and something else. And then the moment was gone.

"Aye, sir. I'm yours to command," she said cheekily and tossed her branch at his feet.

"Oh, I sincerely doubt that," he said, smiling, a deep dimple carved into one darkly tanned cheek, before he tossed his leafy épée away.

"A wise man," she agreed a bit breathlessly. *If a woman only sits and waits for what she wants, then she cannot complain of leftovers.* Drat Francesca!

Lily cleared her throat. "I suppose . . . we'd best go." Without waiting she turned away, hurrying ahead until they emerged from the orchard into a meadow ringed by an ancient hedge and found the break in the thick dog roses that had long since been mended by a tall wooden stile. If she'd been alone she would have climbed the rails and cut across the field.

"I used to cross the meadow on my way to see old Drummond. Saved myself a fifteen minute hike," Avery commented. He plucked a deep crimson rose and twirled it between his thumb and forefinger. His hands were strong-looking and lean, the nails trimmed and clean, the tips blunt and callused. Yet he set the little rose dancing with a touch as adroit as it was heedless.

"Did you?" she mumbled.

He held the rose up, closing one eye and squinting at her through the petals. Probably comparing its color to the blush she felt rising. Drat Francesca anyway for seeding her thoughts with such things.

"Yes." He reached out and poked the flower into the hair at her temple, catching her so completely off-guard that her mouth fell open. "Care to save yourself some time?"

"I . . . well . . . I . . ."

He placed a hand against the top rail and vaulted over, landing lightly on the other side. "Come." He held out his hand.

She wanted to take his hand, to place herself, even in such a small capacity in his care, and so she ignored his offer. Putting her boot on the bottom rail, she clambered ungracefully to the top. She perched on the top rail, studying the uneven ground below for a landing place.

"You really adhere to your 'I can do it myself' code, don't you?"

"Yes, I do." She looked up and found herself just above his eye level. It was a lovely level to be. His razor mustn't be very sharp because a dark cast already covered his chin. For some reason the thought heartened her. It made him seem more human. Less all powerful. A razor had bested him. And she rather liked being taller than Avery Thorne.

She swung her legs, unwilling to give up her vantage. "I take my independence seriously," she said. "You would, too, were you a woman."

He rested his forearm on the top rail, very near her hip, leaned close in a confiding manner, and said lazily, "Happily, I'm not a woman."

It felt as though someone had knocked the air out of her. Her breath came out in a rush. *No. Most definitely not.*

"And, being a man," he continued, "I don't have to protect my independence quite so fiercely. Must be frightfully tiring, always having to be on guard lest someone jeopardize your right to climb a fence unaided."

"It's easy for you to mock," she said. "If you were a woman you would know that any act of self-determination is to be celebrated. Little battles are only a prelude to the larger ones." Like legal equality under the marriage contract, she thought but did not say.

"Rest assured, Miss Bede, I have no desire to thwart

your independence. I simply offered you the aid any gentleman would offer a lady."

"Mr. Thorne," she said, "my father had a pedigree but my mother had none. Her great-grandparents were itinerant laborers. You would call them gypsies, if not tramps."

His brows drew together. "That explains it."

"I suppose you refer to my lack of refinement. You're offended, aren't you?" she said, without any of the satisfaction she should be feeling at having shocked Avery Thorne.

"Not in the least," he said with haughty simplicity. "My comment was made in reference to my discovering where you come by your extraordinary coloring. You, Miss Bede, are a snob. I have encountered your ilk before."

"My ilk?" she sputtered.

"Yes. Those persons with an exaggerated opinion of their lineage and how it affects others. I assure you, I do not give a rip what your ancestors did or did not do for a living. According to Mr. Darwin all of our ancestors swung in trees. Your type will always want to discuss whose swung on the higher branch."

"Oh!" He took all of her fears, her insecurities and dismissed them as snobbery?

"And, Miss Bede, as much as I hate to contradict you—"

"You *adore* contradicting me. In every letter you sent me you—"

"*And much as I hate to contradict you,*" his voice rose,

drowning out her protests, "I insist that I certainly know a lady when I see one. You are a lady."

Having made this declaration, he nodded, as though the matter were now settled and turned, propping both elbows on the rail and staring placidly out at the meadow, apparently content to stay there as long as she wished. Him being a gentleman and all.

He looked absolutely masterful, completely at ease, gorgeously masculine and she . . . she was . . . what had Francesca said? *She* was in a *state*.

He turned his head and smiled benignly at her.

It was the last straw. "Would a lady do this?" She leaned over, grabbed his head between her hands and kissed him.

He jerked back and she grabbed his shoulders to keep from pitching into the ground, inadvertently deepening the kiss. Beneath her lips his were warm as sun-heated plush, an exquisite blend of pliancy and firmness. In an ecstasy of sensitivity her own grew deliciously, dazzlingly responsive.

Her hands crept from his broad shoulders to his neck and finally his lean cheeks, bracketing his face between them. His beard stubble rasped her palms and his skin heated the pads of her fingertips as she explored the slight indentations beneath his high cheekbones, the angle of his jaw, and finally the corners of his lips. With a deep moan, she explored the heart-stopping rush of sensations.

Passionately, fervently, she gave herself completely over to that kiss, growing light-headed, utterly involved, barely aware of what she did, where she was, of anything but his mouth.

Avery wasn't so fortunate.

He was aware, too damn aware, of every inch of Lily and most of it wasn't anywhere near as close as he wanted her to be. And there wasn't a damn thing he could do about it.

God knew why she was kissing him. He sure didn't. One minute he'd been congratulating himself on handling her insecurities with such delicacy *and* managing to pay her a rather nice compliment, the next she was kissing him—with far more anger than passion. At least that is how it started out, but in just a few seconds anger had burned into something a great deal hotter.

In some fascinated, near-panicking part of his brain he knew that somewhere, somehow, this had to be a trick. But he couldn't think, was barely functioning on a conscious level at all. Only a deep instinct for self-preservation kept him from dragging her off that rail and laying her on the ground and covering her body with his own. The craving to absorb her, to feel her melt beneath him, to feel her soft curves accommodate his hardness, nearly brought him to his knees.

He wanted her beneath him, her mouth *open*, by God, not dragging over his with soul-destroying tantalization. He shuddered where he stood.

But the will he exerted to control his limbs could not control his lips. Her kiss teased him, made him hungry, and like a man dying of thirst and bound staked in the desert, his mouth opened, seeking more of the rich flood of sweet sensation. He slanted his head, lining the soft velvet of her lips with the tip of his tongue. On a sigh, her mouth opened. With a throaty groan, he slid his tongue deep within, exploring with sensuous thoroughness the warm, sweet flavor of her, mating his tongue with hers.

Too much. Not enough.

He moved forward, just a step, until her breasts brushed him, sending jolts of furious need ricocheting through him. With each shuddering breath she took her nipples, firm pebbles, traced a line of fire across his chest. Her thighs grew lax in abandon and he took advantage, angled between them, moving closer until the pliant weight of her breasts rested fully against him, the promise of the lee in which he stood drawing him like a magnet.

Her head fell back and her throat arched. God help him, he needed to kiss that slender column, lick the salty sheen from the small indentation at its base, gently suck the delicate tender lobe of her ear as her intoxicating, throaty purrs reverberated in his mind.

But he could not touch her, no, he wasn't touching her. Not with his hands. At least he had that much discipline. But for how long? Panic and desire rode him hard. He wanted her beneath him, by God, not simply to stand here undone by soul-destroying tantalization. Yet he dared nothing more.

Because some tiny piece of his mind that was still

operating sanely suspected that as soon as he actually touched her, she'd send him packing.

So he just stood, his arm muscles bulging with the strain of keeping them from her, his body hard with ungratified want, breathing deeply, accepting her mouth in a dazed attitude of suspension, his own wildly devouring the texture and taste and heat of her.

Don't touch her. Don't touch her. For God's sake, do not touch her.

Suddenly her eyelids snapped open. With a sound of utter horror her lips broke free. "Oh, my Lord!"

She jerked away, tumbling off the rail and landing on her back. For an instant he could not move, his eyes closed in frustration and anger, and then he followed her over, vaulting the stile and standing above her as she stared wild-eyed up at him.

"I didn't touch you!" he shouted.

"I know that!" she shouted back and began thrashing about, trying to get upright.

In her frenzy, her skirt hiked high above her knees, displaying lace trimmed undergarments—Lily Bede, lace?—and improbably embroidered silk stockings. Pins flew from her head and a cascade of gleaming black corkscrew curls fell around her neck and shoulders in an inky fantasy of abandonment.

She almost made it to her feet, but her boot got caught in her hem, upending her once more. Lying flat on her back, Lily's heels drummed the ground in frustration. Finally, after long moments of this utterly fruitless activity she stopped.

With an air of one exercising great restraint, she took a long, deep breath, pushed the hair out of her face and glowered up at him. "Well," she said in a fiercely controlled voice, "you're always going on about being a gentleman. Help me up!"

"Ah. Yes." He eyed her warily. "Certainly." Hesitantly he held out his hand. With a snarl or a sob—for the life of him he couldn't have said which—she pulled herself to her feet.

"You might want to fix your . . . petticoats."

She snapped her skirts down over the tops of her boots and began dusting off the grass and leafy bits clinging to her derrière.

"And your hair."

"What of it?"

"It's down."

"Oh!" Her hands collected the unruly mess. She stabbed some pins into it, utilizing some sort of arcane womanly power to make it look all tidy and neat where seconds before it might have been a talisman for wantonness.

Then with another of those deep breaths, she hitched up her chin and looked him squarely in the eye. Fascinated, he waited to see what she would do next.

"I apologize." Fiery color seared her face.

Whatever he'd expected, it had not been that.

"I have no excuse for my actions. I acted like a complete . . . like a . . ."

"Like a cad?" he suggested, utilizing the name he'd been giving himself.

"Yes! A cad!" She enthusiastically fell on the word. He should have known a gender-crossing appellation, even a negative one, would appeal to her.

"I apologize and ask that we forget this unfortunate little incident."

The way she said it, so primly, so impersonally, made him see red. He'd withstood temptation before but nothing compared to what he'd just withstood. His body still ached with frustration. He could still smell her on him, taste of her, and feel her. Oh, no. She wasn't getting off that easily. Just because whatever little game she'd concocted hadn't come to fruition didn't mean she wasn't obliged to pay the price of playing.

"You might. I certainly won't," he said.

She gaped at him. "But . . . how can I make amends?"

"Amends?" Lily being beholden to him had its definite appeal. "I don't know that you can make amends for having"—he had paused for dramatic effect—"accosted me. But then, since you're a woman, I have no choice but to accept your apology, do I? But Lord, if the roles were reversed we would hear a hue and cry, wouldn't we? Don't let it trouble you that I find this incident hard to forget."

Her glorious dark eyes narrowed suspiciously. "You won't be able to forget?"

God. If she only knew. No. But not for the reasons he was giving out. The vision of countless ice cold baths filled his thoughts, making his voice rough. "Why so surprised? Women haven't cornered the market on sensitivity. Just because I'm a man doesn't mean I can't be offended. But since you, a woman, offer the offense, it shall be summarily disregarded."

"That's not fair," she blurted out and then looked immediately as though she wished to recall the words.

He smiled virtuously. "I agree. But then, surely *you* know that matters between our genders are seldom 'fair.' What you've apparently ignored is that women are not always the ones to suffer from those disparities."

"Surely there must be some way I can make recompense? If a man were to offer you such an insult—"

"My dear Miss Bede," he said, "if a man were to offer me an insult similar to the one you have, at the very least there'd be blood on the ground right now."

"That's not what I meant! I meant that if a man offended you and then apologized, wouldn't you accept it?"

"But Miss Bede," Avery said equitably, "you didn't simply offend me. You took advantage of my assumption that I would be safe from untoward behavior in your company."

For a second he feared he had gone too far. Her eyes narrowed, her brow lowered, and her mouth compressed. But then her hand flew out in supplication and he saw that what he'd taken for suspicion was mortification. He almost took pity on her then, her distress seemed so real, but he reminded himself that whatever game she'd been playing, she'd undoubtedly designed so that he would come out on the losing side.

"There must be some way to deal with this!" she exclaimed.

"Well, if a *man* took a potshot at another man—"

"Potshot?" she asked.

"Yes. A potshot. A blow delivered to one's enemy when his back is turned or he is unawares. Considered very poor sportsmanship."

She paled at his censorious tone. "Yes?"

"Well, should I have received a potshot from a man I would simply warn him that he could expect similar treatment from me at some future date. In the interest of fair play, you understand," he explained. "At least, that's how we gentlemen would do it."

He watched her consider his words. Though he'd kept his tone kind, his thoughts were far from benevolent. He'd thought he knew this woman. That four and a half years of correspondence made her familiar to him. Damn it, that one letter she'd written after Karl's death had spoken to his very soul! He hated being wrong.

He'd expected her to be a girl as unused to male company as he was to female, but her passionate kiss related experience—with how many other men?— which for some reason angered the hell out of him.

"Well?" he said.

She lifted her chin and gave a short, clipped nod. "Fine, then," she said bravely. "I consider myself fore-warned."

Chapter Thirteen

Lily was mortified. She could feel Avery Thorne's eyes on the back of her neck and the answering fire of humiliation spreading up it. She pressed her knuckles to her lips to stifle her moan. With each step she had to restrain herself from breaking into a dead run. She gazed imploringly at the heavens.

What in God's name had possessed her? It had seemed, at least for one instant, to be such a good idea, such a liberated idea. Now it only seemed cheap and tawdry and oh! He'd been so *offended* by her.

What had he said? That simply because he was a man didn't mean he couldn't be offended. True, for a few minutes, he'd responded. Even such concentrated involvement as hers had been could not utterly obliterate the fact that he'd become a participant. Albeit an unwilling one.

She'd spent her life fighting so women would receive the same rights as men and now she'd gone and physically forced herself on Avery Thorne. How shabby. How hypocritical. This time the moan could not be completely stifled.

"Did you say something, Miss Bede?" he asked from well behind her. Which was hardly surprising, was it? He must fear to be anywhere within arm's reach of her.

"No. Nothing."

At least she'd done the right thing in agreeing to his right to seek recompense. She worried her fingers together, wondering what form this "potshot" was likely to take. The only thing she knew for a certainty was that it wouldn't be of a type.

Avery's kiss had most likely been the result of that compulsive sexual drive which was rumored to rule the male gender. Certainly he hadn't contested her statement that she'd acted the cad. And if there had been hunger and desire and passion in his kiss, it was of a reflexive nature. She'd have been ill-pleased herself if someone had awoken impulses that only demonstrated her enslavement to her baser nature. Probably only his much vaunted gentlemanliness—which seemed to appear and disappear as the situation required—had kept him from forcibly removing her. Noting his size and strength, she supposed she ought to be thankful.

She didn't feel grateful. In fact, she wasn't at all sure she wouldn't have preferred that he struck her—preferably hard enough to be rendered unconscious.

She kept castigating herself until they reached the converted stone dairy that housed Drummond's office. She mounted the single step to the worn, poorly hung door and knocked. Loudly. Best get this whole disastrous interlude behind her. She knocked again.

"All right! All right! Curse you to hell you—" The door slit open. One of Drummond's clouded blue eyes gazed balefully at her. "Oh. Sorry. Didn't know who it was."

The old wretch knew exactly who it was. Lily was always punctual for their monthly meetings and Drummond always answered her knocks with vitriolic curses. Today's had been mild compared to some of the verbal blasts with which she'd been met.

Drummond shuffled back into the dim interior, leaving the door hanging on its hinges. At least this time he hadn't slammed it in her face and then blamed his "aged forgetfulness."

Lily pushed the door open, venturing in a few inches. Drummond flopped into a chair behind a scarred desk littered with papers, the chewed stubs of a dozen pencils, and a battered ledger. In spite of the stifling heat in the closed room, he pulled a thin shawl about his hunched shoulders.

The impression of feebleness was a sham. She'd seen this old man carry a calf with a broken leg a mile over rough ground.

"And a good afternoon to you, too, Mr. Drummond," she said. "You do remember we have an appointment this afternoon?"

She glanced at Avery, who eyed her dubiously. He was probably wondering if he would come into possession of Mill House earlier if he could get her declared insane. And if she continued finding him so damnably attractive—because just glancing at him set the heat racing over the surface of her skin—she wasn't at all sure he wouldn't be doing her a favor.

"Are you going to stand there like a half-witted cow or are you going to come in?" Drummond demanded. "And who the hell be yon young behemoth lurking behind you? The new farm manager?" He squinted at Avery. "Nah. I couldn't be so lucky. Besides, you're the wrong gender to be hired by Missy here."

The nasty, vicious old codger. She stomped forward a few feet. "Listen, Mr. Drummond, I didn't come here—"

"Maybe you're daft enough you're gonna marry her?" Drummond asked hopefully, jabbing his thumb in her direction. "That'd be almost as good. Then maybe you could keep her out of my way. At least for a few days." He winked lewdly.

Lily dug her nails into her palm, glad the dim light would hide the blush she felt firing up her face. This was going to be even worse than she'd anticipated.

"I'm not going to take over the farm management," Avery said, "and I'm not going to marry her, old man."

"Well then what are you doing here? I don't give no tours to idlers." Drummond scowled fiercely, his few strands of gray hair sticking up in wiry spikes from his sunburnt pate.

"I came to see how long a man could live on pure meanness."

"Listen, boy!" Drummond popped up from his seat, shedding the shawl and the querulous-old-man tone like a snake sheds dead skin. "You might be big. But you ain't so big I couldn't thrash some manners into you."

He leaned over his desk, glowering at Avery until an expression of incredulity crossed his seamed old face. With a whoop he slapped his big gnarled paw down on the desk. "Avery Thorne, is it? Still an outspoken, cussed rude bugger only now you got the meat to back it up."

"I am never rude."

"Ha!" Something that looked like a smile but was more probably gas since Lily had never seen Drummond actually smile, passed over the old man's wrinkled face. He shot around from behind his desk, shouldering her out of the way and grabbing Avery's hand. He pumped it up and down.

"You've come to deliver me from her ignorance and interference, haven't you, son?" Drummond demanded. "I couldn't be happier to see St. Peter himself!"

"As though there's any chance of that happening," Lily muttered.

"Giving up the game early, is she?" Drummond asked, grinning like a malevolent, gray-haired goblin.

Lord, she hated it when Drummond spoke of her in the third person. Sometimes he did it even when she and he were the only people in the room.

"Well, best for everyone all around." Drummond

finally dropped Avery's hand. "A woman running a farm. Bah! Never heard such a daft thing in my life—"

"I am *not* giving up," Lily declared tightly. "And Mr. Thorne accompanied me here simply to extend his greeting as an old friend."

"What?" Drummond speared Avery with a questioning look.

Avery nodded.

"Well, damn." With an air of betrayal, Drummond turned his back on them and slunk back to his desk chair, treading on her foot in the process.

"Ow!"

Drummond flopped down, mumbling disconsolately. "I suppose that means I get to look forward to more 'appointments,' then? Pah! Well, get on with it. What do you want?"

"*Want*, Mr. Drummond?" Lily hobbled forward and gripped either side of the desk, holding on so tightly she was sure she was leaving gouges in the wood. She leaned over it and fixed Drummond with a glare. "What I *want* is for this farm to be a productive concern. What I *need* is to know when you plan to wash the raddle off the sheep. All portends suggest that this summer is going to be an especially hot one and—"

"What 'por-tends' might those be, Missy Know-All? You been reading them farm journals again? Listen. I been raddling sheep for fifty years, I don't need no one telling me when the sheep needs they raddle washed out."

"No. *You* listen, Mr. Drummond," Lily said, "if that wool isn't dry and ready for shearing before hot weather hits, those sheep will sicken and we will be in substantial financial straits."

Drummond's face mottled over with livid purple splotches. "I know that, you silly gorm—"

"What is raddle?" Avery asked.

Both Lily and Drummond's heads spun around. For a minute there, for the first time since she'd seen him, she'd actually been free of thoughts of Avery Thorne.

"What?" Drummond asked.

"What's this raddle you're talking about?" Avery asked. "I thought I should know since it seems to have prompted such heated feelings."

"It's clay," Lily said, unsure whether he was having her on or not. "Reddish clay used to mark the sheep."

"I see. And why is it you mark them?"

"To tell them apart from the other sheep," Drummond said in disgust. "We got a lot of sheep in this district that graze those hillsides. We gots to know whose sheep is whose now, don't we?" He shook his head. "You wasn't a *particularly* stupid lad as I remembers."

"Carry on with your conversation," Avery said. "It's most informative."

"You really didn't know what raddle is?" Lily asked suspiciously, bemused Avery could so easily claim ignorance. In her admittedly limited experience men never owned up to their limitations. Even her father, as enlightened a male as the world had known, had never to her knowledge actually uttered the words, "I don't know."

"No," Avery said calmly. "Why should I? I've spent only a few weeks at Mill House and those long ago. It wasn't exactly my second home."

From what Francesca had told her, there hadn't been a *first* home. She almost said as much but some quality of guardedness in his face made her hold her tongue. She found herself touched with compassion, which was nonsensical. Avery Thorne had every advantage of his gender and his class. He'd even managed to find a way around his limited finances by virtue of his own ingenuity. What did he lack?

She studied him thoughtfully. Perhaps Thorne wasn't the confident, complacent creature he appeared to be.

Drummond made a disparaging noise. "First a woman. Now another know-nuthin'. Did you have to take a stupid test in order to get into Horatio's will? Still, I'd rather work for a male know-nuthin' than a female know-nuthin'. Better yet, give me the good old days, working for Mr. Horatio."

"Yes, I'm sure the world lost a regular Damon and Pythias when the Almighty separated you and Horatio," Lily said dryly, making reference to the legendary Greek friends.

Avery burst out laughing. Startled, Lily spun toward him. He avoided her gaze but his grin was wide and appreciative.

"That sounds mighty near blasphemy, Missy,"

Drummond said, his face again turning that unappealing shade. "If you think I'll stand by and listen to your godless—"

"Oh, come now, Drummond," Avery said.

Lily stared at him. Of all the corners she would have expected aid from, his would have been the least likely. At least not now. Not after she'd—not after that.

"You make it sound as though you and Horatio stood shoulder to shoulder hip deep in the muck," Avery continued, "battling the foes of animal husbandry or whatever it is farmers battle. The truth is that Horatio spent hardly any time at Mill House and certainly didn't involve himself in the running of it."

"Aye," Drummond said, his eyes misting over nostalgically. "That's right. Mr. Horatio didn't ask to be part of the works and he didn't expect to be. Not like Missy here."

"And what exactly is wrong with the way I do things?" Lily asked.

"Missy here wants to be 'involved.' " Drummond stabbed the air with one blunt finger. "Pah! You're either gentry who don't interfere like Mr. Horatio was or you're yeoman, working the land right alongside your laborers. There ain't *nuthin'* in between, but Missy here thinks that by asking a few questions and studying a few books she can be 'involved.' Well, I'd like to see her involved with a sopping wet three-hundred-pound sheep."

"You can hardly expect her to bathe sheep," Avery said.

"Can't I, now?" Drummond's eyes sank deeper beneath the folds of his eyelids and he glowered like a basilisk. He turned his attention to Lily. "You ain't gentry and you ain't yeoman," he said. "You can't manage things from behind a desk and you won't work in the field. Which in my mind means you're useless.

"Now, when young Mr. Thorne here takes over the running of Mill House, I imagine we'll get back to the proper way of things."

"The *proper* way is the one I set!" Lily burst out.

"Praise be, I only have to put up with another few months of your jabbering," Drummond muttered, rifling through his papers.

Her lips curled back from her teeth and her fingers clutching the edge of the desk grew white with her effort to dent the wood. "Has it ever occurred to you that I might end up owning Mill House? That I might inherit it?"

Drummond didn't even lift his head. "Nope." He waved his hand, like a king banishing an irksome courtier. "Go away. I got work to do. I don't have time to humor you today. Unless . . ." He glanced up. His evil little eyes gleamed with malevolence. "You wants to fire me?"

For the count of ten Lily met Drummond's gaze. She wished she could do just that but Mill House needed Drummond and she would not do something stupid just for a few ecstatic moments of triumph.

But she might if she stayed here much longer. Without a word, she swung around and paced through the open door, slamming it shut behind her.

Drummond burst out into an evil cackle and rubbed his hands together gleefully. He looked up to find Avery regarding him with a chilling smile.

"Drummond," Avery said, "I think we need to have a little chat."

Chapter Fourteen

"Francesca!" Avery shouted through the halls of Mill House just as a peal of thunder sounded far off in the distance. The day had turned unseasonably warm. Since Lily had fled from Drummond's lair that morning, he'd caught only an occasional glimpse of her, and it was driving him mad. There was too much unresolved between them and he was a man unused to biding his time. He wanted—

Damn. That was the problem. He wanted Lily Bede. So much that he could taste it. Something had to give.

"Where the blazes is everyone?" Avery muttered. Even the perpetually keeling-over trio of maids was conspicuously absent. God alone knew where Lily had hied herself off to. Probably devising some other plan to . . . to *what*?

What in God's name had she hoped to accomplish with that kiss? Distract him from illegal activities? The days of smuggling were long gone. Make him so smitten with her that he abdicated his claim on Mill House? She couldn't possibly think that would work. He needed answers.

"Francesca!" he roared again.

A patter of footsteps preceded Francesca's appearance. Shell pink fabric swished around her ankles and her color was hectic. "What is it?" she asked breathlessly. "What is wrong?"

"Wrong? Nothing's wrong. I wanted to speak with you," he said.

She laid her palm flat against the base of her throat. "You gave me palpitations, you young idiot. Shouting down the house like that."

"I 'shouted' because there was no one here to relay my request that you meet me in"—he looked around—"there." He pointed at one of the anterooms. "I didn't feel like running about opening doors looking for you."

"Fine, Avery," Francesca said, entering the room. She settled herself gracefully atop a heavy settee covered in somber maroon brocade and tucked her feet beneath her.

"Where is everyone?" Avery asked, glancing around. He saw now why the family didn't use this room. It was dark, filled with uncomfortable-looking furniture, and there was a draft coming from the hearth.

"Mrs. Kettle is decanting wine for dinner—apparently an arduous and lengthy process and one she takes very seriously—Evelyn is in the sitting room teaching Miss Makepeace to make lace, of all things, and Bernard has gone down to the horse barn."

"It's called a stable, Francesca, and do you think that's wise? What with the boy's lung condition and all."

"Why wouldn't it be?" she asked.

"Nasty drafty places stables. And horses are erratic, excitable beasts. Drink, Francesca?" He indicated the crystal whiskey container.

"That would be nice," Francesca said. "You mustn't worry about Bernard. Lily's nags are long past being a danger to anyone and Bernard enjoys riding them tremendously. The only athletic endeavor he does enjoy, to my knowledge."

"Would that I could," Avery murmured, conjuring an image of Lily Bede, her black hair flying as she cantered across a field.

He dispelled the image, busying himself with the liquor decanter and considering his young cousin. So, whatever triggered the constriction of Bernard's lungs it was not proximity to horses, the agent that had so long bedeviled Avery. Perhaps if he and Bernard researched the matter they could discover under what conditions Bernard was most likely to suffer and thus he could do as Avery had learned to do: avoid those places or events that precipitated the terrifying suffocation.

"Avery," Francesca said slowly, "do *horses* provoke that congestion in your lungs?"

He'd forgotten Francesca. Curled up on the heavy

monstrosity in her filmy, pale draperies she looked like an autumn moth, faded, a bit shabby, but still somehow pretty. "Sometimes," he said in a noncommittal tone. "Not worth discussing. Never go near the beasts if I can help it. Now, about her."

"Her." Francesca's face went blank for a second before clearing. "Oh! *Her*. What about her?"

Avery cast about, uncertain how much he wanted to reveal to his cousin. No one else of his acquaintance was better qualified to judge Lily's proclivities than Francesca. Her expertise in matters of the flesh was a given and had been ever since she'd been a chit.

"Camfield," he finally said, handing her a glass of whiskey and soda.

"Martin Camfield?" Francesca accepted the drink. "What about him?"

"What is the nature of the relationship between Miss Bede and him?"

Her lips made a moue of comprehension. "Well, clearly Mr. Camfield has a high regard for Lily's intelligence."

Avery relaxed. If the strongest feeling Camfield could scrounge up for a woman like Lily was "high regard for her intelligence" the man was either homosexual or a eunuch. In either case Avery felt much more kindly disposed toward him.

He smiled.

"Or that's what Mr. Camfield would like her to think."

He stopped smiling.

"Perhaps Martin Camfield is wise enough to realize that a woman like Lily will find a man who appreciates her mind more appealing than someone who simply ogles her."

"I have *never* ogled her."

Francesca looked startled. "Why, Avery, I never said you did."

"I just wanted to make clear that I'm not that sort of man."

"More's the pity," Francesca said and upended a good half the glass's contents into her mouth.

"And what about Lily?"

"Lily?"

"Her and him."

Francesca sighed. "I do wish you would learn to speak in something other than monosyllables, Avery. It's a habit you had even as a boy. It makes communication confoundedly awkward. And yet, your prose is inspired and I've heard you engage in exchanges with Lily that positively scintillate. Now, try again, dear, what is it you wish to know about 'her and him?' "

Avery's face grew hot. "Does she encourage Camfield?"

"Of course she does," Francesca said, setting her empty glass on the floor beside her. "Whyever are you looking like that, Avery? Are you ill?"

The thought of Lily in Camfield's arms, or worse, of Camfield in Lily's arms, made Avery's jaw ache. With an effort he unclenched his teeth. "I'm fine. I just dislike finding out that a woman of Lily's intelligence would stoop to manipulating men in such a brazen and crude fashion."

" 'Brazen?' 'Crude?' " Francesca frowned. "Just what is it you think I have admitted to Lily's having done?"

"Used her feminine wiles to beguile men into doing her bidding."

"I see." Francesca shook her head. "Men are so fascinating. May I ask what bidding she is supposed to have beguiled Martin Camfield into doing?"

"I don't know," Avery responded testily. "How would I know? What has she gotten out of him?"

Francesca lounged back, her expression deeply contemplative. "Well," she said slowly, "she did rather crow about purchasing seed from him at a good price. I confess, trading one's womanly favors for a ten percent discount on seeds would never have occurred to me, but if that's what she's done, I call it damned enterprising—"

"Don't be ridiculous!"

"*I?*" She rose to her feet. "And here I thought *you* were the one jumping to conclusions. I said Lily *flirted* with Martin Camfield, not *bedded* him, you great fool. There is a difference, you know."

"If you would cease being so damned amused by us lesser mortals and answer my questions in a straightforward fashion I wouldn't be jumping to conclusions," he shot back.

His words had a potent effect. Francesca's suave ex-

pression abruptly disappeared. Beneath its thin pow-
dered layer, her skin flushed.

"Did Lily do something that would lead you to believe that she is, ah, free with her favors?"

"I am a gentleman, Francesca," he answered coldly.

"Aha!" she crowed. "But I don't understand, Avery,
if she and you . . . why aren't you . . . ?" She
peered at him more closely. "You mistrust her . . .
attentions?"

"*If*," Avery said, "there were any attentions to mistrust—and as a gentleman I am not willing to cede
that point—yes, I damn well would mistrust them. I'd
be a fool not to.

"Here's a woman who appears to actively dislike
me, has spent four years trading insults with me,
makes no secret out of the fact that she is trying to
snatch my inheritance from me, and she suddenly up
and . . . *pays attention to me*? What should, er, *would*
I think?"

"You poor dear." Francesca eyed him with horrible
fascination.

"Don't be an ass, Francesca."

At least his response dispelled that nauseating expression from her face. "Humph. Well. If you don't
want my help . . ."

"Your help with what?" he asked incredulously.

"My help in—how does one put this delicately?—
acquiring Lily Bede."

"I don't *want* to acquire Lily Bede."

"There's no need to shout, Avery."

"There's every need to shout! That's the most ridiculous thing I've ever heard. Lily Bede is an obstinate, strong-willed, argumentative troublemaker. She dislikes me. I dislike her. Well, dislike is too strong a word. I don't trust her. She's too intelligent by half and too independent by the other half. Why would any man want to *acquire* such a woman?"

"I can't for the life of me answer that," Francesca said complacently. "I'm not a man. Perhaps you can elucidate?"

"Of course I can," he said angrily, somewhere half-aware that he was just explaining an attraction he'd seconds before been denying. "A kind of magnetism between members of the opposite sex is normal. Just because I've never experienced it to its current degree doesn't mean I wish to acquire Lily Bede.

"My attraction to her is doubtless based on my sudden immersion into the absolutely foreign company of women, a chronological receptiveness, and certain chemicals in the body." He scowled. "And her eyes."

"I haven't any clue what you just said, Avery. Perhaps you'd best stick with the monosyllables," Francesca suggested.

"I mean," Avery said, "that knowing that this infatuation is simply an unfortunate combination of mental, chemical, and sociological coincidences, I know full well how to deal with it."

"Oh?"

"The mill pond," he stated, well-pleased. "I looked

it over very carefully on my walk with Lily. It appears to be quite deep and I know it to be quite cold."

"You're going to take cold swims?" Francesca burst into laughter.

"What else am I going to do?" He knew he was speaking more loudly than he ought, but he couldn't help it. "The woman obsesses me. It's unhealthy. It's ridiculous."

"You just said it was normal."

"I was wrong. No. I was right. Blast it! I can't even make a simple statement where she is concerned. She's ruined my ability to make a rational judgement."

He pulled his cigar case from his jacket pocket, snapped it open and withdrew one. "I need to get away from her. This trip to London will do me good. Obviously, I must have entered the time in my life when I should be looking for a wife. I'll . . . I'll arrange to meet a few friends. Some of them have sisters. Fine, docile, creatures. Good wife material. Damn it, she won't even let me smoke in the house!"

With a savage movement he jammed the cigar back in its case and shoved it back into his jacket's breast pocket.

"Poor dear." Francesca didn't sound particularly sympathetic. "Why not accept the inevitable? Believe me, Avery, I have much experience with your situation. Some things are invincible. It does no good trying to resist them. Such attractions are as strong as an ocean's rip tides. You may as well just drown and enjoy it."

"I will not drown," Avery declared emphatically. "I will take swims. Long, invigorating cold swims. Daily if need be. Twice daily."

"You're a fool, Avery." Francesca sighed. The fact that he suspected she was correct, but could not fathom why this would be, destroyed what was left of his temper.

"Damn it, Francesca, *she wants my house!*"

Her nostrils flared delicately as if she scented something she disliked.

"Lily," she said in a deceptively soft voice, "has given five years of her youth to this house. The same five years that other young ladies generally spent being coddled and cosseted and feted, Lily was straining her eyes over accounts, studying late into the early hours of dawn so she could discover a way to eke another penny from the farm, cleaning the floors on her hands and knees—" At his look of amazement she stopped, disgust making her lips thin.

"Dear me, Avery," she said, "you didn't imagine three pregnant, overindulged little maids did all the work in this house, did you? Man, *look at her hands!*"

"Why?" he asked in bewilderment.

She misunderstood his question. "Because that is the only way she will be able to secure the future she wants. I believe that after all she has done Lily considers Mill House *her* house." Francesca lifted her eyes calmly to his. "*I* would certainly not contradict her."

Her words brought back to him in full force the

dilemma that had been plaguing him. He raked his hair back from his face.

"I know," he said. "I see what she's achieved. I would never have thought it possible." His voice hardened. "But, Francesca, *I* did not present that challenge to Lily. It was through no offices of mine that she was offered my home."

Francesca watched him silently.

"Mill House was promised to me when I was younger than Bernard, Francesca," he said. "I dreamed of it, I planned for it. I counted on it when there was nothing more to—I counted on it. It was to have been my *home*. *She* knew that when she fell in with Horatio's scheme. Don't tell me that she didn't realize that in securing her future she would be doing someone else out of theirs."

"I can see how her act might seem callous, Avery," Francesca said, her look of contempt turning to confusion. "I can only say that five years ago your prospects looked much better to her than her own."

"I don't give a bloody damn. She accepted a challenge which, if she won, she knew would result in my disinheritance. Badly done, Francesca. Badly done."

"Perhaps it was less than gentlemanly, Avery—"

"Damn right," he said harshly. "If she did that, what else is she capable of? Just what would she be willing to do to secure Mill House for her own? And how can I allow myself to be attracted to her?

"Yet," he went on, "when I see those dilapidated nags she cares for, I wonder why would she risk her future for some broken-down race horses? What makes a hardheaded, unsentimental opportunist do something so utterly insane? And then, most importantly, nearly a year ago she wrote me a letter that—" *that saved my soul*, "that meant a great deal to me. It seems impossible that the woman who wrote that letter could be so callous."

Francesca had no answer for this enigma.

Suddenly Avery felt tired. Tired and drained and bitterly aware that the one woman he wanted was the one who he most mistrusted. "I appreciate that Lily has worked hard and long for something she wants. But I hope like hell that she fails. Simply wanting something does not give you the right to it."

"Is that what you're telling yourself when you look at her?" Francesca asked. "That she doesn't deserve your house? Or are you thinking about other things?"

Avery groaned. Francesca could take a debate on monetary reform and turn it into a sexual one. The fact that her words brought back with renewed impact the hunger he felt for Lily did not make the matter any less ironic. He sighed, rose, and went to the door. "As I said, Francesca, that problem I know just the cure for."

He yanked open the door. Bernard stumbled into the room. Avery closed his eyes and counted to three, when he opened them it was to find a garishly red-faced Bernard shuffling before him.

"I was passing and I heard Miss Bede's name," he stuttered miserably. Yet, Avery had to give him credit.

The boy met his gaze squarely, even defiantly. "I didn't hear much. The blasted door's too thick—"

"Don't curse, boy," Avery chided him severely. "It's not gentlemanly."

"Yes, sir," Bernard bit out. "But as a gentleman, I feel . . . that is, I have a duty to Miss Bede, an obligation to see to her welfare. I'm naturally concerned. . . ."

Another Thorne male under the sway of that black-haired witch? Avery narrowed his eyes on the boy's fevered-looking face, trembling body, and heated glare. Damn!

He seized Bernard's bony shoulder, spun him around, and propelled him out into the hall. "Fine, Bernard. I have just the thing for your 'concern.' "

"Where are we going?" Bernard squeaked.

"For a swim, lad. A nice, long swim."

Chapter Fifteen

"Jump in!" Avery shouted. "It's six or seven feet deep here, not shallow like the north end."

"All right." Bernard dropped his boots and stood up to drop his trousers.

Avery experienced a moment of intense déjà vu. He might have been looking at a photograph of himself taken over a decade earlier.

Bernard's broad, bony shoulders spread beneath his linen shirt like a clothes hanger. From under his shirt-tails stuck long white stick-like legs ending in feet that looked like some monstrous duck's paddles. With a body like that, Avery thought, Bernard should swim like a selkie.

"Come on!"

"I said, 'all right!' " Bernard shouted back irritably. Avery's grin spread.

His young jaw tensing with determination, Bernard took a step back and then launched himself off the embankment. Limbs gyrating madly, he sailed

through the air, landed in the water and promptly
sank. A second later he burst from beneath the surface, sputtering fiercely and noisily gulping air. Avery
swam closer, concern supplanting his amusement.

"Don't swim much, do you?" He kept his tone
light, remembering how important it had been to him
to mask his physical infirmity. Listening carefully for
the telltale wheezing but hearing nothing besides loud
clear gasps, he turned over on his back and floated
nearer, ready to give aid if necessary.

"I learned to swim in this pond," he commented
conversationally.

The boy's breathing was settling back to normal
now. He began paddling around inexpertly. "Oh?
Who taught you?"

"No one," Avery said. "I fell in while I was fishing.
It was a matter of swim or drown. I decided to swim.
Who taught you?"

"Miss Bede."

The boy's reply caught Avery off-guard. Bernard,
correctly interpreting his expression, laughed.

"I didn't realize you'd spent so much time with
her," he said.

"I don't," Bernard said. "Not at all. Mother likes
me to stay near when I'm home." His brows v'd over
the bridge of his nose. "Mother worries. Fact of the
matter is that when she found out that Miss Bede had
taught me to swim Mother was so distressed that Miss
Bede promised not to do anything like it again."

From the boy's sigh Avery deduced that further escapades with Lily hadn't been forthcoming.

"It's hell, isn't it?" he said.

Bernard didn't pretend to misunderstand. "Yes!" he exclaimed. "I hate it! The way the deans look at you every time you cough, all frightened and resentful, and how the other lads snicker behind your back, and wondering if you'll ever be well enough to do anything."

Avery nodded. The usually reticent lad had found his voice. He knew how cathartic that could be.

"And how it feels when your chest is all collapsed-feeling, like some invisible monster is sitting atop you, and you're sure you won't be able to draw enough air to live?"

Avery nodded. He knew.

"Sometimes"—Bernard's head bowed but then he looked up defiantly—"a few years ago, I used to think that it wouldn't be so awful if I didn't."

"Bernard—"

The boy looked up, his face angry. "I know. It was cowardly. But I got so tired of worrying Mother and Miss Bede, of being afraid myself."

"And how did that change?" Avery asked quietly, relieved when he realized that Bernard was speaking in the past tense.

"I just got tired about worrying about whether I'd live through the night or not. You know what the funny thing is?"

"What?"

"The less I cared about dying, the easier time I've had of it. I mean, I used to stew a bit." He looked away, coloring slightly. "You know. Lie abed and worry whether I'd be around to wake up the next morning."

Avery's heart ached for the boy.

"Then I'd remember how Aunt Francesca said you'd had the same thing when you were my age," Bernard continued, "and think about how you are now, and I'd swear I'd get strong, too. And then I'd feel better. Not just in here." He tapped his head. "But in here." He thumped his chest. "At least that's the way it seems. Tell me, did you . . . did you really have this thing, too?"

"Yes." The relief the boy felt was palpable. "And it stopped?"

"Not entirely," Avery said, picking his way carefully. "There are still situations and places I eschew. Things I won't attempt. I avoid them like the plague."

"You?" Bernard said incredulously. "Like what?"

"Horses. A few minutes anywhere near them and it feels as though I've a steel band tightening around my chest."

The boy took a few strokes closer. "Really?"

"Really. And I think you should avoid whatever things bring on your attacks."

The boy snorted. "There's no reason for my attacks."

"I disagree. You just told me the reasons. Upset. Worry. Fear. I know it sounds preposterous to think that one's thoughts can so profoundly affect one's body, but I've seen things that not only suggest this to be true, Bernard, but offer categorical proof of it."

The boy didn't look too convinced and Avery knew better than to press the issue. Bernard, like all Thornes, must come to his own conclusions. "Tell me about your swimming lessons."

It was the right tack to take. "It was the second summer Miss Bede was at Mill House. Mother and Francesca had gone to have tea with someone and left me in Lil—Miss Bede's care. It was hot and Miss Bede had spent the morning in the stables—"

"Is she really so devoted to those nags?"

"Oh, yes." Bernard flipped over on his back and let the water buoy him up. "She quite dotes on them. Anyway, she was hot and I was, too, and we sort of ended up here at the pond and she asked if I knew how to swim and I said 'no' and she said I ought to and one thing led to another. . . ." The lad's gaze grew dreamy. "She was so beautiful," he whispered.

Yes. She was, Avery thought.

"When she's wet her hair gleams and her eyes shine. She'd have me float on my back and then hold me up and I'd feel . . ." Bernard's voice trailed off as his eyes glazed over.

Avery felt a bit glazed himself. No wonder the boy was so entranced by the black-haired termagant. Lily Bede, wet. It made his mouth go dry and the icy water seem tepid.

He turned over and plunged beneath the surface of the water, pushing down toward the bottom and through the ropy tangle of waterlily roots. The cool silky water filled his eyes and ears, muting sound and blurring shape. Shimmering bands of sunlight pierced the greenish gloom with golden corridors. Minnows darted past, losing themselves in the forest of weeds. He gave himself over to the calm, cool, *reasonable* beauty of it—in direct contrast to another heated, dangerous beauty. A few minutes later, he swam back to the surface.

"Where were you?" Bernard's frightened voice demanded. Avery turned. The boy stood waist deep in water. "You were down so long. I thought—"

The boy had worried about him. When was the last time someone had fretted over him?

"I'm sorry, old chap," Avery said mildly. "I learned to swim here, but I refined my skills on a Polynesian island. I never could hold my breath for as long as the pearl fishers, but I could match any European there. My comrades used to make wagers on that talent." For drinks mostly, but the boy didn't need to know that.

"You were in the French islands?" Bernard asked. "I don't remember you writing about them."

Avery shrugged. "Only there for a month or so. A stopping off point to Australia."

"You haven't talked about your adventures hardly at all since you've come here."

"Hmm." Avery swam lazily toward him. Above the sky was clotted with thick ivory-colored clouds. A robin sang from a nearby hawthorn. It was so beautiful here. So familiar and healing. He wanted it. The beauty, the calm, the very *Englishness* of it, more than he'd ever wanted anything in his life.

And so did she.

"No need to bore the females with my—what is it Miss Bede calls my stories? Oh yes, 'tales from a superannuated childhood.' "

"She's wonderful, isn't she?"

"It's not the word I would have used, but I'll agree she's a unique woman."

If Bernard noted a lack of respect, he ignored it. "I don't think I've told you how smashing I think it is that you'll let Miss Bede live here at Mill House if she fails to inherit it."

Live with Lily? Under the same roof? The idea transfixed him . . . hell, it scared him. "Now, Bernard, I don't recall ever saying that she could actually live—"

"Yes, you did," Bernard insisted. "You said you would guarantee her welfare. I would never have taken you for a man who would shun his respon—"

"*Don't* say it," Avery suggested, rising from the water like an irate Poseidon. He'd give the boy credit, he stood his ground. A little shakily, but he stood it. "I said I will see to her future and I will."

"Seeing to her future is not the same as seeing to

her welfare. Welfare means happiness and her happiness is here, at Mill House. She loves it."

"I know that. And I have every intention to see Miss Bede is cared for and yes, that she is happy though I'd venture to say that if *she* inherits Mill House I doubt she'll spend any time worrying after *my* happiness! I'm fond of the place myself in case you haven't noticed."

"Well, then the answer to what you should do is simple."

"Oh?" Avery raised his brow sardonically. "Pray, enlighten me."

"You should marry her."

Lily had returned late after spending the afternoon in town arguing over the greengrocer's bill. Pleading a headache, she retired to her room where she spent the evening once more desperately trying to muster an attitude of indifference regarding Avery Thorne.

The next morning she forced her hair into a tight braid and marched resolutely into the breakfast room.

Avery was not there. Good. She didn't want to see him anyway.

Francesca, too, was absent but Evelyn looked up from her place next to Polly Makepeace's wheelchair and smiled as she finished pouring the invalid's tea. Lily studied Polly closely. Polly definitely looked better . . . more relaxed. Even pleasant.

"Good morning, Miss Bede." Bernard scrambled to his feet and pulled out her chair.

"Thank you, Bernard, but really such ceremony isn't necessary," Lily said, slipping into her seat.

"Oh, but it is, Miss Bede," Bernard said. "I mean I hate to disagree with you but as a gentleman—"

"Just what *is* it with you and that cousin of yours?" Lily burst out. "It isn't even as if he was very good at it, is it? He's loud, dictatorial—without troubling about being the least diplomatic—and blunt. He's not suave or charming or even very polite!"

She looked up. Everyone was watching her in open bewilderment. "Well, he isn't, is he?" she demanded.

"Of whom are you speaking, Miss Bede?" Polly asked.

Lily snapped open her napkin. "Avery Thorne! Who else?" She dumped several sugar lumps into her teacup and stirred.

Evelyn and Polly exchanged glances. Bernard, if possible, looked even more confused.

The door from the kitchen opened and Merry came puffing in behind a cart. Without ceremony she began unloading chafing dishes brimming with rashers of bacon and ham, scones and biscuits, coddled eggs, smoked fish, and steaming bowls of porridge.

All this for Avery Thorne. Who wasn't even here to appreciate it, the ungrateful wretch!

"Remind me to speak to Mrs. Kettle about the amount of food she's been cooking lately, Merry."

"There now, Miss Bede. Boys like Master Bernard here"—she gave the lad, who was staring at her bulging stomach in amazement, a saucy wink—"not to mention men like Mr. Avery—need plenty o' good food to grow on."

"Bernard, perhaps, but Mr. Avery looks quite grown enough to me," Lily said.

"Don't he just?" Merry enthused with a sigh and began spooning porridge into Bernard's bowl. "Last night he carried Kathy up three flights of stairs to her room like she were a babe instead of carrying one."

"He carried her all the way to the attic?" Evelyn asked.

"Yup. He was walking by and the tart topples over like a pole-axed cow, so he hauled her to her room, her smiling all the while just like a drunk that's got 'er 'ands on a jug," Merry said in righteous disgust.

"And," Lily said in a voice she congratulated herself on keeping quite calm, "remind me to have a little discussion with you and Kathy and Teresa about this strange inability of yours to remain upright in the man's presence!"

"All right." Merry nodded absently and then turned back to Evelyn. "And you know that big table in the kitchen? The one with the marble slab top what Mrs. Kettle is always banging into on account of it being set too close to the door?"

"Yes?" Evelyn asked.

"He moved it." She leaned over Bernard's shoulder and began pouring molasses over his porridge. "And that ain't all. You know the huge, colored window up under the attic gable?"

"I do," Francesca said as she sailed in. "One of the

only things of true architectural value in the place, I'm afraid."

Bernard leapt to his feet and pulled out Francesca's chair. She sat.

"It's really valuable?" Bernard asked, returning to his seat.

"I should think so," Francesca replied. "But lest that avaricious look take up permanent residence on your face, remember that Mill House and its contents will either be Lily's or Avery's. You were never even in the running."

"I know that. I was just interested in why someone would put an expensive window in a farmhouse."

"Pretentiousness, I'd imagine." Francesca smiled fondly at Bernard. "Anyway, what of the oriel window, Merry?"

"Mr. Avery cleaned it."

"What?" Lily asked.

Merry nodded, adding cream to the concoction in front of Bernard. "Swung himself out from top of the roof on a rope. Said he'd learned the trick in the Him-ee-lay-ahs. Go on, eat up, Master Bernard." She gave him a friendly pat.

"That's dangerous!" Lily exclaimed angrily. "He could have been hurt. Killed. Of all the fool things to do."

"I'm sure Avery has survived far more perilous adventures than cleaning a window, Lily," Francesca said.

"Besides, who else could do it?" Evelyn took a

pause from her conversation with Polly Makepeace to point out.

Polly entered the fray. "If I weren't stuck in this cast, I'd be more than happy to wash your windows for you. There's no reason why a woman can't hang from a rope just as well as a man."

"I'm sure you could do anything you set your mind to doing." Evelyn patted Polly's hand soothingly drawing Lily's startled attention. She'd thought Evelyn detested Polly Makepeace and yet lately the two of them seemed as tight as ticks.

"I agree with Miss Makepeace," Lily said. "Anything that needs doing around here we, or the servants, are capable of doing. I suspect Avery Thorne is simply trying to show me how much better suited he is to run Mill House than I. Well"—her eyes narrowed—"let him."

Lily glanced up at the clock. It was getting late. Perhaps she could avoid Avery for another day. No. She straightened. Better get it over with. It was just a kiss. Certainly it had been very unsettling and, yes, she had spent too many hours reliving it—the feel of his mouth, the muscles hardening beneath her hands, the heat of his breath and—

She cleared her throat. "One would think a gentleman would make care not to inconvenience the servants by being so late for meals."

"Are you asking where Mr. Thorne is?" Polly asked.

"No," Lily said. "I'm merely making an observation. I'm sure I couldn't care less where Mr. Thorne is, except when he discommodes my household."

"He ain't discommoding no one because he isn't here," Merry piped up. "He's left."

"Oh?" She felt as though she'd stepped into a precipice she hadn't known was there, plummeting into painful darkness. Had he been so disgusted with her that he'd felt himself unable to continue living under the same roof? "Is he gone," the words came out in a whisper, "for good then?"

"Oh, no," Merry said, clearing away Bernard's plate and moving on to collect Evelyn's. "He's just gone to London for a few days to visit a tailor. Lord knows he needs some new clothes. Me and Teresa taken the seams out of the ones what he's got as far as they'll go."

To a tailor. She had forgotten. She forced her breathing to an even pattern but there was no hiding from herself the relief that washed over her, the pleasure that surged through her at the thought that she'd not seen the last of him.

Good Lord. She had to fight this. He wanted to take Mill House from her—Mill House for which she'd fought and worked and struggled because it alone could guarantee her future, her security . . . her independence.

"You sounded downright wistful for a moment there, m'dear," Francesca said.

"May I be excused?" Bernard asked.

"Yes. That would be fine," Evelyn said. Bernard

tossed down his napkin, passing Teresa at the door. He had to stop as her bulk pretty well filled the door-frame.

"Oh, miss!" wailed the distended maid. "Something awful happened. That Chinese vase, the one in the drawing room? Someone broke it! It's shattered into a hundred little pieces. I swear I didn't do it, miss. I swear I didn't!"

"I didn't either!" Merry promptly added her wail to Teresa's.

"*That* will be enough," Lily said. "I don't care who broke the vase. It doesn't matter in the least."

"Oh, Lily!" Tears welled up in Evelyn's pale eyes. "The Sevres vase is worth hundreds and hundreds of pounds. The bank officials have a list of all Mill House's assets. And they'll demand that you replace it before they begin tallying up the pluses and minuses of your guardianship. How can you possibly afford to replace it?"

Lily rose calmly. She'd better see about clearing up the mess in the drawing room and attending to whoever was responsible for its breaking. "It's not the Sevres vase," she said. "Years ago, when Bernard first visited Mill House, I arranged with a local craftsman to have a facsimile made. The real Sevres vase is in storage and has been for nearly five years."

She looked around at the quintet of bemused faces. "Considering Bernard's earlier proclivity for toppling things over and shattering glassware—which he has thankfully outgrown—any other course would have been stupid. For all my faults, I am *not* stupid."

Except where Avery Thorne is concerned, a silent voice taunted.

Chapter Sixteen

Sheep stink. Not as much as, say, a sloth, Avery thought, but close to it. And wet sheep, like wet sloths, stink even more.

Cold swims hadn't done it, moving things around the house hadn't done it, and his trip to London where he'd spent two nights immersing himself in a society that seemed unaccountably delighted to meet him—particularly the females, and in particular one Viscountess Childes—certainly hadn't done it. But if he just perservered, really exhausted himself out, then he *would* be able to get Lily Bede out of his thoughts.

He grabbed the huge ewe around her middle and heaved her from her foothold at the edge of the mill pond into deeper water. She thrashed madly in protest. Burdocks and bits of bramble floated to the top of the churning brown water. Beside him another man released his captive and shoved her toward the far bank and the fenced pasture that waited as a reward.

Drummond stood post, scrutinizing each sopping

sheep as it emerged. Every now and again, alternately cursing and cackling, he would push some hapless victim back into the churning pond.

"You, Ham!" Drummond shouted. "That sheep's dirtier than your grandfather's bunghole! Cob, you're supposed to wash that sheep, not drown it! And, Master Thorne," his voice dropped to a sickly, sycophantic whine, "begging your pardon, sir, but would you kindly consider moving yer blue-blooded arse? We've got five hundred sheep to wash!"

Avery released the ewe and grabbed another startled-looking sheep that came hurtling down the mud slide. He shoved her into the water, burying his hands in her wool.

Raddle. He was covered with the stuff; it coated his arms, his chest, and most of his face. His pants were shredded by sharp hooves; his shirt, which he'd carefully draped over a shrub, had been found by a lamb and partially eaten; and his boots—wonderful, custom-made Moroccan leather boots that had crossed from one hemisphere to another—might prove unequal to being soaked for five hours in raddle-poisoned water.

The ewe bucked violently but Avery grimly held on. He ached with his exertions. His muscles burned with strain, his head swam with fatigue, and his body cramped up each night as he took his dinner in his room. And yet, damn it all, every night when he dropped exhausted onto his bed, still she danced before him, her dark, glossy hair a veil slipping through his trembling fingers, her mouth an erotic memory tormenting him.

"Marry her!"

Of course he'd immediately turned Bernard's ears red for making such a suggestion but it hadn't stopped his traitorous thoughts from replaying it time and again.

Marry Lily Bede? Madness. He'd have to give up any notion of comfortable, temperate pastoral bliss because there'd be no bliss with Lily Bede, pastoral or otherwise. There might be other compensations perhaps. . . .

What the *hell* was he thinking? Just because some boy had made a ridiculous suggestion didn't mean he had to entertain it.

The sheep twisted suddenly, flinging muck over his face. "Ach!" He let it go, swearing vociferously.

"You certainly do swear a great deal. For a gentleman," a woman said.

He should have known. The air should have crackled, lightning should have struck, the crickets should have fallen silent, at the very least he should have been visited by some sort of mental seizure. *Something* should have telegraphed her advance. It didn't seem right that nature could create so powerfully stimulating a force and then not warn lesser creatures of its approach.

He squinted up. She was standing on the very edge of the bank, surrounded by placidly grazing sheep. Her hands were on her hips, one booted foot tapping out a message of irritation. Behind her the dark sky threw her ridiculous man's white shirt and buff bloomers into a reverse silhouette, throwing the swell of her bosom and flare of her hips into sharp contrast against the cobalt colored clouds piling up on the horizon. His body tensed and in spite of the cold water in which he stood, he hardened.

Lightning strikes were too subtle a warning for something like her; birds should have dropped from the sky.

"What are you doing here?" he asked, all-too-conscious of the slick, reddish ooze streaming from his torso and the same slippery mud half coating his face. Anticipating the next round of battle, he began sloshing slowly toward the edge of the pond.

"What is *she* doing here?" Drummond shouted from the opposite bank. He snatched his hat from his head and snapped it angrily against his thigh. "This ain't no damn picnic, Mister Thorne, and I'd as soon you sent yer woman back where she come from."

Avery winced. Sure enough, like a bull taunted with a red cape, Lily glared at Drummond. The tapping of her toe turned into a single, emphatic stomp. The ewe grazing next to her lifted its head and blinked.

"First of all, *Mister* Drummond," she said, "I am not anyone's woman except my own. Second, I am not here bringing anyone lunch."

"Then be off with you," Drummond said. "You're the one what was nagging me to get the sheep washed and here I am doing my best to get it done and you're jabbering away, distracting my men, causing problems just like you always—"

"Shut up, Drummond," Avery said.

Instead of a look of gratitude he could have anticipated from any normal female, Lily scowled. "I don't need your help, Mr. Thorne," she said. "I am well able to handle myself—and Mr. Drummond."

"You're not going to leave?" Drummond demanded.

"No!" Lily shouted back.

"Then *I* will. Break for lunch, lads! Now!" Drummond lifted his chin in the air, daring her to take some action.

How would it feel to have one's authority not only constantly challenged but openly denigrated? Avery wondered, unable to quell the sympathy he felt as Lily's face paled. He, too, had experienced the frustration of being disregarded, of his opinions and suggestions being ignored because he was physically unable to command others' respect.

And sure enough, the other workers, without a look at Lily, their ostensible employer, released their sheep and began tromping up the berm. They headed toward the copse of trees at the far side of the meadow where their lunch pails waited.

Drummond strode away, a victorious troll king surrounded by his entourage, his jaunty gait clearly relating that he considered he'd won the encounter. Lily watched them go, unable to mask her anger and frustration before returning her gaze to him. She hitched her chin a degree higher, daring him to voice his sympathy, ready to fight yet another skirmish with another adversary. He understood pride, too.

Suddenly he didn't want to fight her.

"Lily." He extended his hand.

She looked down at it as if he were offering to paint her with raddle.

"Lily." He tried again, keeping his tone soft and unthreatening. He could see that she was trembling slightly.

She took a step backward. "I came to tell you that you have visitors," she said.

"What visitors?"

"The Misses Camfields, who *happened* to be passing by with their *dear* friend Viscountess Childes, whom you met in London, and *her* dear friend Miss Beth Highbridge and her brother, Ethan Highbridge, whom you knew at Harrow."

"Oh?"

"Yes. Mr. Highbridge is rabid, simply *rabid*," she said sweetly, "to have you as his houseguest. He and some of his *lads* are getting up a party next week."

Avery narrowed his eyes on her. "Don't remember any Highbridge. Where does he live?"

Lily waved her hand in a general southerly direction. "A few miles the other side of the Camfields. I am told the house is quite beautiful and well-appointed. No dust covers on any of their furniture."

"So?" he said, trying to ascertain what she was

about. "I'm perfectly happy right here at Mill House. Dust covers and all."

She deliberately let her gaze travel over his mud-covered body. "I understand."

"And what is that supposed to mean?"

"Only that you might as well accept the invitation and desist with the he-man exhibitions. These transparent attempts to illustrate how much better suited you are to be the owner of Mill House impress no one but yourself."

"My *what*?" he exploded.

"All these projects you keep undertaking." Her voice rose as she stalked to the edge of the bank. "Don't think I don't know what you're doing. Merry and Teresa and Kathy and Bernard are full of your daily muscle-flexing antics. I will not bow out of the running simply because you've rearranged some furniture and moved a few shovelfuls of silt from the pond—"

"Wait!" He had no idea what she was talking about. He knew only that if she inherited Mill House all the backbreaking labor he'd been putting in could very well end up benefiting *her*. And instead of being duly appreciative of his effort—not to mention his manly sovereignty over dirt—she was upbraiding him! "A few shovelfuls? I've moved at least two tons of that muck!"

"It looks like you're wearing most of it."

He took a deep, steadying breath. "You, Miss Bede, are an ungrateful, sharp-tongued shrew."

Impossibly, astonishingly, as he uttered that last adjective Lily's lower lip began trembling and her startlingly dark eyes turned black behind a veil of liquid. For one awful second he thought she was going to cry. But then she mastered whatever emotion assailed her.

"And you, Mr. Thorne, are a loud, filthy, domineering lout and *no gentleman*!"

Before he could rebut, she turned, promptly colliding with the sheep behind her. Startled, the ewe swung its giant hindquarters around knocking Lily sideways and sending her sprawling headfirst down the steep clay bank. She landed in the deeper water at the far end with a loud, satisfying splash and disappeared under the opaque waters.

She didn't come up. He waited. A few seconds under some cold dirty water could only improve her disposition.

She still didn't come up. With a sigh, he sloshed over to where she'd gone down and fished about until he found her head and then her neck and then the back of her shirt. With a grunt he grabbed her collar and yanked her up. Sopping wet, clothed in a half dozen yards of heavy material, she weighed a lot, even though the water here, nearly to his shoulders, bore much of it.

"No fair hiding at the bottom of the pond," he said.

"I wasn't hiding," she said. "I couldn't get a foothold and—get your hands off of me!"

"Gladly." He released her. She went down like a ton of bricks, her soaking bloomers billowing out a second before dragging her beneath the surface once more. This time he counted to five before reaching under the mucky water.

She wasn't there.

He dove under the surface, finding the bottom with his hands and sweeping his arms out in great circles. He tried opening his eyes but the mud stung them, blinded him with darkness. He made himself act, moving in quick, ever-increasing circles. She'd been under half a minute. A minute.

Panic gibbered in his mind. He forced it away, forced himself to remain focused on the next stroke, the next sweep of his arm. He made the edge of the lily pads and began groping frantically through them. If she'd unsuspectingly swam into them she could be caught in a net stronger than any fisherman's . . . and drowned.

No!

A minute and a half—his hand brushed through something silky. Hair. He reached down just as her arms came up struggling weakly.

Thank God.

Blindly he ran his hands over her body, quickly finding the net of weeds that wrapped around her upper torso. Feebly she tried to help him as he tore at the lilies imprisoning her, finally rewarded when she slipped free of their deadly embrace. He grabbed her under the arms and with one last jerk, thrust her toward the surface.

She came up choking and thrashing. He looped an

arm around her waist. She kicked weakly, still gasping, her body quaking in the cold water as he hauled her toward the shore.

As soon as his feet hit the silt bottom he scooped her up in his arms and carried her up into the meadow. Dropping to his knees, he lowered her to the grass. She was breathing harshly, her eyes shut.

Tendrils of hair clung to her face. Gently he pushed them away, studying her with increasing concern. Had she fainted?

He straddled her hips and leaned over her, his forearms bracketing her face. Tenderly he wiped the mud from her soft mouth, her cheeks and nose. Her lids fluttered open. Jet black irises stared up at him, unreadable, preternaturally calm. He became acutely conscious of the rise and fall of her breasts, their shape and form as clearly revealed by the slick coating of mud as if she'd been naked, the feel of her hipbones jutting against the inside of his thighs, her open hands flexed above her head, vulnerable between his forearms.

Concern died and desire erupted, surging through him with painful force. She murmured something, so softly he could not hear. He dipped his head closer, his gaze traveling from the fascinating pool of russet water that had collected at the base of her throat to fixate on her full red lips.

His own breathing grew labored. "What?" he managed to rasp out. "What did you say?"

"I asked if you were planning on taking that pot-shot now?" she whispered weakly.

He pulled himself back and rolled off of her.

It would have been better, Lily thought watching Avery's face grow blank and cold, if she hadn't sounded so hopeful. But when she'd opened her eyes and found his mouth so close, she'd wondered if he—

She closed her eyes again. Mortification at having to be rescued by Avery Thorne made her want to disappear. She'd thought only to teach him a lesson, show him how well she could swim after he'd dropped her. So, she'd struck out under the water, thinking to emerge with a triumphant sneer on the opposite side. Only she'd gotten turned around in the muddy water and ended in a snare of water lily roots.

When she peeked through her lashes, he was sitting beside her, one arm nonchalantly draped around his knee. One would think he was simply enjoying the view if not for the muscles working in his jaw and throat.

In fact, a lot of muscles were working. His biceps bulged beneath the sheath of slick mud, and his belly muscles rippled beneath his glistening tanned skin. It was like watching an oiled bronze statue come vibrantly to life and it took her breath away.

"Thank you," she said.

He didn't even turn his head to look at her. She was alive. He'd done his duty. Instead of answering he rose, deliberately turning his back on her and took a

step before hesitating and looking out across the pond.
She followed his gaze.

Off in the distance the workers had begun to stand.
"Let me help you up," Avery said, reaching down. She
ignored his hand, struggling to her knees. "I—I suppose I can carry you back to the house if you can't
walk," he said.

He could not possibly have made a more grudging-
sounding offer. *Touch her? Carry her? Like Merry and
Teresa and Kathy and God knows how many other women
in that house?*

As much as she wanted that—and Lord, she was
beyond self-deception—she would not steal his impar-
tial touch through trickery. She still had some modicum of pride left.

"No," she said, shaking her head.

"Don't be an ass," he grated out thrusting his hand
out to help her up.

"No!" She slapped his hand away.

"Fine," he snapped out. Without another glance,
he snatched a shirt from atop a nearby bush and took a
step. He stopped. Froze.

"Damn it all to hell!" she heard him say under his
breath.

"Did you say something, Mr. Thorne?" she asked
sweetly. He spun on his heels, bent over, grasped her
arms, and jerked her to her feet. His mouth descended
on hers like a falcon on a dove.

It made their previous kiss seem fraternal. His
stance broadened, his arm coiled with steely strength

around her ribs, crushing her to him and bringing her hips into the lee of his wide-spread thighs. His tongue swept between her lips, greeting hers in a deep, lush carnal stroke.

Nothing had ever felt so good. She opened her mouth further, letting his tongue play against her own, and his hands roved her back with long sweeping caresses she wanted desperately to return. She strained to get closer.

Abruptly she was free. He practically thrust her from him. For a second he faced her, breathing deeply, his extraordinary eyes glittering behind their lashes.

"Now we're even," he said and retrieving his shirt, turned around and strode off across the field toward Mill House.

Confusion and sensation making a muddle of her thoughts, she watched him go. The dramatic sun rays slanting from beneath the storm clouds glazed his torso with gleaming light, revealing each detail of his long, lean body, every ripple, every sinew, the prominence of heavy arm muscle, the lean hardness with his belly, the breadth of—

She looked down and immediately slammed her eyes shut. Her sodden muddy shirt made her own body just as public. Anyone—her head snapped around.

The men were returning from lunch and were halfway to the pond. With a gasped oath, Lily scrambled to her feet and, hampered by the heavy wet material of her mud-weighted bloomers, stumbled off in Avery's wake. If she could just catch up, she could use his shirt to cover herself.

"Wait! Avery! I say, wait!" she called, looking over her shoulder at the goggle-eyed men. Avery kept eating up the distance with his ground-covering stride and she kept tripping.

"Wait!" she wailed as laughter and catcalls followed her across the field.

He didn't wait. He didn't even slow down. That kiss . . . that had been his "potshot." His revenge.

Her steps slowed as she approached the house and started round toward the servant's door in back. She stopped. He mustn't ever know what that kiss had meant to her. To him it had been nothing. He probably kissed women all the time. He mustn't suspect that what he'd doled out as a punishment had been to her something wonderful.

She wouldn't slink through the back doors like his . . . his doxy, like she'd done something wrong.

She marched up to the front door, stepped through, and gave it a good hard shove. It slammed closed with a gratifying sound. She smiled grimly just as the front door reverberated with a loud crash.

Alarmed, she opened the door again to see what had happened. There, on the granite steps, lay thousands of shards of brilliantly colored glass, all that was left of the oriel window from high above.

Chapter Seventeen

"One hundred pounds? Is that all?" Francesca took a sip of her port and laid her head back against the divan.

"That's what the glazier said," Lily answered from the deep overstuffed chair across from Francesca.

The lighted candelabra between them guttered in a sudden draft, making shadows leap across the sitting room wall. The storm that had been brewing all day had arrived, disrupting the house's lighting. The relative darkness had driven Evelyn, Polly, Bernard, and Avery to their separate apartments soon after dinner.

Lily, unwilling to retreat to her room and thoughts best left untended, had spent the evening in the sitting room where Francesca slowly and steadily and silently made her way through what wine was left from their meal. She'd recently started on a decanter of port.

Francesca gave a little snort of amusement. "No wonder Horatio didn't have it wrenched out and sold as salvage."

"Thank heavens, it wasn't more expensive," Lily said. "I can find a hundred pounds. I couldn't find a thousand." The shutters outside banged noisily in a fresh blast of wind.

Francesca cocked her head to listen to the wind moan in the chimney and then snagged the crystal port decanter from the pie crust table beside her. "How long is it before the bank vultures swoop in and start tallying up your capital?"

"Six weeks."

"You'll make it?" Francesca asked, pouring a healthy dollop of liqueur into her glass.

"If nothing else untoward happens. Two potential disasters in as many days rather challenges one's belief in a benevolent deity."

"Doesn't it though? I wonder"—Francesca tilted her glass back and took a long draught—"if those incidents were accidents? What if someone deliberately broke the vase and shattered the window?"

Lily shook her head. The storm, the dark, and the port were giving the older woman fancies. Lily had seen Francesca yield common sense to her imagination before—mostly when she drank and was feeling "sentimental."

"What if someone broke the vase on purpose and then crept up to the attic and loosened the casements around that oriel window so that a good rattle from say, a storm or even a slamming door, would send it crashing down?" Francesca mused.

"Why would anyone do such a thing?" Lily asked

reasonably. "Who would even *have* a reason to do such a thing?"

"Who do you think?" Francesca said owlishly.

"Avery Thorne?" Lily asked incredulously and burst out laughing. Francesca's knowing expression crumpled in indignation.

"I never suggested him." Francesca slouched further down in her chair and nursed her glass close to her chest. A sly, conspiratorial look came over her face. "But Avery Thorne, in case you've managed to forget, has a vested interest in seeing that your expenditures far exceed your ability to pay. Maybe you should go and have a little talk with him."

Lily tried not to laugh again—after all, Francesca had her best interests at heart—but it was difficult. "I'm sorry, Francesca," she said, "but the idea of Avery Thorne *creeping* anywhere is absurd. He can't even walk without the floors shaking and really, sneaking about is hardly his style."

She held up her hand to still the protest she could see forming on Francesca's lips. "I do not deny that Avery Thorne has a good motive to vandalize this house, but if he decided he wanted to break a window in order to gain Mill House, he'd simply pick up the nearest piece of furniture and heave it through the glass. And be damned to who witnessed it."

"Hmph. I still think you should confront him. Right now."

"In the middle of the night?" Lily asked. The thought of Avery Thorne and darkness made illicit images leap in her mind. "Besides, I tell you, Avery Thorne would never do such a thing."

Francesca shook her head, blowing a gusty little sigh. "So much faith. So much confidence in a man's honor. *I* was never so naïve."

"I know the man's temperament," Lily assured her.

"Or his heart," Francesca suggested.

Her words sobered Lily. She didn't know anything about Avery Thorne's heart. She knew only about her own. His kiss had destroyed her peace of mind and given her a glimpse of her own unsuspected capacity for passion—and perhaps something even more improbable.

She'd fought a losing battle with her infatuation, except she wasn't certain she could call it infatuation anymore. Now, her only defenses against Avery were his own lack of interest in her and his aggressive, self-assured masculinity, something that fascinated her almost as much as it provoked her.

What must it be like to be so confident, always certain you were right, never doubting yourself, your place in the world, or your ability to hold it? Who wouldn't find such power seductive? She sighed and caught Francesca watching her with a sidelong glance.

"You're a romantic, Francesca," she said, winning a crooked smile from the older woman.

"Am I?" she asked.

"Yes. A rather tired romantic right now," Lily added.

Francesca held her glass up to the light and stared

at the candle through the faceted surface as though it held the mysteries of the universe.

"Why don't you go to bed?"

"Why don't you?" Francesca rejoined absently.

Lily rose. "Because I've ledgers to balance and bills to pay and numbers to juggle."

"And I've a past to balance and debts to repay and memories to juggle." She glanced fleetingly toward Lily. "The business of being a failed romantic is an arduous one."

"I never said you were failed," Lily said softly.

Francesca smiled. "I know. I did. Be off with you, child. I like my own company tonight. Something rare enough that I think it warrants investigation."

"You're sure?" Lily asked, not wanting to leave Francesca here alone with a full decanter and an empty past.

Francesca waved her away and Lily finally left her, walking the short distance down the hall to the library and the stack of waiting bills and accounts that never seemed to grow smaller.

Avery couldn't concentrate. He flung down the magazine that carried his latest serialized story and stared broodingly out of his bedroom's rain-lashed window. She danced through his thoughts; she overwhelmed his sanity; she played havoc with his reason. She was simply there. In his mind, in his blood . . . in his heart.

When she'd lain beneath him today, her eyes devouring his soul, her hips pressed intimately between his thighs, and asked him in that throaty, breathless little voice if he was going to take his potshot, he'd almost done it. Only his stellar code of conduct had saved her—for all of three minutes.

Because as soon as she'd whispered her taunt, he'd taken that flimsy excuse and the equally bogus one of reciprocation and taken his kiss. Her body had been as good as naked. His own had been rock-hard with urgency.

As soon as she'd struggled he'd let her go, afraid of what he would do next, of what he would say, and fled.

He never did see the Camfield chits and their dear friends. He'd been on his way to clean up in the kitchen sink when he'd heard an enormous crash heralding Lily's arrival. He'd raced to the front hall where she stood wild-eyed and dripping mud, then the others had arrived.

At dinner she'd avoided his eye, keeping her lovely, fierce countenance lowered to her plate, testing his resolve to behave in a civil manner. She was in his blood far more intimately than a mere fever. She was like malaria, lying dormant and seemingly harmless for weeks, months, and sometimes years before recurring with virulent, devastating intensity. And like malaria, he doubted he'd ever be cured. He could only hope for some measure of control.

He rose from his chair and prowled restlessly to the window, looking out. Two stories below light spilled from the library window. He pulled Karl's gold watch from his pocket. Even this, which should have been a reminder of his dear friend, reminded him more of her.

He closed the gold lid. Who would be up at this hour? Bernard? The boy had once mentioned how he liked to read late into the night. Perhaps he wanted company. Avery would welcome some distraction from the uneasy path of his thoughts.

He pulled his shirt on without bothering to button it and headed out the door and down the staircase. He didn't light a candle. He'd excellent night vision.

At the bottom of the stairs his attention was drawn to another, fainter light coming from the sitting room. He frowned. Was the whole blasted family nocturnal? Perhaps it was Lily. Cautiously, so as not to startle her, he looked in.

Francesca lay half-sprawled in the corner of the divan, one arm tucked beneath her cheek, her mouth open, gently snoring. On the table before her two candles flickered uncertainly in a pool of wax. Her hair had come undone and her expensive gown was crushed and twisted. On the floor next to the divan stood a half full decanter and beside that a crystal wineglass lay on its side, a small dark stain on the carpet beneath.

He angled his head, studying her. Even in sleep she looked worn and exhausted. Once, not so many years ago, she'd stood up to Horatio's expectations and criticisms and stipulations with a valiance he couldn't hope to emulate. Now he saw what it had cost her and he wondered if she counted the price worth it.

Oddly, in her faded dishevelment he found her much more appealing than he ever had when she'd played the naughty, wild, and irresistible siren even his schoolmates had whispered about.

He approached quietly and bent down and picked her up. Gently, he bore her down the hall past the library and into the apartments she used. Even more gently he deposited her on the big down-filled bed and lit a candle so that if she woke disoriented, she wouldn't be afraid. He pulled a blanket over her shoulders and brushed the hair from her face.

"Good night, Miss Thorne," he murmured and turned.

Lily stood in the doorway, her dark eyes reflecting the candlelight. He raised a finger to his lips and moved by her, taking her wrist and pulling her into the hall. Quietly, he closed the door behind them before leading her back into the library.

"Is she like this often?" he asked.

His voice was soft, not a whit of censor to it, only sadness. She'd never known, never even imagined, that a man could have so kind a heart. She'd watched as he looked down at his cousin. She'd waited for the sneer of contempt for someone older and weaker than himself, at the very least an expression of frustration or disapproval. But there had been only tenderness.

He filled her with dread. Power *and* compassion.

"Is she?" he asked again. He was standing close, so

close she could see the tiny flecks of copper forming a starburst at the center of his eyes.

She shook her head, as much to clear her thoughts as to answer him. "No. Not often. The summer storms seem to bring on these moods."

He ran his hand through his hair and for the first time she noticed that his shirt was undone and hung open over his chest. It said much about his preoccupation with Francesca that he himself did not appear to notice his unclad state.

He was beautiful. His chest was broad, covered with an inverted triangle of fine dark hair. The skin cleaving tightly to hard muscle beneath was fine-grained and clear except for four thick, ragged purple lines running roughly parallel up his left breast and disappearing beneath his shirt.

She touched the scar before she realized what she was doing. He flinched back as though she'd stroked him with a white-hot poker, his hand flashing up as though to ward off an attack. She ignored his hand and his step back, moving forward and touching the raised, damaged flesh again. This time he went utterly still.

"There really was a tiger."

"What?" He looked down at her fingertips pressed lightly above his left nipple and prayed for composure. "Tiger. Yes. There really was a tiger."

"And he really did maul you."

"Yes. She. It was a she."

She had to take her hand from him. He couldn't

think. The scent of her, always a pleasant, illusive thing, thickened in his nostrils, making his head spin. He could damn near *taste* her scent. It filled the small space between them, using up the air, underpinned by another subtler fragrance. He backed up again and this time she didn't follow.

"Why did you do it?" she asked, returning to her desk chair and sinking down on it wearily, as if she'd just given up a fight.

He shrugged, finding her problematic and enigmatic and wholly desirable. "I don't know," he answered honestly. "There was nothing much else to do. It was a way to fill the time, I guess. I couldn't see sitting around London for five years waiting for Mill House. I'd already waited long enough."

She clasped her hands between her knees, allowing the guilt she'd held at bay for five years to finally surface. She'd known, of course, that somewhere in England a young man's inheritance had been ruthlessly wagered away by an old, egocentric man. But she'd never let herself think of what he must have felt when he heard what Horatio had done to him. She did now. Even if she still had every intention of fighting for and ultimately attaining this house, *her* home, she had to acknowledge the monumental unfairness—no, the *wickedness* of it. If only there were some way both of them could win.

"I can't . . . I won't let you have it, you know," she said tiredly, meeting his eye.

"I know," he said. No ranting, no invectives, a simple acknowledgement of their positions on opposite sides of an unspannable breach. "And I wouldn't let you have it if I could possibly stop it."

She nodded. He began buttoning his shirt as he wandered toward the desk, his gaze traveling over the furnishings and paintings with the same tender expression with which he'd looked at Francesca.

"You love it, too," she said.

"Yes," he said quietly. "Mill House is like a friend you knew as a child and aren't sure you'll still like, but then you meet again and you discover that the changes the years have wrought in both of you rather than separate you, draw you even closer together. When I arrived, it wasn't to the house I remember visiting as a boy. That was a palace set in a green park. But the Mill House I've discovered since I've been here is even better than a fairy tale castle.

"It's real." He glanced at her to see if she understood. "It's like a person, with quirks and oddities—the ivy that refuses to give up its place above the front door, the way a northeast wind causes the sitting room fire place to hum. It even has its own affectations like the oriel window and that ballroom on the second floor." His smile was wry.

"It's simple and well-built, solid and enduring, without the weight of too much heritage pressing down on its tenants, or the sheen of newness masking its underlying quality. It's a place where one can live and work and rest." He shrugged. "A home.

"I never had a home. I never had a family," he went

on. His tone held not the least bit of self-pity; it was a simple recitation of the facts. "Mill House is going to be both. My home and my legacy. A place to raise my children and for them to raise theirs."

She didn't take umbrage with his assertion. She would have used the same words. "You want a family?"

"That surprises you? Oh, yes. I want children. Many children, enough to take the dust covers off all the bedrooms up there."

She smiled.

"Every child should have an older brother to emulate and a younger one to teach," he went on, "one sister to admire and one to tease and a baby to coddle. I used to listen to the lads at school complaining about their siblings and I'd curse them for fools I was so jealous. I wanted a family so damn much."

He looked over at her. "And you? You're an only child, too, aren't you?"

She spoke before she thought, the words, like her guilt, finding voice after what seemed a lifetime of silence.

"No. I have a brother and a sister I've never met."

Chapter Eighteen

"I don't understand," Avery said.

It was too late to recall the words, too late to smother the hurt that came from a lifetime of witnessing her mother's torment.

"My mother was married when she was sixteen." At Avery's expression she shook her head. "Not to my father. To Mr. Benton, a bookbinder. She had two children with him, a boy and a girl, Roland and Grace. She left him when she was nineteen."

"Why?"

"I don't know," she replied. There was so much she didn't know. Too much she did. "My mother wouldn't say other than she could not live with him. If you knew my mother, her strength, her commitment and principles, you would accept that her reasons for leaving must have been good."

He nodded. He did not know the mother, but he knew her child. If Lily had inherited her character, her mother had been a woman of courage.

242 Connie Brockway

"Where are your half-siblings?" he asked. "Why haven't you ever seen them?"

"I don't know where they are." The emptiness with which she spoke those simple words bespoke a void of long standing. "After she left, Mr. Benton found her and took the children. He swore she would never see them again. He didn't lie."

He could not conceive of a mother allowing her children to be taken from her. "Why didn't she care enough to fight for them?"

"Care enough?" she echoed. "She broke her heart with caring. She stood outside the door to his home each day for weeks and each day the police came and took her away and each day she came back. She kept coming back until Mr. Benton found a magistrate and had her committed to an asylum."

She placed her folded hands on the desk, too carefully. "My father was among the directors overseeing the asylum. He met her there and immediately realized she was not insane, or perhaps insane, but only with grief and he made it his *cause célèbre* to have her released. But by the time she'd been freed, Mr. Benton had immigrated to Australia with the children."

It was inconceivable, barbaric. "They can't have put her in asylum simply for wanting to see her children."

Lily's sad, answering smile was much wiser than her years should have allowed.

"Laws have changed," Avery protested. "Today a woman has the right to sue for divorce, she can enter contracts, she can own property—"

"But not her children," Lily broke in. Seeing his uncertainty she continued. "Legitimate children *are* property, property a man owns. Should a man decide his wife is unfit he can remove her children from her and the law stands behind that decision."

Yes, he thought numbly. How could he have forgotten? The long school months, the even longer weeks of vacation when he and other aristocratic orphans haunted Harrow's empty yards. He'd been property, all right, paltry property. Dross goods.

Lily's gaze was fastened on her hands. They were clasped tightly now, with the white-knuckled fervency of a religious zealot at prayer.

"There has to be something she could have done," he insisted.

"No. A woman can't even seek redress. She has no recourse except—" She broke off abruptly, flushing.

He understood then, as clearly as if Lily had explained. He recognized in Lily's confused abashment the legacy of sadness and bitterness left by her mother, a woman falsely imprisoned in an insane asylum, her children stolen from her. He looked at Lily and knew as certainly as if she'd told him her mother's mode of revenge. She had made sure that Mr. Benton never had a legal relationship with a woman again.

Outside the rain fell softly. Inside the candle lights studded the night-dark room with stars. "They were never divorced."

She shook her head. Didn't Lily understand what

had been done to her? The selfishness of it appalled him.

"Why not?" he asked. "She could have easily rid herself of him on the grounds of abandonment. Why didn't she marry your father?" He had no right to ask these questions, no right to demand answers.

"Can't you understand?" Lily lifted her gaze. Her eyes caught the candlelight, reflected back the golden flame like a cat's. "An unwed mother retains sole custody for her child. My mother had already lost two children. She'd never risk losing another."

"But your father, surely he must have wanted—"

"My father was an extraordinary man. He accepted her decision." Her words cut coldly through his passionate renunciation of her father's consent to such an intolerable situation. "*He* understood."

Understood? Understanding shouldn't have meant condoning. The wrong of it affronted Avery, hurt him. He would never have made Lily's father's choice. And Lily knew it.

He paced restlessly about the room, the candles guttering silently with his passage. "She tried to find her children?" he asked.

Lily's combative posture eased, leaving evidence of weariness in the bow of her head. He wanted to reach across and smooth the lines from her brow, but he couldn't. She was marked too deeply and the distance was far greater than a span of mahogany.

"She did what she could," Lily said. "My father sent out agents looking for the children. But my father was never wealthy and he was only a younger son, and his inquiries met with no success."

"He must have loved your mother very much."

"Yes."

He studied her bowed head, the deep shadows beneath her jaw and cheeks, her black, glossy hair rippling like silk, and he wanted more than anything in the world to protect her. The need overwhelmed him, confounding him and filling him with rage that no man had done so before, that her own father had failed in this most basic of principles. He did not doubt for a minute that Lily's father had loved her mother and that her mother had never ceased grieving for her two children but where had Lily fit into this quagmire of pain and loss? Who'd loved *her* best?

"He should have loved you more," he muttered roughly.

"Don't judge him. Don't judge either of them." The warning was harsh.

He ignored it. "He should have made certain that you were afforded all the rights and privileges, the property and the respect, that his name alone could have guaranteed. Instead, he allowed you to be an outsider, without legal recourse for your birthright. *He should have married your mother.*"

"As you would have done?" she asked.

"Yes."

"Don't you understand?" Her words, beginning angrily, became entreating. "She couldn't risk having her heart broken again. She wouldn't have survived it. She *couldn't* marry." Her voice trembled, dropped to no more than a whisper. "Any more than I could."

Why should he care? Why should it feel as though she'd just reached into his soul and torn out its center? It wasn't as though he'd entertained the slightest hope . . . he hadn't imagined any sort of future. . . .

"You will never marry, Lily?"

"No." Her voice had dropped to a whisper. "Not until the laws are changed. Not until a woman's safety and health and future are deemed as important as a man's. Not until she has the same rights regarding her children that her husband has."

"And if you should fall in love, couldn't you trust your future to your husband's care?" he asked. "Isn't that love?"

"Would you entrust your future to a wife?" she answered bitterly.

"It's not the same thing."

"No. It's not," she agreed with cold deliberation. "You'd only need to demonstrate your 'trust' until a time it's proven unjustified. Then the law grants you the means to rid yourself of your wife while keeping that part of the union you still value, your heirs. Of course, whether those children are better left in their mother's care than in yours is a matter never considered, much less addressed."

"And you think it better for them to live with the stigma of illegitimacy?" he asked incredulously. "To have doors shut in their faces? Their futures left to uncertainty? To be deemed unworthy because of their birth?"

"Is . . ." She lifted her chin. "Is that how you see me?"

"Damn it to hell, Lily," he said harshly. "It doesn't matter how *I* see you. It matters how society sees your children. I would never allow my child to suffer like that."

"I assure you I have not suffered. I have enjoyed a liberal, interesting, no, a *fascinating* upbringing," she said. "I had loving parents to shelter me from bigotry. I have had an education most men would envy and enjoy a position of respect amongst my sister—"

"You don't have any sisters, Lily. You have an organization," Avery cut in, "your causes, your education, but as for family, you have no more of a family than I. Less." He saw her flinch and felt as if he'd slapped her. Yet, he went on, desperately seeking to force her to reexamine her beliefs.

"Even your presence here," he said, "in this house, is conditional. As little as I have, I can legitimately claim Mill House. In spite of what Horatio did, in spite of his will, I can claim it with a right that you will never be able to claim because your father never gave you his name."

She was breathing heavily, and for a minute he thought she would raise her hand and strike him. He would have welcomed it, seen it as a sign that on some level she agreed with him and must do him violence as a denial.

"It's a house," she said, tasting the betrayal in the words. "A thing. A possession. I don't need stone walls and wood floors to know who and what I am."

"The hell you say," he ground out. "It's not just a house. It is a bell jar keeping a family's history, their lives and stories."

"It's a house, not a cathedral," she insisted but her cheeks were ruddied in the dim light. "Do you think if you have Mill House you'll somehow acquire the family you never owned? Well, a family doesn't come with the deed, Avery."

Her words cut with the fine incisive pain of truth, but then, she knew they would. She'd counted on it stopping his tongue. Not so easily done.

"Family, Lil?" He leaned far over the desk, his lips curling in derision. "You wish to speak about families? Why not? We'll be rather like the blind men describing an elephant, won't we?"

He frightened her. "No, I—"

"Yes," he insisted. "Perhaps between the two of us, we might be able to piece together something of a notion. You, after all, had the adoring parents—or were they? Never matter, parents nonetheless. I, lacking the parents, had the trappings, the name, the house, the auxiliary relatives—"

"I don't want to speak about this," she said, panic touching her voice.

"Damn it, Lily. Can't you see what you're doing here?" he asked. "You've adopted my family, *mine*, as well as these suffragists, these servants, all these people who want something from you, whose fealty you secure with jobs and sanctuary and bribes. Fealty isn't love, Lily. These people aren't your family."

"They are."

"No." He shook his head and at that moment she hated him. He looked big and hard and commanding and what little nature had not equipped him with the ability to take, English law did.

But most of all she hated him for making her question her parents. How much had her father's family's refusal to have anything to do with them been their choice and how much her father's? She would have suffered much to belong somewhere, anywhere, in some capacity.

Hostility snaked within her, anger that her mother's life had so unalterably affected—no, *damaged* her. With anger came guilt. She *knew* the torment her mother's choice had caused her. She *knew* her decision not to marry had not been made lightly and still she could not help her anger.

"You have no right to stand above me and tell me what my father should have done and what my mother should have been willing to sacrifice," she said in a fierce, low voice. "You've never had a child taken from you, as good as murdered—no, *worse* than murdered! My mother died not even knowing if her children were still alive. I saw what it did to her. I heard her at night, torturing herself with questions she could never answer."

He remained silent.

"Can you imagine? She fretted over wounds she should have been there to prevent, the comforting hugs she could not give. Each morning and every night she pantomimed the kisses she could not bestow. She imagined them asking for her and wondered what their father answered, if he told them she was dead or simply hadn't cared enough one day to come back."

His mouth was set with resolve, shadows hid his eyes. "And what about you, Lily?"

"Me?" She carefully unwove her fingers. "I wonder if they even know I exist."

"Lily—" He reached out and touched the back of his fingers to her cheek. She didn't even notice. She simply gazed up at him with stark and empty eyes.

"If the laws had been different . . ." she mused. "If she had had the right to her own children . . . but they aren't. Nothing protected her." Her voice hardened.

He could think of nothing to say. Bitterness pulsed through him, for Mr. Benton and Lily's cowardly mother and spineless father and yet he could not hate them.

"You have to admit, Avery, I have every reason to distrust marriage. Any woman does. Only a fool would enter into it when the laws that govern that union see a woman's children as 'products' of her body which her husband owns."

"But if there were love on both sides. If a couple respected and trusted—"

"Ephemeral feelings," she said. "Hardly worth risking one's children for. It's a matter of logic, Avery. I thought men appreciated logic. A woman cannot afford labile emotions."

She was tearing him apart and like any wounded animal he reacted savagely, instinctively striking back.

"Logic? Labile emotions?" His laughter was mocking. "You're a coldhearted creature, Lily Bede. You would have made a successful general with willingness to sacrifice all for your 'principles.' I salute you. I'm just damn glad I don't have to bed you lest I get chilblains."

"Yes"—her head jerked up and her gaze was like polished ebony—"count yourself fortunate."

She would not be provoked and he needed—God how he needed—to find some answering heat to match the fire raging within him.

The sound of running footsteps sounded above the pelting rain. The library door crashed open.

"Mother of God! Help!" Merry shrieked.

Chapter Nineteen

"Teresa's having her babies!" Merry said breathlessly. Outside a peal of lightning struck close to the house. As if on cue the rain began a torrential downpour. The oil lantern she held in her hand knocked against her skirts, sending her shadow capering across the wall.

"Where's Mrs. Kettle?" Lily asked, rising and moving past the distraught girl. Mrs. Kettle had played midwife before to women whose birthing had come early.

"At her daughter's in the village."

"Drat." With Francesca fast asleep down the hall that left Merry, Kathy, Miss Makepeace, Evelyn, and herself.

Miss Makepeace was bound by her wheelchair and Evelyn fainted at the sight of blood. Merry kept crossing herself and muttering prayers.

"For heaven's sake, Merry," Lily snapped. "She's having a baby, not a demon."

"I can't help it, ma'am," Merry mewled. "I'm sorry, but I can't. I can't bear to see her what with my time's comin' so soon. I don't want to know what's going to happen! I'll be where she is soon enough and oh, miss, she's screaming out like she's being ripped apart! Don't make me go in there, miss! Please!"

"Quiet, Merry," Avery commanded. "No one's going to *make* you do a bloody thing. Just do as Miss Bede says. Without the noise."

His implacable tones had the desired effect. Merry dabbed at her eyes and sniffed loudly but nodded and turned to Lily for instruction.

"Where's Teresa?" Lily asked.

"In her room."

"And Kathy?"

"Last time I seen her she was, ah, heading for the stables, miss," Merry said.

"In the middle of the night, in a storm?" Lily asked.

Merry nodded meekly. "She, ah, she"—she swallowed—"she frets after the horses."

"It's Billy Johnston, isn't it? And last month it was that wainwright in town," Lily said, already striding through the door toward the servant's staircase. "It's not enough that she's already pregnant. What sort of idiot flits from one failed relationship to another? What can the girl be thinking?"

She was all too aware of Avery following silently behind her, like some paladin guarding her. In front of them Merry silently held the lantern aloft to light their way. Silently. Merry. Incompatible terms.

"Merry?"

"Not much thinking going on, I 'spect," Merry offered sheepishly. "That what starts up between a man and a woman is a powerful thing."

Lily paused and stared at the little maid in dismay. "Not you, too, Merry! Has every woman in this household taken leave of her senses?"

"Well, Todd Cleary down to town says he wouldn't mind having a baby in his house if it come with me as its mum. . . ." She trailed off into a blushing, head-ducking, spasm of giggling delight.

" 'Wouldn't mind?' I can see it would be difficult to refuse such a marvelous offer," Lily spat out sarcastically. Only the loud, angry wail echoing down the narrow servant's stairs saved Merry from further scurrilous remarks.

"Be off to the kitchen with you," Lily said. "There's enough light to find your way." She took the lantern from Merry's hand. "I want hot water and soap. Clean linens, lots of them, the sharpest knife you can find, and a brazier full of hot coals."

"Yes, ma'am!" As soon as Merry disappeared down the hall Lily began climbing the steep stairs. She'd gone halfway up when Avery bumped into her.

"Where do you think you are going?" she demanded.

"You seem a bit shorthanded. I can help. I've . . ." For some reason he stopped and when he spoke again his voice sounded odd, doubtless from the acoustics of the narrow stairwell. "I've been present at childbirths before. I may be able to assist."

"That won't be necessary. I can handle it," she said.

He didn't argue. He simply scowled fiercely as though engaged in some internal argument and finally said, "I'll wait outside her door. If you should require any assistance, anything at all, a strong arm, more water, a sharper blade, you'll ask."

She met his level gaze with her own. "I'll ask," she answered and climbed the rest of the stairs.

Another loud, unhappy wail shook the walls as Lily pushed open the door to Teresa's room. The poor woman lay atop a sodden mattress propped up on her elbows, the mound of her belly so high it nearly obscured her face, her hair sticking straight out from her head like the braids of a rag doll.

"Where the hell has everyone been?" she demanded.

"Excuse me?"

"I've been up here bellowing my head off for an hour," Teresa announced testily. "Am I supposed to have this baby all by my—" Her words dissolved into an angry howl as she doubled up, clutching her stomach.

"Good God!" Lily heard Avery gasp from the open door behind her. "Is she dying? Should I get a doctor?"

"No!" she said impatiently, snatching a washcloth from the rail at the foot of the bed and wiping the writhing woman's brow, "and no. The nearest doctor is in Cleave Cross twenty miles away and she's not dying, she's having a baby."

"I am so dying!" Teresa howled in protest. Lily ignored her. She'd been present at quite a few births in the last five years, enough to know that feebleness was far more worrisome than wrath.

"I thought you said you'd been present during childbirth before," Lily said, looking over her shoulder at Avery.

"I was." He shuffled in the doorway, his big, broad frame bright against the back hall. His shirttails were still outside his pants. "I did. But she was . . . she was a great deal quieter than her." He pointed at Teresa.

"Could we possibly have a bit less chatter," Teresa panted. "In case you haven't noticed, I'm trying to have a baby here! And what the hell is *he* doing here anyway? He's nothing but a filthy, slimy *man*!" She snatched the damp cloth away from Lily and hurled it at Avery. He ducked. With a splat it hit the wall behind him.

Avery stared at the maid in shocked offense. He'd always thought Teresa rather liked him. He'd carried her up and down stairs, he always asked after her health and greeted her pleasantly and here she was, wriggling her way back up on her pillow and glaring at him as though he were personally responsible for her current distress.

"He'll stay in the hall," Lily assured her soothingly.

"No," Avery said with a little less assurance than he would have liked. He retrieved the wet towel, edged into the room, dropped it into Lily's extended hand and backed out again. "I'm staying here. At least until you have Merry here should you need any help."

Teresa let out another howl of pain.

Lily glanced at Avery whose face had turned ashen. So much for the intrepid explorer's much vaunted courage, Lily thought unable to hide a grin. She left Teresa, vowing gruesome mass retribution on certain parts of men's anatomy, and shoved a wooden chair across the floor in Avery's direction.

"You might as well sit before you faint," she said.

"I'm not going to faint," he said, sounding as though he was trying to convince himself rather than assure her. "I have never fainted in my life. I will not faint now."

"Hey!" Teresa had rallied once more. "You said he has to stay in the hall."

"Gladly," Avery responded, kicking the chair back into the black hallway and sinking down on it. In the gloom of the hall he looked like some giant, sullen gargoyle.

"Hush there," Lily crooned, returning to mop Teresa's brow. "You're doing a splendid job, darling. Splendid. You are so wonderfully brave."

"Like I have a bloody choice!"

Heels beating a rapid rhythm on the stairs announced Merry. She shoved her way past Avery into the room, water sloshing from the copper kettle in one hand, a small, closed brazier swinging in the other, and linens draping her upper body like a fresh mummy. A hunter's skinning knife hung from the belt at her waist.

"I got everything, Miss Bede," she said breathlessly. "Everything."

She unloaded the brazier and kettle at her feet, tossed the sheathed knife on the foot of the bed and shrugged out from under the winding length of what looked like fresh bed sheets. She took one glance at Teresa, who'd begun moaning again and asked, "Can I go now?"

"Coward!" shrieked Teresa.

"I better go now." Merry's head bobbed up and down unctuously. "I'm just upsetting her."

"Fine," Lily said, unsheathing the blade and holding its glinting surface up to the candlelight, eyeing its lethal edge with satisfaction. It flashed wicked silver.

Avery felt his head swim.

Granted leave to flee, Merry fled.

"You're not going to use that on her?" Avery whispered in horror.

"She won't feel a thing," Lily assured him and closed the door in his face.

For Avery the next hour seemed to last forever. Sporadic bouts of cursing were followed by long, tension-filled silences. On several occasions Avery was treated to graphic and imaginative vows regarding what Teresa would do to the fellow who'd impregnated her if he should ever have the misfortune to cross her path again.

Soon even these vociferous pledges ended and only Lily's low, calm murmurs could be heard punctuated by sounds he associated with incredible exertion. He withdrew Karl's watch from his pocket and noted the time and as he did so he wondered how many of Karl's forefathers had marked the birth of their children by it. He wondered if he, too, would someday watch the minute hand creep around the ivory face accompanied to the sounds of Li—of his wife's labor.

The door swung open. Lily stood in the doorway, holding a tiny parcel in her bloodstained arms. Behind her, Teresa lay on the bed, her eyes closed, her chest rising and falling in shallow breaths. His head swam.

"Here," Lily said. "Hold the baby close, she needs to be kept warm."

She? Avery peered down at the bundle Lily still held out. He couldn't see anything. Certainly not something that resembled a "she," not even a pre-she.

"I haven't got the brazier ready for her yet."

"What," he asked, "are you going to bake her?"

She laughed—a sweet, sweet sound. "No. I'm going to set up a little bed before it for them, to keep them all toasty and warm. Usually we'd put them in the bread warmer in the oven but the oven's gone cold."

"Them?"

"Yes." Lily beamed. "Teresa's having twins."

Teresa stirred in the bed behind Lily. She glanced

over her shoulder. "Here. Take her and keep her close."

Mutely, numbly, he accepted the tiny creature she placed in his arms. She rewarded him with an encouraging smile. "That was easy, wasn't it? Next one seems to be taking his sweet time in making his appearance," she confided, leaning closer. "But it'll be fine. You'll see."

Why was she consoling him? It was just a baby, for God's sake. He could hold a baby.

"Are you going to help me or stand about all night talking to that maaa—" Teresa bolted straight up in the bed and grabbing hold the iron rails on either side, threw back her head and howled.

"Teresa tells me she's Irish," Lily said. And on the enigmatic and casual comment closed the door on him.

Avery stared down at the baby's dusky purple little face scrunched up like a badly darned sock. One of his palms engulfed her entire head and most of her upper body. He'd seen freshly whelped pups as big.

Carefully, he moved some of the linen from around her face. She wriggled and a tiny fist punched its way up from the loose cloth. In amazement, Avery stared at the minuscule hand, perfection in the sliver of nail tipping each minute fingertip, the wrinkled palm, the delicate wrist.

He bent his head nearer. Her lashes were no more than mayfly antennae, mere suggestions feathering a dusky rounded cheek. He closed his eyes and inhaled the warm, human scent of absolute newness, and touched her cheek. Downy warmth.

Her uniqueness, her singularity, the life he cupped in his hands staggered him with awe, suffused him with a primal need to shelter and protect. How much more urgent would that need be if this were his own child?

The door opened once more. Lily stood on the other side of the door, her face relaxed into a triumphant smile. In her arms she held another tiny infant.

He looked down at his charge. "If she were mine," he said, "I'd do whatever necessary to protect her and keep her safe. No one would take her from me. Ever. I swear it."

The smile died on Lily's face. Her dark eyes went flat. Their truce had ended, the hostility and longing that were the cornerstones of their relationship obvious once more.

"As would I," she said.

Chapter Twenty

By next morning the storm had ended. A fresh wind chased the tattered remnants of clouds, leaving behind a fresh washed sky. Lily took breakfast in the library with the door closed.

She'd revealed things to Avery Thorne that she'd never told another. She'd entrusted him with her reasons for her commitment to the women's rights movement and her difficult decision not to marry. She'd been unprepared for his passionate reaction, his accusation that her decision was reckless and irresponsible and selfish—and by extension, so was her mother's. He'd been so self-righteous, so immune to the meaning of a mother's loss, and yet . . . she understood.

She stayed in the library through lunch.

She needn't have bothered. Avery left the house well before dawn, arriving at Drummond's door and offering his services in whatever capacity Drummond saw fit to use him—as long as it was strenuous, exhausting, and kept him away from the manor until after dark. Drummond gleefully obliged.

He sent Avery to work on a haying crew in the meadow behind the stables where he climbed the huge piles of hay, called rucks, and caught the hay tossed up to him from below, heaping it into an ever higher mountain.

For the next week Mill House was singularly quiet. Francesca took to her bedroom without offering any excuse or apology. Teresa kept Kathy and a tearfully penitent Merry busy admiring her babies. Evelyn, feeling obliged to keep Polly Makepeace company while her leg slowly mended, played hostess. Surprisingly, the two ladies began to look forward to their hours together. Their interest in promoting Lily Bede and Avery Thorne's relationship for the moment was on hiatus as it was hard to orchestrate encounters between people who were rarely even in the house at the same time. Bernard kept to his own devices.

When Avery finally mastered his emotions he realized that in fleeing Lily's presence he'd abandoned his young cousin to the company of women.

That being so, on the day before the Camfields' party, Avery went in search of Bernard. The boy wasn't in his room or in the library—his polite query through the closed door had been met with Lily's terse, clipped reply—nor was he in the drawing room. Mrs. Kettle finally steered him to the attic above the second floor servants' wing.

As he walked down the narrow servants' hall he realized he would have to pass Teresa's open door on his way to the pull-down ladder that ascended to the attic at the end of the hall. He approached warily, half-expecting Teresa to start flinging wet rags or something a fair deal sharper at his person.

From within her room he heard a trio of women cooing. Eyes riveted ahead, he strode by.

"Mr. Thorne!" Teresa's voice snagged him a few feet from the ladder. She didn't sound crazed. Still, one couldn't be too careful. "Mr. Thorne, do come see the babies! After all, you as much as birthed them yerself!"

He could not let this rumor go unchecked. He retraced his steps and poked his head through the door. Teresa sat propped up by at least a half dozen pillows, an incongruous and matronly lace bonnet covering her hair, and a fluffy pink yarn caplet around her shoulders. Merry and Kathy, holding a baby apiece, sat on either side of her bed. All three ladies beamed at him.

He cleared his throat. "How are you, Teresa?"

"Oh, I'm fine, Mr. Thorne!" Teresa enthused, her fingers playing flirtatiously with the ribbon of her cap. "Come look at the babies. You all but delivered—"

"No," he said firmly, taking a step into the room. "I did not almost do anything. Miss Bede delivered your babies. I sat outside."

Teresa waggled her forefinger playfully. "Now, that's not how I remember it, sir. You're just being modest, is all. You were my pillar, you were. My tower of strength in my time of need. I'd only to look at you to know that I would be all right, that you wouldn't let nuthin' 'orrible 'appen to me." Her eyelashes fluttered adoringly.

The woman was delusional. She'd been planning on filleting his private parts the last time she'd seen him. Obviously, there was no reason to continue the conversation.

"Lookit the babies, sir!" Merry chirruped brightly and thrust a little creature out at arm's length for his approval. Kathy, giggling loudly, followed suit. He leaned over and gave each of the babes a cursory glance. They looked like tiny, animated turnips.

"Very nice," he said.

"Would you like to hold one, sir?" Kathy asked.

The baby opened its little maw and wailed, a long, reverberating howl of dissatisfaction. He stared at her in bemusement, stunned that anything that little could be that loud. And red—her scrunched-up face was rapidly becoming aubergine colored. And mad—she let loose another howl of discontent. Obviously, she'd inherited her mother's lungs.

Amazingly, Kathy didn't appear to notice that the baby she held had turned into a banshee.

"Here." She pushed the baby further into his face.

"No." He lowered his voice. "No. I . . . I . . . my hands." He pointed at one blameless member with the other and grimaced apologetically. "Dirty. Disgusting. Unfit to touch babies."

All three of the maids' faces fell. "Oh," Teresa said disappointedly and then shrugged. "Well, later then."

"Yes," he agreed, "later. Nice, er, nice babies." He nodded in Teresa's direction and promptly escaped, being halfway up the stairs before they could recall him.

He heard Bernard before he saw him. Grunting, the boy was dragging an enormous yacht's telescope toward one of the windows beneath Mill House's deep eaves.

Avery looked around. The attic was surprisingly free of clutter containing only a few well rummaged steamer trunks; an armoire missing a front door panel; a battered sideboard; and a great, musty-looking four-poster improbably set up in the center of the room.

Bernard, oblivious to his presence, had by now situated the telescope in front of the window and was absorbed in adjusting the eyepiece.

"Hallo, Bernard," Avery greeted mildly, approaching the nook the boy had created for himself. An upturned butter churn acted as an end table, stacks of books banked a battered armchair, and a ceramic jar— from which arose a steam redolent of chicken soup— stood by Bernard's feet.

The boy looked up, caught back a start of surprise, and grinned his welcome. "Cousin Avery! I say, I thought you were out with Drummond's men again. I was just going to try to find you with this." He patted the monstrous old telescope affectionately.

"Come here often, do you?" Avery indicated the evidence of dozens of sandwiches in the gnawed over

crusts and crumpled oiled paper wrappings littering
the area around his chair.

"Yes. I 'spect I do," Bernard said. "Seems silly,
doesn't it? I mean, I so look forward to being with my
family and then once I'm here it's so different from
what I'm used to that I have to take myself off sometimes."

Avery understood. He'd felt the same way when he
was a child, craving the days at Mill House and yet
needing the hours of solitude in which to absorb the
deeds of the day: every detail, every aroma, every inch
of the place. It hadn't been until his adulthood that
he'd learned to be comfortable with others, and then
only a few, boon companions. Friendships had never
come easily for him, and the few he had he'd treasured. Karl's somber face flickered through his memory.

He wished he could have saved him. Sometimes late
at night he would replay the day of his death, rechart
their course over the Greenland snowfields, question
why Karl had been on his right rather than his left,
whether he should have insisted they go in single file.

Guilt came then, an insidious visitor poisoning his
thoughts, denying him sleep, mutating his affection
for Karl into a painful encumbrance. Then he would
read Lily's letter, a zenith of cool compassion and un-
erring wisdom.

Only all her letters, including the one that had
meant so much, had misrepresented the woman.

She wasn't infallibly wise, after all. She was far too

human in her failings. She'd chained herself to a dead woman's grievances and made a crusade of her mother's pain. There was no room in her heart for him. He'd never hold the place of importance in her life that she'd come to hold in his.

"Of course, *you're* always welcome," Bernard said. "I mean, it's not really mine to welcome you to but—" Avery gazed at the boy uncomprehendingly before realizing that Bernard had misread his silence.

"Does that prick?" Avery asked, knowing that as Horatio's heir, the boy had more right to Mill House than either Lily or himself.

"Oh!" Bernard blinked in surprise. "No!"

Relief washed through Avery. He'd have had to convince Lily to give the boy the place should he want it, but then, should he want it, as Horatio's primary heir he could afford to buy it from Lily.

"I mean," Bernard went on, "it's a jolly pleasant sort of place but if truth be told, I fancy a more urban setting myself. No rough and tumble existence for me."

"Really?" Avery considered his cousin. He'd assumed the lad to be like him at that age: eager for adventure, a chance to prove himself, test his physical courage. "You might find you enjoy the 'rough and tumble existence' given the opportunity."

"Definitely not. Not that I don't admire you profoundly. Your adventures are all the crack and terribly bully, but not the sort of thing I'd fancy. A dip in the old mill pond is one thing but wrestling crocodiles in the Nile is another."

He was telling the truth. There was not the slightest bit of chagrin in his expression or tone.

"What do you want to do, Bernard?" Avery asked, sitting down on the arm of the chair.

The boy's head dipped shyly. "I'd like to be an actor."

"An actor?" Avery asked in astonishment.

"Yes," Bernard said. "I should like to try on any number of roles, hundreds of different men, hero and villain. Someday, I might even write plays. I think I could write a decent sort of play." Chagrin touched his smile. "You think it's foolish, don't you?"

"No," Avery said carefully.

It wouldn't have been his choice but after his own youth and the years of Horatio's bullying he knew he would never try to force another into a prescribed mold. Whatever Bernard wanted, he'd stand behind him in his seeking it. "It's never foolish to work toward something. It's only foolish to strive for something you haven't a chance of attaining."

He frowned uncertain of whether he spoke of his desire for Mill House, Lily's desire for Mill House, or his desire for Lily. He could not deny it any longer. She was in his heart. He'd always accounted himself an honest man and he would be honest with himself.

He leaned over and rubbed the glass window with his sleeve. From this vantage one could see most of the Mill House property. Below them the apple orchard spread in a wedge from the mill pond. Beyond, sheep bloomed like ripe cotton in a green pasture. Avery looked south where hay rucks the size of small houses dotted the field close to the stables.

He'd always thought of this place as his. His gaze traveled toward the paddock in which a dappled gray, sway-backed nag chomped contentedly. And Lily Bede thought of this as hers.

"Your ambitions are worthy, Bernard," Avery said. "Mine are not so laudable. I've allowed myself to be forced into a competition with a woman whose future depends on acquiring the one thing in the world I've ever wanted."

"I don't see that you had a choice."

"There's always a choice."

"You won't hurt her," Bernard said quickly. "If you win, you won't let anything bad happen to her?"

He should have taken affront at the very suggestion, but the boy's sincere concern for Lily could not be gainsaid. "I'll do whatever needs to be done," he said wearily. "She shan't be displaced, I promise you that."

"Have you"—the boy darted a quick glance at him and fitted his eye to the telescope lens before continuing—"have you given any consideration to my suggestion?"

"What suggestion was that?" Avery asked.

"That you and Miss Bede marry," Bernard said. "It would solve so many problems."

"I don't think so."

Avery shook his head. "We are as unsuited as oil
and water, as bees and wasps, as fire and ice. I have
little in the way of family, Bernard, but what I do have
is irrevocably bound and represented by the name
'Thorne.' I am proud of that name. It represents
something important to me, something worth sus-
taining. Miss Bede doesn't give a rip for name or station or any of the things I hold dear. She'd burn the
family archives for tinder and call it a fair use of
wasted paper."

"No, she wouldn't."

"She doesn't value any of the things that I value."
He said the words to purge her from his heart and
hopes. To make himself realize how futile his—his
love was. "Lily Bede doesn't value anything I am, anything I have done, anything I will do."

"That's not true."

"Really?" Avery asked, his voice sounding desolate.

Bernard had risen, his young sallow face in stubborn lines. "Come with me."

"Really, Bernard, I don't much feel like—"

"Come with me." His insistence so surprised Avery
that he complied, trailing the lad slowly down the ladder, past Teresa's closed door, out of the servants'
wing and into the abandoned corridors directly beneath his own rooms.

"Where are we going?" Avery asked.

Bernard didn't answer, but simply led him through
the empty wing until they reached a double set of

doors leading into what Avery remembered was the ballroom. The boy disappeared inside.

Avery smiled ruefully. Even as a lad, he'd thought it a charming piece of vanity to include a ballroom in what was ostensibly a working farm. He wondered how many balls had actually taken place there. He entered the room just as Bernard flung back the last of the ivory satin drapes covering the floor to ceiling windows.

In near stupefaction he looked around.

An adult water buffalo was caught forever by the taxidermist's art, pawing the shining floorboards; likewise a stuffed tiger prowled between a mannequin in Maori warrior dress and one in Bedouin clothing; a crocodile basked in the light streaming through the windows, its glass eyes gleaming malevolently. Curio cabinets and long tables carrying row upon row of neatly labeled artifacts surrounded the perimeter.

Everything he'd ever sent to Bernard was in this room. The frailer items were carefully protected by bell jars, and those open to the air were recently dusted. Labels identified the artifacts by year, region, and circumstances of acquisition, written in a familiar, unmistakable feminine hand.

He couldn't speak, had no answer for the challenging expression on Bernard's young face. The lad didn't understand what he'd done to him. No woman through a sense of duty alone would invest such time and effort into chronicling the life of a man for whom

she had no regard. Here was indisputable proof that
Lily Bede cared for him and had cared for him.

But it didn't make a damn bit of difference. What
future could they possibly have? He wanted a family,
one to carry his name.

Without a word, Avery strode from the room, the
enormity of his loss hounding his footsteps.

Chapter Twenty-one

Bernard did not go to the Camfields' party, after all. Pleading extreme fatigue, he nonetheless made his mother promise to attend without him. Unable to think of an excuse to stay behind, the rest prepared for the festivities.

Consequently, the ladies entered the carriage that would take them to the Camfields looking as strained as if they were going to an inquisition not a party, which reflected Avery's own mood to an amazing degree. The ride over was silent, except for his own vexing bouts of sneezing. These eventually escalated to such intensity and frequency that Lily broke her silence.

"Whatever is wrong?" she asked in exasperation.

In just as much exasperation he answered. "It's the damned horses."

"The horses?" He could barely make her out in the dark interior. A deep-hooded cloak shadowed her face, only her dark red lips were illuminated by the lanterns swinging outside the carriage window.

"Yes. I'm allergic to the wretched creatures," he flung out. What difference did it make if she knew of his weaknesses? She already owned his heart, an atrociously defenseless organ.

His admission for one instant shook her from her self-containment. She leaned toward him. "But I thought—"

Whatever she thought he was not to be privy to because her lips clamped shut and she turned away from him to remain stubbornly silent for the rest of the drive.

Upon arrival Lily fled through the opposite door while Avery assisted Francesca and Evelyn to alight and escorted them to the door, by which time Lily had disappeared inside.

Avery entered, looking carefully around. Camfield had obviously done extensive renovation. An ornate staircase curved up from an inlaid marble floor. Banks of flowers stood in great urns on either side of a set of double doors leading into a conspicuously vast drawing room where all the furniture—at least that which Avery could see—had been set against the walls to accommodate the guests.

Too many guests. A good hundred of them jostled and chittered and strutted with the studied self-consciousness of courting cranes—necks high, chins tilted out, eyes rabidly assessing those they passed even as they themselves were assessed.

Amazingly, the herd seemed to be enjoying themselves. Faces were bright with anticipation, lips curved into smiles, and occasional laughter broke out as the tinkle of glass and china played like a backdrop of wind chimes to the racket.

And Lily was nowhere in sight. Glumly aware of his duty, he shepherded Francesca and Evelyn through the reception line, nodding at Camfield, bowing briefly over the hands of his sisters and finally, with much relief, reaching the end.

Now, where was Lily?

He missed her in the receiving line and soon after the Camfield chits attached themselves to his sleeves. Only their brother's intervention freed him from their attentions. He checked his pocket watch. They'd been there an hour and he was already bored.

"I must say, Avery, you look very well in evening dress," Francesca remarked playfully. "And how delightful to find a tailor to fit you out so quickly."

"Hmph."

"Ah! Eloquent as usual. Who *does* write your stories, dear?" She didn't expect a response. Her color was high; her eyes glittered as she scanned the crowd putting him in mind of a cat loosed in a dovecote. "I know this is tiresome for you, but please try and be charming. It will make things easier for Lily if the county knows she has your endorsement."

"I am always charming," he said. "Besides, Lily doesn't need my endorsement. She obviously doesn't give a rap for these people or their approval or she

wouldn't traipse around the countryside in trousers—
don't argue with me, Francesca—and annoy their servants with her propaganda. She's probably wearing the
damn things right now. Only in pink."

"Hmm." Francesca's smile looked suspiciously like
a smirk.

"Where the devil has she got to, anyway? You'd
think she'd spend some time with you."

"Careful, darling," Francesca advised. "You sound
pettish. If you'd just look over there, you'd see her."

He looked around. Across the crowd he saw Martin
Camfield. His face was animated with pleasure as he
spoke to a black-haired woman whose long, svelte
back was nearly naked. No wonder he looked animated. The lady began to turn. Avery only wished Lily
was witnessing Matthew's salivating attention to—
Lily?

It *was* Lily. Lily dressed—no, Lily *undressed* in some
horrifyingly erotic-looking thing of sheer black silk
tissue over a gleaming underskirt of flesh-colored
satin. Jet beads winked in the appliqued black roses on
the skirt and bodice. Her throat and shoulders rose
like moon polished amber above the gown's dusky,
shimmering embrace. Where the hell were her
bloomers?

"Your eyes, darling," Francesca murmured in
amusement. "Strive to keep them in your head."

"Where did that come from? Lily can't afford a
dress like that."

"No. But I can. We had it remade to her figure. I

hate to admit it, but what with all that inky hair, it suits her far better than it ever did me."

"No. It does not."

"Lower your voice, dear. You sound like a husband. And I'm afraid it does." Francesca tilted her face up to his and grinned. "The manner in which the other gentlemen are watching her in no way connotes disapproval."

Other men? Avery's head snapped up and he scowled fiercely as he noted the interested gazes of a half dozen gentlemen in Lily's vicinity. "Impudence. Doesn't anyone in the country have any manners? How dare they stare at her as though she were a— a—"

"Woman?"

For a moment he couldn't answer. He was too occupied struggling to overcome the urge to shrug out of his coat, stalk to Lily's side, wrap her in it, and carry her out the front door.

"She looks delicious, doesn't she?"

Delicious. Damn Francesca, that's exactly what Lily looked. Dark and exotic and gorgeous and as alien in this group as a black swan amongst a flight of egrets.

"You shouldn't have forced her into that thing, Francesca. She's bound to be damned uncomfortable attracting attention like that."

Francesca shrugged. "She doesn't look uncomfortable. She looks as if she's enjoying herself."

She did, damn it. Her eyes glowed and her lips parted slightly as though she were about to speak, or whisper, or be kissed, which was ridiculous because they were standing in the middle of a ballroom, for God's sake. He ran his hand through his hair and compelled by a need to reestablish their previous relationship, and afraid that he would not be able to do so, he excused himself to Francesca and made his way through the throng.

Musicians at the far end of the room began tuning their instruments. He could dance with Lily. Take the opportunity to hold her, clasp her lightly in his arms. She was alone for the moment, though several men watched her surreptitiously.

"Lil—Miss Bede?"

She turned toward him with an expression of relief shaded with apprehension. "Avery."

He couldn't recall her having spoken his name before. It sounded wonderful, intimate, it bespoke knowledge and history, both of which he wanted desperately to continue.

"Your dress."

"Yes?" Her brows rose and when he remained silent she prodded, "What about my dress?"

"It's . . ." *Delicious?* He could hardly tell her that. *Nice?* Too insipid. "Francesca said it suited you better than her. I believe she was right."

An amused spark lit her dark eyes. "You sweet-talker, you."

He felt his cheeks grow warm. "I only meant that you look very nice this evening."

"Like a proper lady."

Proper? In that backless gown? "Well, very feminine."

She laughed and all the wariness he'd felt from her dissolved as she shook her head. "You really are incapable of the least diplomacy, aren't you? I mean, you will always say exactly what you think, when you think it."

He frowned. "Do you . . . do you think that a defect in my personality?"

Again she shook her head. "No. It might make others uncomfortable, and I'm not sure it's proper social deportment, but I'd sooner have the truth from you than lies." Her smile grew bittersweet. "At least I know where we stand with each other."

He moved forward to touch her arm and jostled the woman next to him. "Lily—"

"Mr. Thorne!" the female cooed. "I am so glad to meet you again, though I suspect you'll think me naughty for admitting as much."

Avery looked upon a wealth of white-blond curls and then into the green eyes of a young woman. Who the bloody blazes was she? Behind her stood Francesca, an apologetic look on her face, with Camfield.

"Ah, er, yes? Miss?" he said.

Her rosebud mouth pursed. "Mr. Camfield here introduced us half an hour ago."

He waited.

"Andrea Moore? Lord Jessup's daughter?" the girl said, her expression dancing with amusement. In the meantime Camfield had secured one of Lily's gloved hands in his own and was pulling her toward the dance floor. Blast! Sure enough they began to dance.

"Mr. Thorne?" He looked down at the blond chit. Her lashes were fluttering up and down. Must have a piece of lint in one.

"Jessup? Oh yes. What do you want?" he asked.

She looked at him in confusion. "I . . . I . . ."

Why didn't the blasted girl speak? He glanced over at Francesca, who shrugged. The Moore chit's gaze followed his and latched on to Francesca in relief.

"I am sorry, Miss Thorne," she said, "I didn't see you there. How are you?"

"I manage, Miss Moore," Francesca said sweetly. "Have I congratulated you yet on the numerous placards I see in London's shop windows bearing your lovely image? You've quite routed all the other London beauties."

The girl simpered. Avery looked past her to where Lily and Camfield had been dancing. They were gone.

"Isn't it a wonder, Avery?" Francesca asked.

Where the devil could they have got to? he wondered. Suffragist or not, Lily still should have a care for her reputation—

"Isn't it?" Francesca demanded.

"Isn't what what, Francesca?" Avery asked impatiently.

"Isn't it delightful that Devon's very own Miss Moore is the most popular of all the professional beauties?"

"Professional beauty? Honestly, Francesca, I have

always accounted you a reasonable woman but I haven't a clue as to what you're babbling about. Now, if you'll excuse me, ladies?" He did a nice bow to Francesca and the opened-mouthed blond chit and went in search of Lily.

"Well!" Andrea Moore, Lord Jessup's daughter, London's reigning toast, and the comeliest creature to ever escape Devon said as soon as he was out of hearing range. "What a rude fellow. He's not at all what I imagined him to be from his stories."

"He's looking for Lillian Bede," Francesca explained. "You may have seen her. Jetty hair, skin like buttered cream, eyes black as midnight, figure like a Greek go—"

"Doesn't he know who I am?" Andrea cut in brusquely. "Why, I am told, Miss Thorne, that there are no less than five private gentlemen's clubs in Kensington where I am toasted nightly."

"I'm sure there are, dear." Francesca patted the outraged girl's hand. "But Avery doesn't get to town much. Too bad, isn't it?"

Avery spent ten minutes looking for Lily and Camfield before moving into the hallways. He began opening doors. A few of the smaller anterooms had been set up for cards, one had been secured as a cloak room, and a white-haired dame made him understand in no uncertain terms that the room he'd been about to breech had been reserved for ladies. Though he surprised at least three couples in situations they'd later regret he didn't find the couple he sought.

There was only one more room on this floor he hadn't been in and then—he glanced up at the elegant curving staircase—he couldn't believe she'd be so rash as to go up there.

He opened the door into a dark room and poked his head through. Sure he'd caught a furtive movement out of the corner of his eyes, he strained to listen, moving halfway through the door. If Camfield had her in here, in the dark—

"Let me get the light for you, old man."

Avery wheeled around, nearly colliding with his host. Camfield reached past him for the gas wall sconce. The room leapt into illumination. It was a library crammed full of leather furnishings, hung with heavy burgundy draperies and olive striped wallpaper.

"Won't you come in?" Camfield asked, extending his arm before him. Avery entered.

Camfield pulled a cigar case from his inner breast pocket, flicked the inscribed silver lid open and held it out. "Cigar? Cuban."

There wasn't the least animosity in the man's face. He looked thoroughly benign, the consummate host. If Avery had found some chap lurking about Mill House, opening closed doors and such, he certainly wouldn't be treating him to cigars. Apparently they were going to behave like gentlemen. For once, Avery cursed the role.

"Thank you," Avery said, accepting it and a light.

He drew on the cigar with short, quick puffs. Good cigar.

"Brandy?" Camfield asked.

"No, thank you."

"I suppose these sorts of events seem rather tame and boring after your adventures?" he said, lighting his own cigar.

"Not at all."

"My sisters are, in case you hadn't noticed, smitten with you."

"And you wish to warn me off?" Avery asked expectantly, happily anticipating a nice row. Finally a reason why Camfield and he were having a civilized discussion in the man's library.

"Heavens, no," Camfield exclaimed. "Not at all. I'd be frankly relieved if at least one of them got leg-shackled. Can't think of any objections I'd have to you. Good name, fine old family. By all means, do your damnedest if you're interested."

"Oh." Deflated, Avery took another long draw on his cigar. "Well, I'm not interested."

"No," Camfield said sadly, "I didn't think so." Then, after a moment, "What do you think of my home?"

"Very nice."

"Been in the family . . . four years now." He gave a bark of laughter. "We Camfields are Derbyshire family. My family's manse is entailed. Thus I'm having to begin my own dynasty. Must say, I'm doing rather well. In fact, I'm ready to increase my holdings. Problem is all the land here about is owned. Except Mill House."

"Mill House has an owner."

"Yes," Camfield allowed. "But who is it? Miss Bede or you? I guess in a few weeks I'll know with whom I have to deal."

"Who told you that?" Avery asked.

"Miss Bede."

"Chummy with her, are you?" Avery took the cigar from his mouth and nonchalantly knocked off the ash into a silver tray.

"Chummy?"

"You and Miss Bede. In each other's confidence and all."

"Oh." Camfield blinked as though the direction of the conversation had caught him off-guard. "Yes. Fine woman. Very intelligent and quite up on current agricultural methodology."

Avery wasn't buying it for a moment. He had a duty as Lily's—as Lily's *nothing*, Avery thought angrily. He'd no right at all to be questioning Camfield about his relationship with Lily. Not that that was going to stop him.

There was only one reason a man would pursue a chummy relationship with a woman he knew intended never to marry. For his own good, Camfield had better not know Lily's views on matrimony. Damn him to hell.

"What are your intentions toward Miss Bede?"

Avery ground out, impatient with all this oblique chatter.

"My intentions toward Miss Bede?" Camfield's eyes went round and his lips slack. The cigar drooped from his lower lip. "I don't understand."

"Come now, man. Miss Bede doesn't have anyone to look after her interests and since she's living with my family . . ." he trailed off.

"I don't have a relationship with Miss Bede," Camfield said, still looking dumbfounded. "I admire her and I respect her, that's all."

"Then why did you come round with your family to see her?"

Camfield blushed.

"My sisters came to see, ah, you and that necessitated meeting Miss Bede. I told them they were being insufferably top-lofty," he hurried on. "I mean, it isn't like anyone was asking them to become bosom buddies with the girl, is it? But an occasional visit, invitations to the larger, more egalitarian festivities, that sort of thing could hardly hurt them and might certainly aid me."

"Aid you?" Avery asked in a deceptively mild voice.

"Yes," Camfield said. "I mean. I think you can tell by now that I mean to make an offer for Mill House and its properties. Maintaining friendly relationships with the owner of a place one covets is simply good business." He smiled at Avery. "Either of its potential owners. Care for that brandy now?"

"No." Avery smashed the cigar into the crystal ashtray beside him. "So your courtesies toward Miss Bede have all been a matter of expedience?"

"Yes," Camfield agreed sunnily. "Good God, man, you don't for an instant imagine that it was anything else? I mean, Miss Bede is a fine-looking woman in a foreign sort of way, but she's decidedly not the sort one pays serious court to and for God's sake man, I'm a gentleman, I'd never form anything but a respectable union with a woman. Even a woman like Lillian Be—"

He never finished saying her name.

Lily patted her hair into place and pinched her cheeks to bring color to them before exiting the women's retiring room. Thankfully, one of the Camfield maids had furnished needle and thread with which Lily had been able to stitch the lace flounce back onto Evelyn's dress—a memento from a cow-footed squire who'd insisted Evelyn dance with him.

She glanced at the wall clock as she emerged from the room. It had taken longer than she'd expected. Not that she minded.

Except for a few fascinated matrons who'd cornered her earlier and demanded she send them information on the next meeting of the Women's Emancipation Coalition, she'd barely spoken to anyone. A young man had asked her to one dance, but the manner in which he kept casting smug looks of triumph at his friends quickly robbed her of any enjoyment she might have had in it. When the next fellow had asked to partner her she'd refused.

Evelyn, upon her dress being restored to its previous glory, had been taken with a sick headache and accepted the Camfields' offer to retire to one of the bedchambers; Francesca was dancing through a throng of attentive gentlemen like a firefly through a midnight meadow; and the last time she'd seen Avery he'd been bent over the gorgeous form of Andrea Moore.

She paused at the threshold leading into the ballroom, suddenly tentative, unwilling to see Avery holding another woman in his arms, even for a dance. Stupid. She had no claims on him.

All her sentimental fantasies about his softheartedness and compassion had been built around a case of allergies. She steeled herself to enter when she heard Martin's voice behind the half-closed door directly beside her.

"She's decidedly not the sort one pays serious court to and for God's sake man, I'm a gentleman," he said. "I'd never form anything but a respectable union with a woman. Even a woman like Lillian Be—"

His words were abruptly cut off by a muted thump.

Liquid heat covered every inch of Lily's skin in a wildfire of embarrassment. She whirled around, nearly knocking over one of the Camfield girls—Molly? The young girl's face registered an instant of distaste before setting into the determined smile of a social hostess.

"Ah, Miss Bede. I hope you're enjoying yourself?

Were you looking for a place to freshen? We're using the—"

At this moment the door beside them swung fully open and Martin Camfield stumbled out, his hand cradling his left cheek. Even between his fingers the dark swelling beneath his eye was evident. His startled gaze flickered from his sister to Lily before his pale skin flushed darkly.

"Martin!" Molly Camfield exclaimed. "Whatever happened to your eye?"

"I, er, stupid of me but I walked into a door," he muttered. "I best find the kitchen and see about getting some ice on it." He nodded shortly and hastened off down the hall.

"Well, I have never known Martin to be clumsy! I wonder—" Whatever the girl was about to say was interrupted by the appearance of Avery. He came out of the library scowling. The knuckles of his right hand were red.

"Mr. Thorne!" Molly gasped. "Whatever happened to your hand?"

He didn't even pause but strode right past them. "Slammed the damn thing in a door."

Chapter Twenty-two

"Don't you think we should have insisted that Francesca return home with us?" Lily asked when the silence in the carriage stretched to an uncomfortable length.

"We could have insisted," Avery answered shortly, looking out at the passing countryside, "but it wouldn't have done a damn bit of good. She was being admired."

"And you're certain that Evelyn left earlier?"

She could barely make out his nod.

"Yes. Some neighbor or other drove her home. You didn't think she'd actually leave Bernard alone for more than an hour, did you?"

She had no reply for this and so fell silent, content while hidden in the dark corner of the coach to study him.

The moonlight bathed his face in an icy luminescence that oddly made his tanned skin appear even darker against the stark white collar and snowy tie.

His hair, ruffled by the night air, fell across his forehead.

He was the most extravagantly masculine being Lily could imagine. His stylish clothes did nothing to destroy the image; they only augmented his breadth, his height, and his musculature.

And whether he approved of her or not, no matter how irrational or ill-fated, he cared about her. Pleasure unraveled in her and for once she allowed it.

"You didn't have to hit him," she said.

"Hit who?" he replied so quickly she knew he'd been waiting for her to address the issue. "I don't know what you're talking about."

"Martin Camfield. I was in the hall. I heard what he said, or rather what he was about to say."

"What an extraordinary accusation to make." He sniffed again and sneezed. "I'm a gentleman. I don't go about striking my host. I suggest that you curb this tendency to listen at doors. It only encourages that vivid imagination of yours to run amuck."

But she knew now. And nothing he could say could erase her knowledge.

"You hit him because you thought he'd been toying with my affection," she replied.

He looked around, his features still hidden in the carriage's gloom, but his fair hair gleamed in the moonlight like some alchemist's rare metal.

"If I were to strike someone," he said slowly, "I suppose that would be one of the few justifiable rea-

sons to do so. Fellow woul[...]
hurting a lady."

"Since we're creating [...]
in which a gentleman [...]
gentleman, might I add[...]
tion?"

"Hmm."

"Suppose that the defending gentleman had [...]
read the lady's involvement? Perhaps the lady knew all
along that the fellow who was flattering her did so
only to smooth his way in any future business negotia-
tions? Would the defending gentleman still be justified
in beating up his host?"

"One blow can hardly be construed as 'beating up'
one's host," Avery said.

"I see."

They fell silent except for the sound of Avery's fingertips tapping on the windowsill and his occasional
sneeze.

"You allowed Martin Camfield to fawn all over you
knowing he did so to get into your good graces?" he
finally burst out.

"Yes."

She peered closer but could see nothing of his expression, lit by the bright moonlight from behind as
he was. "Why did you allow it?"

"He's the only man who's ever paid me any sort of
court," she admitted, hoping the darkness would hide
her blush. "And besides, one could hardly call his
tepid pleasantries 'fawning all over.' Your kiss was

stopped, appalled at what she'd just said,
tted. In confusion she moved further into
er.

was overwhelmed by her sense of him, the fra-
ce of crisp linen, the angle of his jaw, newly
aved and marble smooth, just catching the light, his
deep rumbling voice.

"Camfield's a fool," he finally murmured. He lifted
his hand. She held her breath. Gingerly, he moved his
knuckles down the long coil of hair that lay on her
shoulder. "Tepid pleasantries? Were I to—"

His mouth grew nearer and she felt herself pulled
toward him. His fingertips brushed along the curve of
her cheek, skated along her chin and tilted her face up,
exposing her expression in the bright moonlight.

He would see. He would know how very much she
loved him. And what good would it do either of them?

"How could anyone react tepidly to you?" he
mused.

She leaned closer and as if against his will, he
touched her cheek with his knuckles. His hand turned
and a touch turned into a caress.

She closed her eyes and rubbed her cheek against
his fingertips. They trembled against her skin, glided
over her eyelids, and traced her lower lip.

"Lily . . ." His voice held a smile. "You are so
damn beautiful. I wish . . ."

She wished, too. But she didn't want to hear him
give voice to dreams that could never be realized. Too
much stood between them—a house, an inheritance,

and most of all, a future they could never share, he because he would never live in an unsanctioned union, she because she would not live as any man's chattel.

"Hush," she implored, her eyes awash in tears. She didn't want this moment to end. She couldn't let go of it.

She turned her face into his caress and kissed the warm center of his palm. She heard the sharp intake of his breath and then she was being pulled into his arms, enfolded in a powerful embrace to half lie against him in the dark and wonderful carriage, rocking gently in a timeless void.

One hand cradled the back of her head, his other arm looped about her waist. His mouth touched her temple, moved to her cheek, and toward her mouth.

"Dear Lord, Lily. You set me a—"

"Fire!" Hob yelled from atop the coach. "Gawd Almighty! The stables be on fire!"

Lily jerked back from Avery, clambered to her knees atop the seat, and thrust her entire upper body through the window. Her eyes riveted on Mill House's stables. Behind it one of the great rucks blazed like a beacon, wind whipping the huge tongues of flame out to lick the stable's southernmost eaves. Already smoke spewed from the top of the building, noxious plumes streaming into the blacker night sky.

"Hurry!"

But Hob had already laid the whip against the horse's flank. The mare bolted forward and Lily half tumbled from the window only to be caught by strong hands and hauled back into the carriage.

"You'll get yourself killed," Avery said, shoving her into the seat opposite him and shrugging out of his dinner jacket. He snapped the white silk tie from his throat, ruining the stiff collar in the process.

The carriage careened over the rough road as Lily clung to the window frame, her eyes fixed on the stables.

"My horses!" Her voice broke. "My horses."

Her upper arm was seized in an implacable grip and she was spun around to meet Avery's tense face.

"Do not go anywhere near the stable," he ordered. "I need able bodies. Go to Drummond and find the field hands. Find buckets. Pump water. But stay the bloody hell away from the stable. Do you understand me?"

"My horses!"

He shook her. "I'll get your damn horses out. I swear it. Now, promise me!"

She gave one short nod. He released her and opened the door of the carriage just as Hob began dragging back on the hand brake. He leapt, fell and rolled, regained his feet, and raced toward the burning building. By now half the roof was fringed in a border of orange flames, its delicate appearance the gluttonous hiss of fire consuming the wood.

The carriage skittered to a halt. She saw Hob leap from the seat and make for the stables. Somewhere a bell rang out, alerting all within hearing distance to the fire. She pushed the carriage door open and dropped to the ground. Her heel caught in the silk skirt and she cried out in exasperation, tearing the gown and running toward the stable.

She had the ablest body at Mill House. All the buckets were at the stables and the kitchen pump was too far away to be used as a water source. But by the stables was the well that was used to keep the troughs full.

She lifted her skirts and ran.

Thank God the seasonal workers were there. The twenty men and boys hired on for the June harvest were already milling about the burning hay ruck and stables but, like ants on a termite mound, their fervid actions were random and ineffectual. A few beat blankets against the hay stubble leading to the barn. Others flung water where it would provide little good.

If the fire made it to the barn, Mill House would be lost. Martin Camfield could name his price for what was left.

Avery began shouting orders, his face set with determination. Within ten minutes he'd a team digging a firebreak between the stables and the barn, another group containing the flaming ruck, and a water line working on soaking the stable roof. Each passing moment the air congealed in his chest, clogging his throat, a steel vise tightening around his lungs.

The long ride in the horse-laden atmosphere of the carriage, the smoke and hay stubble, the dry, hot air all worked inexorably toward a crisis. He didn't have time for a crisis.

The sound of frantic whinnying rose above the roar of the blaze. Hooves struck stall doors and haunches crashed against box stalls. Lily's horses.

He tore off his shirt, doused it into a bucket of water and tied it around the lower portion of his face. The air staggered into his lungs. He swore viciously, unable to find even enough breath for his curses and, ducking his head against his arm, plunged into the stables.

Around him white smoke swirled, still thin enough that he could make out the bolts latching the doors. He jerked a stall open and stepped aside. The mare within danced, eyes rolling wildly, hooves flashing.

He flapped his arm and the mare shied back, teeth snapping, ear flattened.

"You damn, bloody ass!" Avery gasped, tearing his shirt from his face and flinging it over her eyes. He grabbed the sleeves beneath and twisted tight then jerked hard on the makeshift blinder, half dragging the mare out into the aisle. He jerked his shirt off her head and smacked her hard on the rump. She bucked once and shot out of the stable.

He leaned over, gasping for breath, his muscles trembling from lack of oxygen, his vision swimming.

"No!" he ground out savagely and hobbled, doubled up for the next stall. Thank God the next horse had the sense to flee. He'd shoved the bolt back and the creature skittered out, slipping and stumbling in its haste to escape.

Another stall, another horse. With each step the white blanket of smoke grew thicker. He began coughing, expelling what precious air he had from his paralyzed lungs. He reached out with a trembling, sweat soaked hand for the bolt. Too weak.

Within he could see the phantom figure of a horse lunging madly within its smoke filled prison.

Lily would kill him if anything happened to her horses. He stumbled to his knees. Two more horses. He couldn't hear them anymore, couldn't hear anything. A dull rushing sound had replaced the pop and hiss of burning wood. The last horses' frantic calls had stilled. He fell forward, caught himself on his hands. The straw pierced his palm and the pain brought a second of lucidity.

Lily wouldn't have to kill him. He was already dead.

She saw him enter the stable. His face, even in the reddish stain of the fire looked ghastly above the dirty, sopping shirt tied around the lower part of his face. Sweat slickered his muscular arms and coated his hard torso and he moved in a half crouch as though doubling up against pain.

A minute later India dashed from the stables, haunches low to the ground, hooves beating a heartbeat staccato, and disappeared into the night. A big gelding followed and then in rapid succession five of the seven remaining horses. The rest were in the pasture.

Lily worked on, her arms aching from pumping well water into buckets. All around her, her dreams burned accompanied by the manic chortling of crackling wood and the sweetish, thick aroma of burning grass. Men shouted, the bells rang incessantly calling for aid, and inside the stable a horse screamed.

One of the seasonal workers, his face blistered from working too near the blaze, came over and commandeered the pump, calling to his mates as he drove the handle with a force she could not match. She stumbled out of his way, her feet carrying her closer to the stable, trying to see within the smoky interior.

It had been minutes since the last horse had exited. The smoke roiled slowly, thicker near the ceiling, somewhat thinner near the ground. She bent over, peering inside.

One of the horses ricocheted in its stall, the sound of its frenzied neighing and splintering wood filling Lily's ears. Where was Avery? She stumbled into the stables and flung open the stall door.

"Gee!" she shouted. The liberated horse, foam flecking its mouth, eyes ringed in white, shot from the barn as sobbing, Lily fumbled her way to the last stall and released its occupant. *Avery* . . . dear God, he was allergic. Wildly, she looked around.

She saw him then, lying near the far end of the stable. In seconds she'd run down the aisle and fallen on her knees beside him. She grasped his arms and turned him over. His face was dusky and streaked with grime.

"Avery!" She slapped his face hard twice. "Avery!"

He moaned, his head rolling to the side. He wouldn't be able to get out of here under his own power.

She screamed. As loud and as long as she could, she screamed but the roar of the blaze consumed her voice as easily as it consumed the stable roof and her cries for help turned into spasms of choking coughs.

No one could hear her. There was no time to go for help. Her eyes already stung and her throat burned. She had to get him out.

She snatched India's headstall from its peg beside her stall and crouched down, tying first one then the other of Avery's boots together, leaving a few feet of slack leather in between. She stepped between his legs, lifted the leather straps in both hands and pulled. His dead weight inched forward. She readjusted the leather across her hips and, like a mule in harness surged forward, praying the slender leather straps held his weight.

He moved. She took another step and another, choking and coughing, her eyes streaming tears, her parched lungs gasping for air. Foot by foot she dragged him down the aisle and finally out into the night. She collapsed beside him, wringing wet, her dress in ruins.

She had no time to fall apart. On shaking limbs she crawled to his side and laid her ear against his naked chest. Deep within she could hear his heartbeat, rapid but timely. A whistling like wind in a plugged chimney flue filled her ears.

Still gasping, she crept behind him and hoisted him up into her lap. His head rolled limply against her shoulder.

"Come on, Avery." Fresh tears stained her cheeks. Her voice shook. "Wake up, damn it!" She sobbed, rocking forward and back, her arms wrapping tightly around his big body. "Don't you want to shout at me for disobeying you, you overbearing, domineering male?"

She squeezed her eyes shut and bit hard on her lip. He couldn't die. He was too stubborn, too alive, too vigorous. And she couldn't lose him. She loved him too much.

"I . . . am a . . . gentleman," she heard him gasp. "I never shout at women."

Chapter Twenty-three

Two days after the fire the acrid taint of wet charcoal still lingered in the air. Lily, wandering along the hushed second floor gallery, looked out at the charred stable, smoldering in the last of the afternoon light.

Thank God, Avery was going to be all right. The thought of looking for his body amongst that ruin of timber and ash set her trembling. She forced the image from her thoughts.

Avery would be fine. He was already well on the mend. His breathing was easier and the awful grayish cast had disappeared from his skin. The only visible scars he bore were long angry abrasions on his back and shoulders from where she'd dragged him across the ground.

Somehow they'd managed to keep him abed all yesterday. True, he'd shouted invectives at anyone who braved his room, but he'd stayed abed, nonetheless.

But this morning, long before her, he'd risen, appropriated the carriage, and driven off. She didn't know where he went or when he'd return.

Ah, well, she thought, he'd much to do, much to see to, not least of which was finding someone to rebuild his stables.

His stables.

Lily's gaze drifted to the south meadow. In the failing light, the hay rucks gleamed like piles of gold on a green baize gaming table. Thankfully, two nights ago the wind had been light. The fire had never made it to the barn or spread to the other hay rucks. It could have been worse. The new owner of Mill House might have inherited a ruin.

But for the former owner of Mill House that fire had proved disastrous. There was no possible way she could afford to rebuild the stable or recover the money represented by the loss of that one hay ruck. Under her direction, the estate had gone into debt.

She'd lost Mill House.

She felt disconnected from the knowledge as if she'd read about an unhappy episode in a stranger's life. *Why had it happened?* The question recurred with dulling regularity. *How, so soon after a soaking rainstorm, had a fire begun in the hay?*

It hadn't been warm enough and the hay hadn't stood long enough to spontaneously combust as tightly compacted roughage occasionally did. There hadn't been any lightning that night. There was no reason fire should have been anywhere near that hay ruck, lest someone had purposely set it ablaze. And that notion she simply would not entertain.

A lover's tryst by lantern light perhaps? Or maybe one of the seasonal worker's children sneaking a cigarette where his parents wouldn't find him. An ember falls, catches fire, the frightened child runs, and Lily's dreams—her life—go up in smoke. She'd lost Mill House.

And she'd lost Avery Thorne.

She thought nothing could hurt more acutely than the loss of Mill House, but she'd been wrong. When she left here she would leave behind not only her home, but every reason she had for seeing Avery Thorne. There'd be no pretext for them ever to meet again, no excuse to trade words, either written or spoken. The tenuous bond that had held them together for five years was gone, broken—no, burnt.

A shivering began in the very core of her, spreading, gaining force until she stood shuddering before the window, staring blindly out, tears spilling helplessly down her face as she recognized the desolation enveloping her.

She'd never see him again. Not unless she stood like a beggar on the drive, staring down the shell drive at midnight, watching for his silhouette against the brightly lit window. She would never do that because then she might see her, the woman he would have married, who'd bear his children, be his lover and companion, and that was an anguish she could not even imagine.

She'd lost Avery Thorne. Not that she ever had anything of him except his wit, his eager opposition—and those all too brief moments when she'd held him. And, of course, she had the knowledge that she loved him, a knowledge come by as she'd willed him to breathe.

She'd probably begun loving him soon after their correspondence had begun, she thought. He'd taken up every gauntlet she'd thrown, discussed wholeheartedly any subject she raised. And though he'd often irritated and purposefully provoked her, once engaged in a debate he never treated her opinions with condescension.

Indeed, his respect for her had been evident with every written word. He'd never ignored her observations or discounted her opinions because of her gender. Yes, he sometimes discounted them because of what he perceived to be faulty reasoning or misjudgment or what he termed her "pigheaded obstinacy." But he'd never dismissed *her*.

She pressed her forehead against the cool glass, her shivering having subsided, leaving only emptiness. All lost. All gone.

"Lily?" She heard Francesca.

"Yes?" She didn't bother turning.

"Lily." An elegant hand clasped her wrist and gently turned her about. "Lily, you must listen to me now," Francesca said. "I'm going away this evening. In fact, I'm going in a few minutes."

"Yes?" Lily said disinterestedly. Francesca often left

on the spur of the moment and stayed away for weeks, sometimes months, only to return just as spontaneously.

"I can't help you rebuild the stables," Francesca said. "I won't lie and say I couldn't if I—"

"I would never ask you to!" Lily exclaimed, drawn out of her torpor.

"That's not the point, Lily," Francesca said. "I know you would not ask and I also know that should I offer you would likely not accept."

But I would, thought Lily dismally, I have so little left, what do a few shreds of pride matter?

Francesca placed both her hands on Lily's shoulders, gazing steadily into her face. "If I were to scrape together most of my wealth I would be able to make you a loan to rebuild. But I won't. I need it"—her fingers tightened on Lily's shoulders—"for me. I need to live the way I do."

"Yes," Lily agreed.

"Lily." Strain marked the corners of Francesca's mouth. "All I have are my certain pleasures. Do you understand?"

She didn't, but Lily nodded anyway, answering the older woman's plea rather than her words.

"You have so much, Lily."

Lily shrugged out of the other woman's grip. "Why yes," she said trying to laugh, hearing only bitterness. "Yes. I'm a regular tycoon."

Francesca shook her head, searching for words. "You still have dreams. You still have a future. I've

spent both humiliating my father and I'll end a fool
wasting my life trying to embarrass a corpse."

"I have nothing, Francesca—"

"The boy is in love with you, Lily."

"Bernard?" Lily asked wearily. "Puppy love. He'll
get over it. I'll be careful of him."

"Not Bernard. Avery."

She couldn't speak.

"No. That's wrong." Francesca's voice sounded sad
and musing. "Not *in* love," she whispered. "He loves
you. Simply. Deeply. Unhappily."

"You must be mistaken."

"Sometimes you're allowed only one chance, only a
second, to decide the course of your life. Don't be
distracted by your pride, Lily. Or your common sense.
Or your past. Or anything that keeps you from . . ."
She let out a little laugh that turned into a sob. "Eden.
I'd go find the lad, Lily. I swear to you, I would."

She turned away, moving down the hall murmuring, "And she says she has nothing. . . ."

"I don't know what we can do now," Polly whispered to Evelyn. They were ensconced on the divan in
the sitting room ostensibly tatting lace together while
Bernard, on the other side of the room, was engrossed
in a book.

"Mill House isn't a good setting for romance these
days," Polly agreed. "Stables burning tend to dispel a
cuddlesome mood. Those two have been treading
round each other like two tomcats in one barn. I think

we can forget any notion that Miss Bede and Mr. Thorne will"—she glanced at Bernard, who was concentrating fiercely on a huge leather bound tome—"get friendly."

Evelyn shook her head. "I had such hopes but perhaps for Lily's sake, this is for the best."

"Nonsense," Polly said so emphatically that Evelyn glanced at Bernard, giving the little woman a warning shake of her head.

Polly colored but the tilt of her chin told Evelyn she was about to commit herself to some action or opinion.

"If Miss Bede loves this chap," she said, "and he seems a decent chap, but she does nothing about it, it will be . . . *wrong.*" She paused and cleared her throat. "Love is not a reward, it is a chance. A chance to be something more. When that chance is offered to a man or a woman, it has to be accepted, no matter what the risks. Love is important, Evelyn."

She lifted her gaze, embarrassed and caught for a minute exposed by her words. "Do you understand?"

Slowly, Evelyn nodded. "Yes."

"Do you agree?"

"Yes." Her voice was stronger now.

"Good." Polly released her breath and her momentary vulnerability disappeared behind an expression of consternation. "Miss Thorne was the most obvious person to goad Miss Bede into realizing this, but she's decamped and no one in this room is equipped by nature or experience to play Cupid."

"Too true," Evelyn sighed. "Whatever shall we do?"

Polly clapped her palms against her thighs. Bernard looked up.

"Oh, don't worry about dropping the occasional knot, Miss Makepeace," Evelyn said loudly. "You're doing splendidly well." She lowered her voice. "Quiet. Bernard would *so* disapprove if he knew what we were up to."

Polly nodded her understanding. "Right-o," she whispered. "Back to Miss Bede. The first order of business is to figure out what her plans are for the immediate future. Would you ask her to come in here, Evelyn?"

"Of course," Evelyn agreed, rising and casting a quick furtive glance in her son's direction. Bernard turned the page of his book.

She went directly to Lily's room and tapped discreetly on the door but no one answered. Thinking Lily might be in the library, she started up the stairs when she heard the sound of footsteps in the corridor overhead. She paused, considering who it might be.

Avery had taken a room up there, but the sound was too light to be his. It was far too late for Merry or Kathy to be working and besides, Teresa and her twins held nightly court and would not look kindly on any absentees. That left only Lily.

Lily? Evelyn had to know if she was right. Slowly, carefully, Evelyn climbed to the third floor. Cautiously she peeked around the corner and peered down the dimly lit hall.

Lily paced nervously to and fro in front of the door to Avery Thorne's bedchamber, twisting her hands anxiously and muttering to herself. Every now and then she'd suddenly stop, square her shoulders, and stare resolutely at the closed door. Then, just as abruptly, her shoulders slumped, and she commenced pacing again.

Whyever would Lily—?

But of course!

The smile spreading rapidly across Evelyn's face abruptly froze. The girl would never do . . . anything . . . what with the lot of them cluttering the house. Well then, Evelyn thought with a decisiveness quite foreign to her, they would simply have to vacate the house—noisily and with equally noisy assurances of not returning soon.

Lifting her skirts, Evelyn tiptoed quickly down the stairs and, upon reaching the main floor, for first time since girlhood ran. Snatching her bonnet and cape from the hall tree she flew to the sitting room and burst in.

"What is it? Evelyn?" Startled, Polly began to rise oblivious of the cast she wore.

"We—we need to go to—to town," Evelyn panted.

At this Bernard looked up. "Little Henty?" he asked naming the crossroads that boasted a pub-cum-inn, a greengrocer's, and a dry goods shop. "Whyever for?"

"Not Little Henty. Cleave Cross," Evelyn said.

"But Cleave Cross is twenty miles away," Bernard said in astonishment. "It's eight o'clock at night. Can't we go in the morning?"

"No. I want to be there first light to see the dawn on the harbor. It's a sort of holiday for—for Miss Makepeace."

Polly's eyes widened incredulously.

"She's dreary sitting about here and what with that nauseous smell of wet ash she's bound to feel dismal. Aren't you, dear?"

"Ah," Polly uttered, her mouth gaping. "Yes."

"See, Bernard? Now go and pack a valise, just an overnight bag will do and then find Hob."

"Oh, all right," Bernard said unfolding his long lanky form from the chair and tossing down his book. "I'll tell Miss Bede to get ready, too."

"No!" Evelyn shouted and then smiled nervously at Bernard's astonished expression. "I mean, no that won't be necessary. Miss Bede will not be going."

"Oh?"

"She is having the carpenters in to see about rebuilding the stable tomorrow."

"And Cousin Avery?" Bernard asked, a hint of suspicion coloring his tone.

"He's staying, too," Evelyn said smoothly. Once having lied, she discovered additional lies tripped out of one's mouth rather winningly. "Surely you realize that he will be incurring the cost of rebuilding, Bernard. Of course he will want to stay and help make whatever decisions need be made."

She spoke with far more authority than usual and she could see her manner perplexed Bernard. Silently she prayed he didn't push her too much. There were only so many hurdles she could leap in one day and she felt that for this particular day she'd leapt more than her share.

For a minute he studied her before finally, with what looked like a shrug, making a polite bow in Polly's direction. "I'll get my bag."

Twenty minutes later Bernard, Polly, and Evelyn stood in the center hall making blaringly clear their intentions of spending the night away from Mill House.

Chapter Twenty-four

It sounded as if the furies were departing their lair. Doors slammed, voices called out instructions, and boot heels clattered across floor boards. Venturing out to the top of the stairs, Avery found Merry hastening down the steps, her belly swaying from side to side, a pair of women's boots in one hand and a traveling medicine chest in the other.

"What's going on?" he asked.

"They've gone mad is what's going on!" she said, looking up. "Takin' into their silly heads to go off to Cleave Cross."

"Tonight?" Avery asked incredulously.

"Not only tonight, but right now. Hob's waiting out front with the carriage this minute. Ah, well. Least ways maybe we'll all gets some sleep tonight. Teresa's babes do have right healthy lungs," she said morosely and left him standing alone.

Avery returned to his room, unhappily aware that he couldn't see the drive from here, but determined not to go downstairs and press his nose to the front window and watch them drive away. Still the sense that they'd abandoned him—no, that *she'd* abandoned him—gnawed at him.

He resented her going away without saying a word, even if it were only for the night. Then he realized that soon she'd go away not just for a night but forever and he wondered if she would take her leave like this, silently, without a word of good-bye. Emotion stirred and boiled within him, exasperation and grief dogging his footsteps as he paced the length of the room over and over again. He heard the door slam shut a final time, the gong of the hall clock mark the ninth hour, homely sounds coming from the back stairs and then silence.

It enveloped him, stretched about him, pure and wholly hateful. He settled into a chair and picked up a book lying on the table next to it. With Lily's departure Mill House had become a mausoleum, no longer the home of his imagination but simply a receptacle of funerary items, the mementos of a life already lived.

Ridiculous. He opened the book and began leafing through the pages, his unseeing eyes fixed on the flow of senseless words.

He was simply romanticizing, as any man who has perhaps come a little too close to having taken his last breath might do. Soon Mill House would be his, as it should have been from the first. He would see Lily taken care of, with or without her approval, and he would live here and he would marry some worthy woman who would not have black hair and dark eyes or a mouth fashioned from a dream, but one who would bear him anemic blond children—

A letter fluttered off the table onto his lap. He stared at it, the ragged fold lines, stained with the grit of three continents. Tenderly, he picked it up. It was her letter, of course. He'd kept it with him since the first time he read it. With an oath, he surged to his feet. The letter fell from his numb fingertips. He hurled the book across the room.

He couldn't stay in this room. Even though she'd never been here, he felt her, she was with him, in the words of that letter, in the air that they shared, in spirit and body.

He made for the door, prepared to follow her, and drag her back, to make her say good-bye, but not, please God, not leave him here like this.

He jerked open the door and looked down into Lily's face.

Her courage having earlier failed her, Lily had finally found an excuse to come back. She would see if he'd had his dinner. There'd be no reason to bother Merry or Kathy—

"I can't stop thinking about you," he said.

She heard him and reality crumpled around her. This had to be some sort of dream, one from which she wanted never to wake. His face was strained and intense, his voice pleading and low.

She stepped closer, her chin tilted up as she listened, trying to read what was in his eyes.

"I—" He cast his gaze heavenward as though for strength . . . or inspiration. "I just want to kiss you so damn much."

It was the last thing she'd expected. In fascination, she searched his face. She must have moved closer, carried toward him by pure magnetism. With a dazed sense of disbelief, she waited for the next moment. She was a voyager in her own body: feeling her heart thudding anxiously, listening to the shallow rapid draws of her breath. The promise of his words, the stark hunger in his eyes bedazzled her and left her naked in her own mind's eye, exposed to whatever he wanted, whatever he wished.

This was abandonment. And it never occurred to her to resist.

"Let me kiss you," he whispered. He raised one strong hand and using only the tips of his fingers, tilted her chin up. She rose on her toes. Her eyelids fluttered shut and she heard him make a sound halfway between a sigh and a groan.

Gently, his lips touched hers. They retreated, an absence measured in seconds, and returned for another exquisite kiss and then another and then, again, another. With each kiss, his lips clung an instant longer, moved deeper. His mouth opened just enough to steal her breath, though it felt more like he was stealing her soul.

Soft kisses, warm, moist kisses, kisses that made her light-headed with wanting more. Teasing, promising, leisurely kisses. Dozens of them. Enough kisses to make up for all the kisses that had never been, and all that would never be. And each one taking her heart into his keeping.

His fingertips skimmed delicately along her jaw. He slanted his mouth sideways, nibbling, coaxing her lips apart. With a sense of gratitude, of near relief, she felt his tongue tease the corners of her lips and his tongue glide into her mouth.

Light-headed and breathless, she could barely stand her legs were trembling so, and he only touched her with his fingertips—playing over her face, under her chin, directing the angle of her head with the slightest of touches to afford him better access, a deeper penetration, one with which she eagerly complied.

His kisses grew more demanding, casting her into a vortex of whirling sensation. She clung to him, anchored to the moment only by his mouth, his kisses, and the feather-like touches of his callused fingers. Her knees buckled and she started to fall. He caught her.

He swept her up against him, high up on his chest, breaking off the searing kiss.

She'd stopped thinking. Ideas no longer formed a cohesive pattern, only one image spurred her now, drove her with an imperative lash. She needed to get closer to him, was overwhelmed with the need to be part of him, in him, *one* with him.

Feverishly she worked to rid him of the shirt keeping him from her. Her hands plucked and fumbled at the buttons as he watched, his chest moving in deep uneven breaths, his mouth taut, his face rigid. With a little cry of triumph she finally uncovered him and spread her hands flat against his heated skin. Smooth and hard and tanned, his chest moved powerfully beneath her palms.

"I want—"

He stopped her words with his mouth in another kiss, his shuddering body attesting to the power he held just barely in check. She slipped her arms beneath his open shirt and wrapped her arms around his waist.

With a choked sound, he slid his hands down to cup her bottom, lifting her up against him, making her excruciatingly familiar with the hard bulge in his trousers. Her hands raked down along his satiny skin, through the dark, crisp whorls of hair on his chest to the flat, rippling belly, collecting a wealth of sensation as she searched over every masculine inch of him.

"Kiss me," he commanded breathlessly. Eagerly, fervently she complied.

She'd once disdained his exaggerated masculinity. She'd lied, to herself, to him. She gloried in it.

She loved his strength, the easy power with which he molded her body to his, the taste of his tongue, warm and tinged with brandy as he explored deep within her mouth, the masculine musk of the aroused male animal. He inundated her senses, he overwhelmed her, and she feasted on it; his potency and his aggression; his hunger and restraint.

She twined her arms around his neck and mindlessly, instinctively wrapped her legs around his hips, pressing her mound against the promise of his evident arousal, rocking against him. Sparks of pure sexual excitement ricocheted behind her closed eyelids. Swirling, teasing dabs of carnal pleasure spiraled out from that contact.

Abruptly he broke off their kiss. She fell away from him, half-swooning, but he caught her, one hand cradling the back of her head, one arm tight around her hips, clamping her there. He rolled his hips against her, drawing his breath in a hiss of pleasure.

Her eyes fluttered open. She did not want simulation. She wanted the reality.

He wanted reality.

Each moment had led to this. Mistake upon mistake. He shouldn't have kissed her. He shouldn't have touched her. He shouldn't have picked her up and God knows he shouldn't have spread her against his cock like this.

Her head rested heavily in his palm and her breasts moved beneath her linen shirt, agitated by her shallow pants. Her eyes drifted open and even as he told himself to let her go, her gaze found his.

He held his breath, waiting for reason to return to her gaze, for comprehension to chase the seductive languidity from her black eyes. Deliberately, her gaze still locked with his, she pushed herself against him in a parody of his own instinctive thrust.

He groaned. He should go. She should go. A dark premonition gibbered unheeded in some portion of his mind. Everything he believed himself to be, everything he'd built his life upon, his code of honor, the principles he'd cleaved to when he'd nothing else of value, were being torn asunder in a hurricane of desire.

"Make love to me," she whispered.

Her gaze, always direct, pierced him with candor, dared him to disown the emotion he held silent and still within his heaving chest. He couldn't. He could no more deny her than his own heart, which were one and the same.

He tried. God help him, he tried. "Folly." He kissed her sweet, succulent lips. "Madness," he whispered against their lush promise. "Disaster." His tongue swooped into the sleek warmth of her mouth and returned, leaving him breathless.

"Please," she said.

He breathed his assent into her mouth. "Yes, love."

Their mouths still locked together, he felt her hands seeking between their bodies for his waistband, her fingers cool as they slipped beneath the material, touching his skin.

He dipped down and picked her up, unwilling to take her upright, like a doxy in an alley, and stilling her complaint with more kisses, moved with her to the bed. He deposited her with more haste than grace and with even greater haste wrenched his wretched shirt completely off, and tore the belt from his waist.

She lifted her arms, reaching for him and he forgot everything but the look of her, womanly and wanton beyond beautiful and the molten passion pounding in his veins. He needed to feel her skin on his, to absorb her texture, to taste her fragrance, and to breathe her excitement.

He reached for her as she reached for him, shedding layers of clothes as they rid themselves and each other of every barrier between them until his flesh pressed against hers, and their lips and hands clung and roamed in a ravishment of senses and thought and imagination.

Untutored by vast experience, he followed instinct, licking the under curve of her voluptuous breast, skating his teeth over the silky smoothness of her inner thigh, the column of her arching throat, suckling the tip of her tongue, kissing her eyelids, licking the delicate flesh at the curve of her arm, and finally finding the glistening petals of her womanly core.

Her gasps spurred his pleasure, taunted him with her own unfulfilled crisis. He was an adventurer on a spiritual quest, his thoughts murky and distant, his body a vehicle on fire, her own body his pilgrimage.

Her eyes, dazed with the sensual assault, looked wildly for an anchor and found instead his glittering eyes. She recognized the primal power, felt his masculine exultance, and answered it with a feminine one.

Innocent of expectation, she flung her leg over his hip, toppling him against her, and felt the thick hard prod of his masculine part. Instinctively, she hitched her hips upward. Instinctively, he rolled his own forward.

For a second they froze, joined as intimately as two
bodies can be, hearts beating in tandem, mouths open
in astonished sensation. And then he was moving in
her, muscular arms enveloping her, each thrust pene-
trating deeply, filling completely before withdrawing
and surging back within her again. She caught fire
from the rhythm, squeezed her eyes shut, her heels
digging deep against the mattress as she strained for
the lifeline of repletion that danced just beyond her
reach.

"Yes," he urged in her ear, his words a low, hoarse
purr. "Love. There. Sweet, sweet Lily. My love."

His words drove her into a climax. Wave upon wave
of pure pleasure spun out from the point of their
union, rioted along her nerve endings and then she
felt him tense, his big, masculine body adamantine.
He pulled slightly away, the muscles in his neck cord-
ing, his jaw clamped and then the sound of him reaching his own crisis incited a surge of echoing pleasure
in her.

It was all gone too fast. The little aftershocks, running through her body, pooling in her loins. Dimly
she became aware of the laboring sound of his breath
close to her ear. With a shaking hand she reached up
and smoothed the dark gold hair from his forehead.

"Avery?" she whispered.

He gathered her closer, his eyes still closed.

"Avery?"

"Shh." His voice was low and infinitely sad. "Hush.
Tomorrow's waiting outside this door. It's crouching

there in an ocean of words and uncertainties. But it's not here yet and we are. Lily. Lillian. Love. I'm begging you. Let me love you again. Let me love you all night long."

She answered with a kiss.

Chapter Twenty-five

Dawn arrived armed with doubt. Avery watched its approach stoically, his heart a doomed sentry set against legions of inescapable facts.

Lily lay nestled against him, sated on passion. The dark threads of her hair spilled over his shoulders and arms, her breath fanned his chest and her hand lay relaxed upon his thigh. He closed his eyes against the sight of her, as sequestered in slumber as she would be in her constancy to her mother's cause.

For hour upon hour he'd devised speeches and refutations, anything that would make her his wife. Because he could accept no other relationship and he feared there was no argument that could persuade her to marry him.

The laws governing the disposition of children were as atrocious as the thought of voluntarily making one's own child a bastard. She would not stand for one and he could not consider the other. God help him.

Bitterness spiked his grief for her dead mother, the

woman Lily loved so well she was willing to sacrifice
her life—no, *their* lives—in a memorial to her
mother's bereavement.

As if she felt his animosity, Lily stirred in his embrace, a shadow crossing her features. He gathered her
more closely, careful not to wake her. He opened his
mouth against the cool rumpled veil of black hair,
breathing deeply the scent of sleep and sexual satia-
tion, intensely aware that this moment may well be the
last of its kind. How could he lose her, his sweet antagonist and carnal fantasy, his adversary, his heart?
Yet what could he say to win her?

From the depths of the house unrolled a long,
piercing cry of frustration, like a bad-tempered imp
thwarted in its haunting. One of Teresa's babes was
hungry.

He felt Lily wake. The very air seemed to take on a
shroud of watchfulness, destroying his vigil. He trembled under the weight of an execrable choice.

"Stay," he heard himself say. "Stay with me, Lily."

She rustled, her arms withdrawing from their casual
intimacy, her head turning as she gathered the sheet
about herself. She'd heard the baby, too. Just as he
heard in the innocent cry a reproach for his willingness to bastardize his own children, she would hear a
warning sent by her mother.

She wound the sheet around her shoulders, her
cheeks flushed delicately, her eyes averted demurely
against his nudity. He sank back against the pillows,
his physical exposure an incidental thing compared to

the monumental nakedness of his soul. She rolled away and sat on the side of the bed, lowering her long legs. Even now desire, like some separate beast occupying his body, prowled close.

The baby wailed again, louder, demanding. Lily's head lifted and in profile he saw the frozen look of recognition on her face. He flinched from her withdrawal, understanding it to be the precursor of a far more mortal wound.

"We should wake every morning like this, close in each other's arms," he said, unable to keep the slight desperation from his voice. "We should be wed and spend the next decade waking to the sound of babies—"

"Avery, please . . . I can't marry you." Her words came out in a rushed whisper. "You know I can't."

"Yes, you can," he said with tamped anger. He caught her wrists, demanding that she at least face him. "Tell me, Lily. What can I say? What words can I utter which will make you believe that I am not going to ever leave you, ever stop loving, that no power on earth would cause me to hurt you by stealing our children?"

She swallowed, a look of intense longing on her face. "There are no words, Avery. There are laws and if those were different—"

"Damn it, Lily!" he exploded, releasing her wrist and pushing away from her. "You trust a set of laws more than me?"

She shook her head. "It's not for myself. It's for any children I may have."

He snatched his trousers from the floor and thrust each leg in, stood and buttoned the fly, refusing to look at her. But he couldn't abandon so easily what he'd found and treasured so late. He'd learned to fight when he was young and now he'd fight for her. "Then just stay with me, here, at Mill House."

Her head turned quickly in his direction and all the gorgeous corkscrew curls danced across her shoulders, settling along her spine like a black river.

"Not as my wife, if you refuse that, but in any capacity you want, as my companion, my housekeeper, my lover, my mistress. Any role you wish to play, but be in my life, Lily." His voice was strained, pleading. "Don't go."

Her eyes were soft with pity and unfathomable tenderness and a deep sadness. But she was mute and while she was silent, he had a chance. "You want Mill House. I want you. We can both have what we want, what we need. We'll spit in Horatio's eye," he said with a fierce grin, "damn his soul for placing us in this position."

She clutched the bed linen closer. Her eyes were huge in her face. "And children?" she asked through stiff lips. "What of them?"

He could give her anything of himself, but he could not harm any children they might have, could not deny them his protection and name and the wordly benefits that came with it. And no matter how desperate he was, he could not promise her that, he could not lie to her. He sat down beside her and took her hand and brushed his finger across the knuckles. "We won't let there *be* children."

She recoiled, rose, and backed away from him. Pain made her eyes black embers.

"Stay with me and I promise a full life, Lily. A rich and rewarding one." He stretched out his hand, flicked his fingers in a commanding gesture, calling her back to him.

"I can't. You want children, Avery. A huge, rambunctious family. One for each bedchamber in this house, remember? I can't . . ." She shook her head violently. "I won't do that to you."

"Yes. We can—"

"No!" she nearly shouted the word. "Don't tempt me. Don't! At first maybe you would have recompense in my company, maybe for a few years, maybe for many. But eventually, with the birth of your friends' children, the christening of Bernard's first child, the emptiness of this house would grow into a maddening din. You'd come first to resent and then hate me for it."

"Never." But his tone lacked some depth of assurance, some ringing truth, because the anxious watchfulness in her eyes bled away, leaving only calm despair.

"Yes," she said softly. "And I could not . . . I would not live if I'd made you hate me."

"Lily." He stretched out his hand pleadingly.

"I must leave," she whispered, gathering the enveloping sheets and twisting them about her. "I must go today."

Even Karl's death had been less wrenching, an appetizer compared to the heaping platter of pain before him. "No," he clipped out. "I'll leave. I could no more stay here now than a charnel house. It reeks of the death of my dreams."

"Forgive me, Avery!" With a sob, Lily turned and bolted from his room, disappearing into the pale, dim hall.

Lily turned the key in the lock and stumbled into her room. Tears coursed down her cheeks and her hands, engaged in the task of pulling on her dressing gown, shook violently. With a sob, she gave up trying to fasten the silk frogs and sank blindly to the floor.

She'd woken to the feel of his hand gently winnowing through the hair at her temples, heard the steady beat of his heart beneath her ear, and been suffused with contentment. She'd raised her head and seen a tender lover who'd spent the long night hours worshiping her with his body.

For the space of a minute, she'd considered answering yes to his proposal that they create a life together without marriage or children. But then she'd looked at him and known she could not ask that sacrifice. Avery should have a family, a brood of tall children with gem-colored eyes who would adore him.

And, truth be told, she did not know if she could

live with him knowing that the potential for those children existed, but was never realized. For the first time, she questioned her mother's choice, looked at it coolly, as an adult, examining her motives objectively, and not as her mother's companion in a life of remorse.

She still understood her mother's choices. She just wasn't as sure as she'd been yesterday that she agreed with them. And wasn't that simply a convenience to give her permission to do what she wanted to do? Marry Avery Thorne?

She didn't know, God help her, she didn't know. She had only her past to guide her and right now that seemed a very suspect guide indeed. Alas, the only one she had.

And he was leaving. Perhaps forever.

Lily lowered her head into her arms and when her tears began, they flowed like an ocean of regret.

With the only carriage being in Cleave Cross, Avery chose to walk to Little Hentley. Merry, her brows rising like gulls on an updraft, offered to send his valise and trunk later on her brother's wagon. He accepted, thanking her before going in search of Lily.

He found her in the library, bent over the ever-present ledger. He reached up and knocked on the lintel. She lifted her head. He could not stand to see her so hurt and know that there was nothing he could do to alleviate it; that, in fact, he was the source of her pain.

"I'm going now," he said, stopping just inside the doorway.

"Yes."

"I'll be at the Hound and Hare in Little Hentley for a few days should it be necessary to reach me."

"Yes." She studied him carefully. "What would you like me to say to Evelyn?" she asked.

He shrugged. "Whatever you'd like. Tell her my wanderlust is once more in ascendance." His gaze touched the thick ledger opened near the last page, reminding him of their relationship as contenders for Mill House; he as victor, she as loser. He did not feel like a survivor, much less a victor. "I expect I'll see you at Gilchrist and Goode next month."

"Where?" she asked, momentarily distracted from her wary pose.

"At Horatio's solicitors. The end of your 'test' is near, remember?"

"Oh." She scanned his face for some sign of the man whose muscular arms had held her buoyed above him as he thrust deep within her body and saw a man clinging to the frayed edges of self-control.

"In London, then. I bid you good day—"

"No," she said, panicked by the thought. "I don't think we will meet in London."

He raised one dark brow askance.

"There's no reason for me to go there. I've lost the challenge and I certainly have no plans to make a public statement disclaiming my association with the suffragists."

"Of course not." His smile was desperately unhappy. "Now, if you'll pardon me?" His bow was perfectly courteous, a gentleman's bow, as if he were taking leave of a stranger.

He turned, preparing to walk away from her forever.

"Wait!"

His back stiffened.

"Bernard," she blurted out. "What about Bernard? He'll wonder . . . would you have me tell him, too, whatever I like?"

It looked to her as though he took a deep breath but when he faced her, his expression was composed. "I'd forgotten about the boy," he murmured.

In the habit with which she was well-acquainted, he withdrew his gold timepiece from his pocket. Idly, he snapped the lid open and shut with the rim of his thumbnail, his brow lowered in concentration.

Watching him carefully consider the best way to deal with a sensitive boy, she felt her heart overflow with love and understanding.

She blinked rapidly, fighting the threatened onset of tears. He looked up and saw the single escapee fall from a lower lash. He jerked forward, one involuntary step, before his jaw locked and his gaze went abruptly blank.

"Send word to the inn when they come back," he said. "I'll stay until his return and then I'll come and see him."

She bit down hard on her lips, nodding her understanding.

"Lil—"

She looked down, unable to look at him, so controlled—men always had control—accepting that which threatened to rend her life apart. Oh, he was undoubtedly very sorry for what had occurred and yes, he'd warned her even last night that this morning would bring recriminations. But he hadn't told her they'd tear her apart, that he'd survive and she—

She would not . . . she would not give in to it. She would be as strong as he.

"Yes," she said. "I will tell him."

When she looked up, he'd gone.

Chapter Twenty-six

Mill House's drawing room and antechambers were empty, its hallways hollow. A messenger had arrived with a letter from Evelyn stating her intention to remain in Cleave Cross with Bernard and Polly Makepeace through the weekend.

With Lily's appetite destroyed and no one else to cook for, Mrs. Kettle had abandoned the kitchen. The only other occupants of the huge old house, Merry and Kathy, settled into Teresa's room to coo over babies and compare bellies. They treated Lily with kindly contempt, a society of expectant motherhood from which she was excluded.

Harrowed by memory, counting down each hour to her last in Mill House, Lily fell to cleaning. She spent hours rubbing brass and scrubbing marble mantles, polishing windows and buffing woodwork until even the fragrance of Francesca's sweet-scented sachets faded. Only the scent of Avery's tobacco clung to the library curtains. Lily avoided the place, as she avoided the third floor of the house, and the sitting room, the mill pond, and—

It was just as well she had lost Mill House. In just the space of three weeks he had made it his. The house which over the course of five years had become her home was suddenly a prison, sleep an exhaustion, memory a torment.

With the house as vacant and pristine as a waiting sarcophagus, she then started putting her guardianship in order. She began in the early morning and was still at it by late afternoon. She'd seen to the maids' futures by writing letters of recommendation and character references, noting names of people who would help them find employment, and organizations that might see them placed. Finally, she'd begun writing a note to Avery, pleading with him to keep her horses. For her sake, she knew he would.

She'd almost finished when Kathy appeared, panting and wide-eyed. "Gentleman to see you, Miss Bede."

Avery? She half rose and caught herself. No. Kathy would have said as much. Indeed, had it been Avery, he'd have appeared without announcement, probably carrying Kathy. "If it's a tradesman, Kathy, tell him I've no need for him."

"Ain't a tradesman. A gentleman, I said and a gentleman I meant. And a foreign gentleman, at that."

"Foreign?"

"Aye. Dark, slim chap with a great hat and an odd way of speech and what's more he come to see you specific like. 'Miss Bede, please,' he says. So, I put him in the sitting room."

"Very well," Lily said dully and setting her pen down beside her letter, followed Kathy to the sitting room.

A slender young man rose as she entered, his tall, oddly shaped hat clenched in one dark fist. A huge grin split his darkly tanned face. He swept forward in a deep, courtly bow and when he rose his brown eyes sparkled.

"Lillian Bede!" He eyed her with evident gratification. "I am delighted, positively delighted, to make your acquaintance."

Why, the fellow was an American. "I'm afraid you have the advantage of me, sir," she said.

He laughed, a deep rumbling sound. "Forgive me, Miss Bede. You'll think me a mannerless cur, indeed. Allow me to introduce myself, I'm John Neigl."

Seeing the name offered no illumination, he went on. "I had the honor, well, *sometimes* it was an honor." His kind eyes sparkled even brighter, inviting her to share his amusement. "Sometimes it was just dam—er, darned fortunate, and on occasion a right ordeal, to be Avery Thorne's companion for most of the last five years."

Avery's companion? She thought. Of course, he'd written about the American leader of their expedition who'd contracted malaria and later joined them on other ventures. Impulsively, she held out her hand, smiling warmly. He stepped forward and took it, pumping it up and down enthusiastically.

"I arrived in England two days ago and I made immediately here. I simply had to meet the redoubtable, the one, the only Miss Lillian Bede."

Her smile faded and her brow puckered. Had the malaria affected the fellow's mind? "I'm afraid I don't know what you mean exactly," she said.

She indicated the seat from which he'd risen. "Please. Won't you be seated and Kathy," she said sending a sharp look at the maid, who was fussing about with a feather duster in a patently ineffectual manner, "if you could get Mr. Neigl and me tea?"

Kathy sent her a sour look, and with a little huff of annoyance flounced out of the room.

"Avery tried to tell us you were a scarecrow with a mustache and an eye that could fry an egg, but I knew better. You're exactly as I pictured," John said, taking his seat and balancing his ten gallon hat on his knee. "I knew you'd be a beauty from your letters."

Her brows climbed even higher. "My letters?"

"Avery didn't tell you?" Again the unaffected laughter. "Just like him. He used to read us your letters, ma'am. Not every one of them, of course, but bits from here and there. He kept them, all of them, through every journey and every adventure. Sometimes when things got a mite rough"—his eyes flickered away and she knew that the roughness had been more than a "mite"—"Avery would read something you'd written, to sort of bolster us up."

She stared at him in shocked silence, unable to believe what she heard. Avery had kept all her letters? She'd kept his of course, but that was for Bernard—or so she'd told herself. She bit the inner lining of her cheek. She would not fall apart. John Neigl prattled happily on, unaware of the effect of his words.

"Why, I remember once, in Brazil, when the guides had been run off by some hostiles and we were left to flounder about on our own for, oh Lord, at least a month." The memory brought a flash of teeth. "I don't mind admitting that we were pretty despondent, but Avery used your words to cheer us.

" 'Here now, chaps,' he said, 'If Miss Bede does not worry about our welfare, why should you?' At which someone, probably myself, asked why you were so stingy with your concern and to which Avery replied, 'Why, and I quote Miss Bede, God takes care of fools and children thus, being men, you are double safe-guarded against misadventure.' "

Lily's face flamed. John chuckled.

"Another time we were in Turkey as guests of this nomadic prince. One of the chap's sisters, an authentic princess mind you, developed a tendre for Avery. Actually wanted him to marry her. Surprised the hell out of us." John grinned hugely.

Lily in the process of feeling jealousy set torch to her heart, blinked at the man. "Why is that?"

He blinked back, just as perplexed. "Come now," he said. "In spite of his claims to be the picture of gentlemanly graces no one would ever mistake Old

Avery for Oscar Wilde, would they? I mean, he's witty as all hel—witty as can be but—"

"He has very nice manners," Lily cut in.

"He has no manners at all!" John guffawed without a trace of malice. "Brusque, intolerant, as subtle as a club on the old noggin, that's Avery Thorne."

She had no answer for this monumental piece of disloyalty and could only frown.

"Anyway," John went on, thoroughly unconcerned with Lily's frown, "Avery would have none of the girl and when the prince asked him why, Avery said, 'I am unsuitable husband material. I am childish and immature and irresponsible. I have it on the best authority, that being Miss Lillian Bede of Devon, England, that what I have defrauded the reading public into believing is an exploration of the world's last unknown corners is in actuality nothing but a quest to find the world's largest primate and then challenge him to a chest thumping contest.'"

John burst into an unfettered laughter that lasted a full five minutes and finally ended with him wiping tears from his eyes. "You should have seen the prince's face."

"Confused?" Lily asked coolly.

"No!" John burst out. "That's what's so funny. He understood perfectly! He nodded very sagely, sighed, and said you sounded like his wife!"

"I'm glad my words afforded so many so much amusement."

"Oh, they did. I assure you, they did!" He smiled

brightly through tears of amusement. "It's no wonder Avery loved your letters."

She froze.

Kathy chose that moment to reappear, huffing under the weight of an elaborate silver tea service. John jumped up, took the heavy platter, and set it down on the table.

"I can't begin to tell you how much we anticipated the next salvo in your correspondence," John said blithely. "I don't know who was more eager for your letters, Avery or the rest of us."

"I'm sure—" she began, darting a glance at Kathy.

"I am, too. Avery was." His smile went from one of amusement to admiration. "It pleased us."

"You can leave, Kathy," Lily said.

"I'll just open the windows here, it bein' such a fine day—"

"*Leave, Kathy.*"

With another flounce, Kathy disappeared out of the door. As soon as she left, Lily stood up. "Mr. Neigl, I'm afraid you've made—"

"I'm sorry. I guess I'm not much better housebroken than Avery, am I?" he asked in chagrin. "Barreling in here and making free with your history and all, but I just feel I know you so well, like a member of the family. I owe Avery more than I can ever repay and more than that, I really *like* the big son-of-a—the big guy."

"I'd say that Avery Thorne is like my brother, but that would be a lie," he continued, his tone for the first time sobering. "Avery Thorne is my leader. He has been from the start though I was the one who put the original party together. If I were one of your Scotsmen he'd be my laird. If I were an Indian, he'd be my chief. There's no man I would rather be caught with in a rough patch; no man I'd sooner trust my life with and I have," he assured her gravely, "a dozen times over. He never failed once. Though he thinks he did."

Her fingers plaited themselves restlessly together.

"You saved his life there, you know," John said.

She shook her head. "I don't understand what you mean."

"Karl's death." For a second his amiable expression disappeared in sadness. "Avery was killing himself with self-recrimination. Not that he said anything. No, then we might have been able to answer. He wouldn't have burdened us like we burdened him."

He sighed as though still carrying the weight of his thoughts. "We shouldn't have put so much on him, made him feel so responsible, but he made it so easy, you know?"

She nodded mutely.

"Always doing what needed to be done, always found a way—across a river, through the diplomatic uncertainties of hostile nations, whatever.

"After Karl died . . . well, you could see it was eating at the man. He became silent and guarded. Hesitant in small matters, reckless in ones of personal safety. And then your letter came." He reached over and patted her hand companionably. "Bless you. I

don't know what you said. He never read it aloud—
nor did we ask him to—but for a while I'd see him
reading it when he thought no one was about, after a
particular bad bout or something occurred that would
set the haunts in his eyes again. Your letter eased him,
you know?"

At her silence, John seemed to recall his manners,
and that they were in fact, strangers. His dark face
flushed and he twisted the brim of his hat in his hands.
"I didn't mean to come over all morose and such. This
is a great day for me, finally meeting the woman who
married Avery Thorne."

"What?" This new shock supplanted the old.

"Where is he anyway?" John asked. "Rechanneling
a river? Man has more energy than is healthy." He
finally noticed her stunned expression, her agonized
eyes. Immediately, he recognized his faux pas.

"You aren't married?"

"No!" The word shot out, falling between them
with all the grace of an ostrich in a dovecote. "We're
not."

"I am sorry," he choked out, mortified. "It's just
. . . well, after the letters, I'd assumed. It seemed so
obvious that you were both . . . *courting*. And when I
got his address and realized it was the same as yours, I
assumed. Well, it wouldn't have been unlike Avery—
or even what I knew of you—to run roughshod over
the niceties and just get married! I'm sorry I've embarrassed you. Really," he finished miserably.

"It's all right. You simply took me by surprise," she

said, her thoughts whirling around the honest mistake he'd made, perhaps because it hadn't been a mistake. Those letters had been a courtship. "Mr. Thorne is at the Hound and Hare in Little Henty."

"I see." John's abashed gaze settled on his shoe tips. "Well, I'd best go find him then. Thank you for the tea and the pleasure of meeting you. You're prettier than I could have imagined," he said smiling, "and a lot quieter."

His smile faded. "Though that's my fault, eh? I can't say again how sorry I am to have prattled on like that, I—"

"Really, it's fine. Think nothing of it."

"Good day then, Miss Bede." He stood up, slapped the huge hat against his thigh, and started for the door where he turned and gave her a little bow. When he straightened the self-assured grin was back in place, a devilish gleam had entered his eye. "Since you wouldn't have Avery, Miss Bede, perhaps you might consider me?"

It said much about Lily's state of mind that she didn't respond to this absurdity. Indeed, she might not have heard it all. "Good day, Mr. Neigl."

She went upstairs to his room and opened the door and memory and sensation rushed in on her. She stood at the threshold gasping slightly as though being caught in an unexpected gale. Here he'd picked her up. Here he'd kissed her, hundreds of sweet, tender, hungry kisses. There he'd carried her . . .

She brushed her hair back and moved cautiously into the room. It smelled like him. A touch of rich tobacco, the scent of sandalwood soap, the clean linen scent, the subtle woodsy aroma of his travel battered clothes.

She spied a book on the floor near the far wall and she started toward it but a sheet of paper lying on the carpet near an armchair caught her attention. Its edges were frayed to soft velvet by time and much handling. She picked it up and turned it over, unfolding the creases carefully lest it rip.

It was from her.

My Dearest Enemy,

I am concerned.

Your last letter did not contain your usual compliments and flattery, but was terse. What am I to think? Have I lost my most valued foe to his grief? No. You simply must not allow your loss to ripple across the oceans and continents to become mine. It would be most ungentlemanly.

Allow me for a minute to take hold the flail which you have lain against your back. You mustn't castigate yourself for your friend's loss. Even for you, this is a bit overweening.

Would you stand in Charon's boat forever, wresting his oars from him to keep your comrades on these living shores? And who would do that service for you, Avery, and would you want it done? Or would you resent anyone who barred you from taking even one step on a path upon which you'd set your foot? I daresay we both know the answer.

You say Karl Dhurmann died homeless, without country, and alone. I know this to be patently untrue. You were there, Avery. Karl Dhurmann sustained many losses: a house demolished, a family killed, a country destroyed.

But in your company he'd found not replacements for those things, but alternatives. Did you not call him "brother"? Who knows better than you and I how closely that word resembles "home"?

You tell me Karl had chosen me for his wife; well then I refuse to lose both antagonist and suitor. I have too few relationships to relinquish any of them—most especially those which have demanded such an intellectual investment as ours.

So, let me claim his widow's role and say that which a loving wife would surely avow. Karl died as the result of an accident which no one could prevent. He died in the fullness of his years, in the course of pursuing his own life, not fleeing it, and leaves behind those who have wept for his loss. May we all have so satisfactory a eulogy.

Now, my dearest enemy, I have done more than smile, I have shed my tears. It is past time that you shed yours, too.

Your own,
Lillian Bede

The letter John Neigl had told her about. Those damned, wonderful, impossible letters. Why, oh dear Lord, why couldn't they have continued that way? She put the letter on the table and cried.

Chapter Twenty-seven

They returned last night.
Lillian Bede

Avery folded the note. "They" were undoubtedly Evelyn, Bernard, and Miss Makepeace. With that short sentence Lily had fulfilled her obligation. For a woman who'd penned voluminous letters on no weightier topic than "a footman's livery" you'd think she would have something more to say. Some cautionary word, some indication . . . my God! he thought, crumpling the sheet into a tight ball, they'd shared their bodies; she could have shared more than four words!

He dropped the letter onto the narrow cot that one borrowed for six shillings a night at the Hound and Hare. He missed Mill House. No, he missed what Lily had made of Mill House, the uncluttered, homely comforts and relaxed atmosphere.

He missed Lily. The odd, stunningly beautiful

woman who challenged his preconceptions and had wrested his wholehearted respect. He missed her sharp tongue, her crafty penuriousness, her ridiculous campaign to save race horses, and her honest bewilderment in dealing with Bernard's adolescent crush.

He did not know how he could live without her.

He certainly couldn't live at Mill House without her. It was hers. From the cheap reproduced Sevres vase to the comfortable sitting room, it bore her stamp. Even the bloody portraits in that embarrassingly pretentious gallery somehow belonged to her. It was a home only as long as Lily was its mistress.

He bent down and extracted from beneath the slumped mattress a battered valise, withdrawing a tightly bound bundle. He could at least make something come right of this ungodly coil.

He snagged his coat from a peg and headed out of the inn, nodding at the blushing girl scouring the whitewashed steps. He began walking the dusty road that led to Mill House.

"Here. This will rebuild the stables and put you in the black once more." Avery dumped the thick packet of bills on the desk.

She looked composed and remote and cool. Her impeccably clean bloomers and stiff man's shirt had more starch in them than a Chinese laundry. She glanced down at the money. "What is this?"

"Your money."

Her gaze, flat and wary, slid up to meet his. "I don't have any money."

"You have this. It's the money you've been sending me for five years. It's the allowance. I kept it."

For a second, surprise kindled a gleam in her dark, empty eyes. He'd only one thing now to offer her— one thing that she might be convinced to take, but he must do it carefully, lest even this small token, this tiny thing he could do for her, be thrown back.

"I don't believe you," she said.

"I don't really give a damn whether you believe me or not," he lied. "Stop reacting like some self-proclaimed misused debutante and *think*."

His words had the desired effect. The pain and wariness disappeared from her expression. Her flesh smoothed tightly to the bone. If she'd been a horse her ears would have been lying flat.

"I do *not* think I have been misused," she said loudly, coming round from her side of the desk. "I am sure that you consider you have acted in a most noble manner by offering me your money—"

"Listen, Lily," he cut in, pulling his cigar case from his jacket pocket and taking his time in making his selection. "I made a bid for you," he murmured. "I lost it. I may be selfish but I hope I am still a gentleman."

"Oh, yes," he heard her say softly. "One cannot say you weren't a gentleman."

He fumbled a cigar free of the holder, in doing so taking a short reprieve. He took his time nipping the end off it, jammed it between his teeth, and finally looked at her.

She hadn't moved. Her body was tense with caution.

"Anyway," he said around the cigar, "if you take a moment to consider, you'll realize this is the money you sent. Think of my pride, Lily. You have always gone to lengths to point out my surfeit of the stuff. Can you imagine a more likely gesture for someone like myself to make? Someone with my tendency for— what is it you once said?—'Dumas inspired histrionics'?"

"I wrote that because I was angry," she said, blushing. Too beautifully. He looked away. "I didn't want you to get hurt and you were always rushing rashly into danger—"

He didn't want to hear. He couldn't bear to hear that she'd been concerned for him, that she'd cared for him. "You know I would never accept the allowance you sent," he said. "There was only one thing I could do with it; give it back to you." He flicked the packet with his fingers, sending it skidding to the edge of the desk toward her, and smiled.

She backed away to a position on the other side of the desk and picked up the packet of money by the corner, like a soiled thing.

"And what am I to do with this?" she asked.

"Rebuild the stables. Balance your books. Win the *game*, Lily," he advised. "Take possession of Mill House."

"Why?"

"Because it's yours." His voice was calm now. "You worked for it, you sacrificed for it, you struggled for it. You deserve it."

"And don't forget," she said chin up, "I whored for it."

The blood drained from his face; his hand grew cold. He did not trust himself to speak, nor to move.

"That's what this is, isn't it?" she asked, her voice unutterably wounded. "Payment for services . . . or is this conscience money?"

She picked up the stack of bills and ruffled through them. "My. Your conscience must be hard-pricked."

She set the stack down. "This isn't my money. It's yours. I lost Mill House, but I'd like to leave knowing that I met my obligations here and one of those obligations was seeing you received an allowance. What you do with that allowance is in no way my concern. Build yourself a new stable, buy an automobile, burn the stuff for all I care, but I won't take it."

"Don't be an ass." He snatched the cigar from his mouth.

"Don't sweet-talk me."

"You want Mill House. I'm offering you the means to secure it."

"I no longer want Mill House."

"That's a lie." The cigar broke between his fingers, the two halves dropping unnoticed to the floor.

"How do the women resist that silver tongue of yours, Mr. Thorne?" she asked sarcastically before becoming suddenly mindful that she had not resisted. Heat swept up her chest and throat. Avery's stance remained rigid. Her pulse pounded in her temples.

"Where will you go? What will you do?" he demanded.

"That need be no concern of yours—"

"The hell it isn't!" he shouted. "Everything about you is my concern."

She opened her mouth to deny this but the look of him stopped her. For a long tense moment he studied her and when he spoke his voice was low and furious and yearning.

"I don't give a bloody damn if I never share your bed, your name, or your house—you are *still* my concern. You can leave, take yourself from my ken, disappear for the rest of my life but you *cannot* untangle yourself from my—my concern. *That* I have of you, Miss Bede, for *that*, at least, I do not need your permission."

His words shocked her. She looked decades hence and she saw a specter of what might have been haunting her every moment, her every act, for the rest of her life.

"Your concern is misplaced."

"It's mine to misplace," he said steadily.

"I can't . . . I can't be a party to such nonsense," she said faintly, damning the quiver in her voice. "I won't tell you anything of my plans. They are mine. You need know only that I'm leaving here by week's end." She was breathing too hard. Her gaze skittered over him.

He loomed where he stood, his broad shoulders capable of bearing any weight, his face set with determination. Who could stand against him? He'd always win what he sought. She backed away.

"Don't bother," he sneered. "I'm leaving. Neigl is setting off for the African interior. He needs someone to see to his bags."

Once more Avery was imperiling himself, taking ungodly chances? Her heartbeat raced under the spur of fear.

"No!" she shouted. "Didn't you hear me? Are you incapable of understanding? You can't have your way because you are stronger, because you are male, because you want it. *I* am leaving!"

He leaned over the desk, both arms braced and stiff. "This isn't about me being a domineering male and you being a helpless victim. This is about—"

The door swung open and Bernard, his face awful, burst into the room. "I heard," he said. "I was coming to meet Avery . . . I heard what he said, how you answered. You can't go, Miss Bede. You can't!" His skin was pale, his eyes feverishly bright.

Lily caught back a sob. The choked sound shattered the last of Avery's restraint. With a muffled oath, he snatched his jacket from the back of the chair and shouldered his way by the gasping boy.

"Oh my dear, deluded lad," he grated out as he strode from the room, "but she can."

356   Connie Brockway

* * *

On the verge of betraying her for ten minutes,
Lily's legs finally gave out. Gracelessly, she sank into
the desk chair. Bernard raked a big hand—so like
Avery's—through his hair, setting the dank brown
strands on end.

"You can't leave. There's nowhere for you to go!"

"That's not true, Bernard," she said, trying to reas-
sure him. "I've friends, my sister suffragists—"

"So?" he said, stopping abruptly. She could hear
him panting slightly, overwrought and miserable.
"You'd be a houseguest. A visitor. This is your *home*!"

"No," she said. "It's Avery's home. He won the
challenge. I lost. It's all been fair and—"

"He must have offered to let you stay!" Bernard
exclaimed. "As a gentleman he couldn't ask you to
leave. He swore he wouldn't."

"No one asked me to leave and yes, he asked me to
stay," Lily said. "I assure you I am leaving because I
want to leave."

"You *love* Mill House." Bernard's tone was edged
with desperation. He was gulping for air now. In concern, Lily rose and came round the desk.

"Yes," she said, calmly taking his arm and tugging
him toward a chair. He shook her off, his eyes fierce.

"Mill House may have been my home for five
years," she tried to explain. "But it's not mine and
I . . ." She could hardly tell the boy that the thought
of living with Avery as neither lover nor wife, with the
memory of one passionate night ever burning between

them, seemed a far darker hell than any of the torments Dante envisioned. "I do not want to live here as a guest."

"Why not?" The boy wheeled about, this time both hands playing havoc with his hair. "You were supposed to welcome the idea," he muttered. "It was the ideal solution."

"Solution?"

He threw up his hands in a gesture begging her understanding. "Yes! If you lost grandfather's challenge Avery would inherit Mill House. He has the wherewithal to see it restored. No one would have to sell Mill House or any part of it. You were *both* to live here. He promised he wouldn't make you go."

"Oh my God, Bernard," she whispered with dawning realization. "What have you done?"

"I'm sorry!" he cried, stumbling toward her. He plucked at her hands. "I only wanted you to stay. I did it only to make certain of your future. To take care of you."

"You broke the vase," she said tonelessly.

He nodded, tears spilling from blue-green eyes, so like Avery's. "Yes!" he gasped.

"And the window. And set fire to the—"

"I only meant the ruck to burn. I didn't know it would set the stables ablaze. I wouldn't have endangered the horses—"

His sobbed confession ended in a thick, hoarse cough. The air whistled like a rusty squeeze box in his chest. He fell heavily into a chair and his head dropped forward. He buried his face in his lap.

Dear God, Lily thought, he'd destroyed everything she'd worked toward. She'd never taken Francesca's suggestion of a saboteur seriously and if she had she would have picked Drummond, who hated working for women. Even Polly Makepeace, with her animosity and fears, was a more likely candidate for saboteur. But this boy . . . to have worked clandestinely for her downfall . . . and, for her own *good.*

How utterly masculine.

She throttled the impulse to hysterical laughter. The lad was miserable. His head was still bowed, his narrow back shuddering. "Please, Bernard. It's all right. Bernard?"

He didn't move. She touched his shoulder and he slumped bonelessly to the ground. His eyes rolled back in his head and a sound like a breaking violin string burrowed up from his chest.

"Bernard!" He was unconscious. Panic sent her flying upright, instinct sent her dashing for the door and racing down the empty corridor toward the front door. She snatched it open, immediately spying his tall broad form cresting the dusty road.

"Avery!" she shouted at the top of her lungs. "Avery! *Help me!*"

His reaction was instantaneous. He spun about and raced toward her. Within minutes his long, strides brought him to the stairs. He vaulted up them and she snagged his sleeve, dragging him in.

"Bernard!" she said. "In the library. He's passed out."

He pushed past her, speeding to the library. By the time she reached the door he was already on his knees, Bernard's slack body doubled over his forearm. The boy's fine hair swept the carpet, his hands lay limp, the nail beds tinged with blue. With his free hand, Avery thudded on either side of the boy's spine.

"Bernard?" He choked out his cousin's name in low, fervent tones. "Bernard?" He lifted him closer, careful to keep his head down, his chest uncompressed.

"What can I do?" Lily whispered.

Avery turned toward her, his face stripped of hauteur and confidence, the amazing eyes stark with terror. "I don't know," he answered hoarsely. Tears streaked his bronzed face. "I do not know. Pray."

She knelt down beside the pair, her lips forming silent entreaties, as she watched helplessly as Avery continued thumping on Bernard's back, jostling him every now and then, always calling him softly back to the world.

Long moments passed and more followed. Finally, at long last, after what seemed like an eternity, Bernard gave a deep rattling gasp and moaned. Avery's gaze flew to meet hers, hope returning some of the brilliance to his eyes. The boy coughed.

"Water," Avery rasped.

Lily splashed a glass full of water and handed it to

Avery. Gingerly, he eased Bernard up, bracing the lad against his chest and tilting his head.

"Drink this, Bernard. Careful. Slowly now, breathe deep, from the stomach. Count five in, five out. Ah, there. Fine." Avery's self-possession had returned. His voice was assured, slightly cajoling, but Lily could see his eyes. They were still defenseless; the mask had not yet covered them.

For the first time, Lily saw Avery not as a preternaturally competent man who wrung from life exactly what he wanted, but as a man beset by the same needs and doubts and fears as herself.

She saw a man desperately vulnerable, assailed by the knowledge that no matter what he did, in his own mind it would never be enough where the safety and happiness of those he loved were concerned. Even here, even now, he dared not lest Bernard see how very much he cared, lest his worry translate itself to the boy and cause a relapse.

A man like Avery would be destroyed if someone took away his child.

"Good," he was saying, his large hand gently massaging the boy's back. "A few more like that and I'll allow you to sit on the sofa. Yes, Lily's here. Scared her a bit, you did."

"Did I?" Bernard asked, blinking bewilderedly, the whistle still singing lightly in his lungs. "I'm sorry. I didn't mean to burn the barn. I just wanted her to stay here, where she belongs."

"Hush." Lily knelt down beside him, smoothing

the hair back from his brow. "You must trust me, Bernard. I know where I belong."

He seemed to take her words as a promise and with a faint smile, closed his eyes and relaxed in his cousin's protective embrace.

Chapter Twenty-eight

In the end it was Polly Makepeace who took command. The daughter of farmers and with practical experience in many medical matters, she calmly directed Avery to carry Bernard to the sea-facing southern nursery on the topmost floor. There she swung the windows wide open, letting the fresh, clean air scour the thickness from his lungs.

She stayed in the room, ostensibly to keep Evelyn company, but it was soon apparent that it was her unperturbed and watchful eye that offered both mother and son the peace of mind they needed in order to relax and finally rest.

Avery, haggard and drawn, went searching for his own respite in the orchard. That is where Lily finally found him, his back settled against an ancient tree trunk, his wrists on his knees, his hands lax and his eyes shut. Quietly, she sat down a few feet from him, breathing deeply of the sweet, cidery scent of ripening apples. How long she watched him sleep she'd no idea but by the time his eyes opened the mid-morning air had lost its tang.

He saw her and immediately straightened. "Bernard?"

"Is fine. He's still resting. I came to find you."

He nodded and slouched back against the tree trunk. "I see."

With the moment upon her, she didn't know how to begin. He took the initiative, by beginning what he must assume would be one more painful, impossible conversation, because she did not want to and, as John Neigl had said, Avery would always do what needed to be done, no matter what the cost to himself.

"I know you said you'd leave Mill House, Lily. I can't very well make you stay, but I sincerely hope you'll reconsider." His gaze was steady, fatigued. "It wasn't fair for Horatio to put either of us in this position, but it was least fair to you. He assumed you'd lose, he counted on it, and yet he was willing to let you bleed sweat into this place for five years just to prove that a woman was not as capable as a man."

"I knew. I accepted anyway," she said quietly.

"Who wouldn't? What self-respecting, intelligent, slightly desperate"—here his wry smile robbed the word of its sting—"person wouldn't accept such an opportunity?"

"You wouldn't."

"The hell you say," he scoffed and laced his fingers around his knees.

"You wouldn't," she insisted. "Because you would

see it for what it was, a challenge made not to offer a homeless, uppity young woman a chance to win a home but to shame a young man. And, too, you wouldn't have accepted the challenge because if you'd won it would have been dishonorable, unfair to the dispossessed heir."

"But no one expected you to win."

"That wouldn't have mattered to you, Avery. Tell me if you can, that I'm wrong. Would you have accepted the conditions of that challenge?"

He met her eye squarely. "No."

She blew out a shaky laugh. "At least you haven't claimed that honor is the sole province of men."

"I might have at one time. Before I knew you."

"And I taught you its presence in others through its omission in myself?" she asked, aware that the bite of her tone cut her more deeply than him.

"Don't berate yourself for accepting Horatio's challenge five years ago, Lily," he said gently. "You've fretted about it, stewed about it, and now you've finally got an excuse to walk away from it. You can finally satisfy your honor."

"My, we *have* been busily cogitating away, haven't we?"

He looked past her. She followed the direction of his gaze and saw Mill House, a mellow, square edifice basking in the warm summer sun, its ivy mantle just acquiring a claret tinge in readiness for the coming autumn. The windows gleamed and the shell drive sparkled. It was gorgeous.

"It's a house, Lily. It will not be easy for either of us to walk away from. It's what it means that's so hard to abandon."

"Oh?" She bit on her lip.

"Family," he said quietly and when she did not answer, he went on in the same steady voice, stripped of arrogance and force. "I love you, Lily."

He smiled again, as sadly and kindly as if he'd just dashed her hopes instead of fulfilled her dreams. She waited, mute with confusion. They sat only a few feet apart, he'd just told her he loved her, and yet they might as well have been separated by an ocean.

"I have loved you for a long time, long before I laid eyes on you, I think. When I saw you, I was confounded by your appearance, and all the old insecurities came rushing back, because then I wanted you, and it seemed extraordinarily unlikely that you could want me, too. Then you kissed me and I can't begin to tell you the havoc that played with my heart."

She leaned forward drawn to him as she'd been from the start. "Avery—"

He drew back, just a trifling movement but one that hurt. "I've never been a lady's man, Lily. What with desire and love and this onerous contest mucking things up between us, I have done incredibly stupid things. But none was stupider than making love to you."

"No," she said, reaching out to him, "it wasn't wrong. It was . . . wonderful."

He looked at her hand but made no move to take it.

"Wonderful?" he echoed, testing the word. "Yes and yes and yes but also stupid, Lily. And hurtful. Because you'd already told me that you wouldn't marry me and I knew you would never say something you did not mean." He laid his head back. The sun glanced off his eyes in prisms of blue-green light. "I love you, Lily. But I can't live with you unwed."

She listened carefully, finding more than promises and hopes in his voice, finding truth.

After a moment he continued. "I would not be worthy of the name 'father' if I were to give any child created out of our love anything less than all the protection and benefit and advantages I could bequeath it. You wouldn't ask me to love our child less than I love you."

His brow furrowed and his gaze fell to his hands, clasped now between his knees and Lily was startled to see that his knuckles were white. "Lily, you are center of my heart, my lodestone, my companion, and my lover. Can't you trust me as I trust you?

"The only way you would ever hurt me is by leaving me. But know this, Lily, it will be a mortal wound. Because I'll never find the likes of you again. I've wandered all over this world, Lily, waiting to come home. I'm here. Now. Please. Don't send me away."

He did not look up as he spoke and she saw that his eyes were squeezed tightly shut and realized that he was waiting, in strained silence for her answer.

As though her spirit discovered wings, a sense of release, of heart's ease, of pure and soft joy suffused her. She crept to Avery and put her arms around him, and laid her cheek against his chest. His arms seized her, clasped her in an iron embrace. "Foolish Lily," he said. "Don't you know why I haven't touched you? Didn't you guess that once you were in my arms I would never let you go?"

"Don't. Because I won't release you, Avery. I love you."

"Dear God," he whispered. He gathered her closer, pulling her onto his lap while murmuring endearments in a soft, shattered voice.

"Here is my heart, Avery," she whispered. "Here is my past. Here is my future. They've been yours all along. I was just too blind to see."

Epilogue

The back lawn at Mill House overflowed with children. Teresa's twin brats and a few of Kathy's older girls were chasing Merry's eldest boy. All were hooting with unparalleled delight. Under strict orders from their mother, the twins left Merry's youngest girl—who had a tendency to tears—alone. This so enraged her that in order to impress her older, god-like companions, she decided to climb the ancient cypress tree at the corner of the house.

She'd reached the top and begun shouting her bravura before it dawned on her how very high she'd climbed. Her gleeful shouts became a frightened wail.

When it became clear that no one else was going to rescue the gooey faced six-year-old, Karl Thorne ungraciously succumbed to his genetic predisposition for chivalry and began climbing. This attracted the attention of his youngest sister, Pamela, a bossy eight-year-old. Dropping Kathy's newest infant in her aunt Evelyn's lap, Pammy posted herself beneath the boughs of the giant cypress and offered advice to her brother, who'd already climbed halfway up. This munificence went unaccountably unappreciated by Karl whose pithy response to her encouragements would have made her mother gasp—possibly with laughter.

Pretty soon the rest of the children appeared shouting encouragement to the gallant, albeit grumbling, Karl.

Only Jenny, the oldest of the Thorne children and the most serious, seemed disinterested in the nearby proceedings. Spread out on a blanket by the edge of the mill pond, a furrow creased her brow as she read through the first edition of her uncle Bernard's *Biography of a Romance: The Unabridged Letters of Avery and Lillian Thorne.*

Around her the adults chatted. Aunt Evelyn, Kathy's drooling infant cuddled against her neck, was waxing eloquent about the advances in the laws governing child labor while Aunt Polly patched up Karl's rugby bat.

Cousin Bernard was staring at Jenny's mother—but then Bernard always stared at her mother—and her father was trying to convince Great Aunt Francesca to come to Egypt with them that winter. So far he'd made no progress, but from the look on Great Aunt Franny's face, she'd soon capitulate. Her father could charm the sun into shining.

"Don't be a fool, Francesca," he was saying, "London's a cesspool in the winter and you came down sick

with the influenza last year. Best thing is to escape. Or
did you like puking your guts up for three weeks?"

"You just want me to come along to act as nanny to
your three brats."

Father glanced over at Mother and what the family
universally knew as "that look" came into his eye.
"Hmm," he said. "There is that."

Great Aunt Franny laughed. "Perhaps, I will. But
only if I get an occasional night off . . ."

The rest of what she said was lost because Jenny,
who'd just finished the year 1891 in the book, shut it
with an emphatic sound of disgust.

Bernard looked over as she scrambled upright and
began folding up the legs of her trousers. "Going
somewhere, Puss?" he asked mildly, his glorious dark
gold head turned thoughtfully in her direction.

"To the mill pond. I'm going wading."

"Oh? Cooling off, are you?"

"Yes," she replied trying to ignore him, which was
hard when one was ten and a Greek god was address-
ing you. And that was what Bernard was, a bloody
Greek god.

Tall, slender, and remote, he had an intellect nearly
as keen as her father's. Therefore it had disappointed
her extremely to see he'd so misrepresented her
mother in the pages of his latest book.

"Might one inquire why?" he asked.

Her detachment crumpled. "These—these letters
you say Mother wrote Father."

"Yes?" he said. "What of them?"

"They aren't from my mother."

"I am extremely sorry to contradict you, Jenny beloved, but they are indeed. Your mother kindly allowed me to copy them verbatim for this book."

"And why the hell she gave you leave I will never understand," her father said, having overheard them. "Why would anyone want to read someone else's letters? None of their damned business."

"Come, Avery," Bernard said, giving one of his rare smiles. "You're not exactly a nonentity. The courtship of one of England's most celebrated explorers and one of the suffragists' most celebrated orators? Who could resist?"

"I could," Jenny said firmly.

"And why is that, Puss?" Bernard asked.

In answer she fell to her knees and began rifling through the book until she came to the spot she wanted. "Here. Listen: '*My Dearest Enemy, Allow me to respond to the imbecilic notion that women should content themselves with being 'the spiritual hearth by which men warm themselves.' If a man's flesh is cold, I suggest investing in a good furnace. If his spirit is cold, I suggest a shot of whiskey.*' "

Her father threw back his head and laughed and Bernard smiled more broadly. "That's your mother for you," he said.

"No, sir," Jenny said. "My mother would never have been so mealy-mouthed. My mother would *fillet* any man who made such a ridiculous statement."

Both men glanced at Lily who, having seen Kathy's

son restored to her, had regained her seat, and was listening quietly. She lifted her dark eyes to her daughter's.

"Quite right, Jenny," she said serenely with a smile at her husband. "But when one finds the rare gentleman worth the trouble of instructing, one can afford to be gentle."

If you're looking for romance, adventure,
excitement and suspense be sure to read
these outstanding romances from Dell.